C000075867

THE
ONES
WHO ARE
BURIED

BOOKS BY KERRY WILKINSON

Kerry Wilkinson

THE ONES WHO ARE BURIED

bookouture

Published by Bookouture in 2023

An imprint of Storyfire Ltd.
Carmelite House
50 Victoria Embankment
London EC4Y 0DZ

www.bookouture.com

Copyright © Kerry Wilkinson, 2023

Kerry Wilkinson has asserted his right to be identified
as the author of this work.

All rights reserved. No part of this publication may be reproduced, stored in
any retrieval system, or transmitted, in any form or by any means, electronic,
mechanical, photocopying, recording or otherwise, without the prior written
permission of the publishers.

ISBN: 978-1-83790-138-8
eBook ISBN: 978-1-83790-137-1

This book is a work of fiction. Names, characters, businesses, organizations,
places and events other than those clearly in the public domain, are either the
product of the author's imagination or are used fictitiously. Any resemblance
to actual persons, living or dead, events or locales is entirely coincidental.

ONE

DAY ONE

Millie Westlake's foot went through the top of the feathery moss and squelched into the hidden puddle underneath. The muddy water seeped instantly into her supposedly waterproof shoes for the fourth time in barely fifteen minutes. The silt was between her socks and the sole, making her foot slide squishily around within the shoe.

The man at Millie's side slowed a pace to let her catch up. 'How are the feet?' he asked.

'Wet,' Millie replied. A pause. 'Aren't waterproof shoes supposed to be... *waterproof?*' She spoke quietly enough that the smaller group of men up ahead wouldn't hear.

'I think if the water goes over the top of—'

'I was being rhetorical.'

'Ah.'

Of the men ahead, four were wearing wellington boots, with murky splash marks pebble-dashed across the rubber. The other was in some sort of plain black shoes, that were likely wetter than hers. The ground was a sponge – and not even a fresh one from the packet. One of those grim, slimy things that live at the back of a draining board, spreading cholera and herpes.

Millie slipped her hands deeper into her pockets as the wind howled around the desolate moor. She shrank into her coat, trying to shield her neck and cheeks from the gale that fizzed around them. It wasn't raining, not yet, but the sky was a gloomy wash, and there was a general sense that it might lash it down at any moment.

As well as the five men ahead, there were another two behind. Millie and Guy were holding the middle ground, the odd ones out in their regular day-to-day clothes. Six of the seven were wearing rubbery fishing-style wading trousers. The other man was leading the line. He'd walk for a few minutes, stop, and look into the bleak distance. After a moment or two, he'd slightly change direction, and then walk for a few minutes more. Their odd little group had been on this strange, slow dance for fifteen minutes.

'What are you doing for Christmas?' Guy asked.

His question came from nowhere, still quiet enough that only Millie could hear. A distraction from whatever grim sight was to appear in the coming minutes. She suspected he was trying to take her mind off such things.

'I have friends coming over on Christmas Eve,' Millie replied. 'Christmas itself should be quiet, then I've got Eric from Boxing Day. He's staying until new year.'

Mentioning his name brought Millie's eight-year-old son's little face into her mind. She blinked it away, not wanting his image to be with her here. Not with what they were about to find.

'Come over, if you want,' she added, trying to sound cheery. 'Bring Barry.'

She thought they'd been talking quietly enough for only each other to hear but perhaps the breeze was carrying their conversation. The odd man out ahead, the one without the waders and wellies, missed a pace and then stopped to turn. The men at his side were alert and instantly on edge, hands poised next to hips, as if about to leap into action.

'Who's Barry?' the man asked.

Guy and Millie stopped together, as did the other two men behind. The wind whipped up further, somehow seeming to come from all sides.

'My labradoodle,' Guy said.

'Didn't you used to have a black lab? I remember you having him in the old office. Used to lie near the door.'

'That was twenty-five, thirty, years ago, Kevin,' Guy replied.

Kevin Ashworth nodded slowly as a hint of a frown creased onto his shadowed face. He pulled his coat higher onto his shoulders, though it slipped down almost immediately. It was at least three sizes too big for him – and clearly not his.

One of the two police officers at his side muttered something to the pair of prison guards. Millie didn't catch it but Ashworth did. He turned and scanned the grim horizon, before dipping his head and carrying on in the same direction they'd been heading.

A second later and the rest of the group was off again, stomping across the moss and slipping over the rocks, all guided by a man who'd spent the best part of three decades in prison.

It was quite the group. Two police officers and two prison guards on either side of Ashworth. Then Guy and Millie. Then, further back, two massive blokes who each looked like a cross between a Rottweiler and a wall. Millie didn't know who they were: enforcers or bouncers, something like that.

Ashworth had been locked up when Millie was barely a teenager. She'd had no interest in the news at that age – she wasn't mental – but that didn't stop everyone at school knowing his name.

His face, too.

His mugshot had been front and centre of every newspaper

and TV report for months. Kevin Ashworth was their town's
Freddy Krueger or Jason Voorhees. Except Kevin was real.

And now, he was a couple of metres from her, limping along
a moor in sodden shoes and someone else's coat.

'Stevie, he was called,' Guy said, shouting towards Kevin.
'That black lab was the love of Carol's life. Lived 'til he was
seventeen. Nobody I know has heard of a lab living longer.'

Millie wasn't sure how she felt about Guy calling amiably to
the monster ahead of them, even if the police wanted something
from him. Something only Kevin knew.

She was less sure how she felt about Ashworth *specifically*
requesting Guy be on the moors.

Why him?

Her own presence was less cryptic. She and Guy had
somehow fallen into being something of an informal investiga-
tive duo – even if he was close to forty years older than her.
Ashworth requested Guy for this expedition but Guy wouldn't
do it without Millie. The mystery of whatever they were
walking into had been too much to ignore.

And here they all were.

Ashworth maintained his pace but shouted back over his
shoulder: 'How is Carol?'

Guy answered without hesitation, or emotion: 'She died a
couple of years back.'

Ashworth stopped again and turned. So did the other men
at his side. 'She... *died?*'

'Cancer,' Guy replied. 'It was quick. She didn't suffer.'

Millie had barely known Guy talk of his former wife, let
alone so matter-of-factly.

'I'm sorry to hear that,' Ashworth added.

There was a silence for a moment, punctured only by the
whistle of the breeze.

'It's OK,' Guy replied.

Ashworth nodded again and then turned. He led them

forward for a wordless minute or so and then stopped once more. He wiped the sweat, or damp, from his eyes and then stared across towards the trees in the deepest horizon. Everything seemed so flat and lifeless. He twisted further, towards the way they'd come.

A fair distance back was the three-way road junction from which they'd set off – and, beyond, Whitecliff. The town was out of sight, at the bottom of the hill, but the ocean was there, raging in the winter storm.

Ashworth mopped his brow with his sleeve and turned again. Millie heard his feet squelch. There was moss and heather, grass and rocks. Mud and puddles. Lots of nothing.

One of the police officers spoke: 'Are we stopping... or...?'

Ashworth crouched and touched his fingers to the damp earth. He stood again and then pointed to a large rock embedded in the ground.

'It's there,' he said.

TWO

Nothing happened for a moment. Everyone was staring at Kevin Ashworth. As if the enormity of what he'd announced was too much to take in. Almost thirty years of silence and now... *this?* A random patch of moss near a big rock?

Surely there was more to it than that?

It was the human Rottweilers behind who jumped into action. They strode through the group, shovels under their arms, and then one of them placed the tip of the spade on the ground. Not bouncers or enforcers, after all. Diggers.

'Here?' he grunted, talking to Ashworth.

'More or less,' Ashworth replied. 'It'll be close.'

That was enough for the two brutes to begin work. Ashworth was ushered a few metres away from the scene, sandwiched between the various officers. Millie and Guy stood on the other side, hands in pockets, elbow to elbow.

The shovelling was rhythmic and relentless. The men heaved huge spadefuls of earth from the spot Ashworth had indicated, then dumped it in what quickly became a large mound. The steam of their breaths spiralled and swirled as everyone else watched.

'They look like they've done that before' Millie said quietly to Guy.

'I used to know a professional gravedigger,' Guy replied. 'He was on the council payroll. He'd dig all the graves around the district. Would drive around day after day, week after week, visiting the cemeteries to dig holes. I did a feature on him one year. Had shoulders like you wouldn't believe. I've seen weightlifters that didn't have the physique that fella did.'

Millie wasn't surprised. Guy had spent decades on the local paper, before being made redundant. Despite being almost seventy, he was determined not to retire and had set up his own news website. He'd been relying on his years of contacts and his mountain of old papers – his archive – to report what he called 'real' news.

'What happened to him?' Millie asked.

'Got made redundant. The council hired it out to some private company that charged them three times as much.' A pause. 'I think he had heart disease in the end.'

That was how too many of Guy's stories ended. Heart disease here, cancer there. Someone was hit by a car, someone else had a stroke. Millie never felt her own mortality more than when she spent an afternoon with Guy. He knew too many dead people.

'Why you?' Millie asked, quieter still.

Things had happened too quickly in the previous day or so for this conversation to have taken place.

Guy didn't need to ask to what she was referring. He raised himself onto the tips of his toes and then back down. 'I used to report on the football club,' Guy said. 'Not the matches – sport was never my thing – but I knew the chairman.'

Millie allowed herself a gentle, inward, laugh. Of course he knew the chairman.

'I'd write things about their various charity events,' Guy added, 'or the after-dinner speakers they'd host. The auctions and the jumble sales to raise money for a new stand. That sort of thing. Kevin was one of the youth coaches at the club – but also a teacher at the primary school. I knew him from both places.'

It didn't answer Millie's question – but it was getting there, which was Guy's way.

'When they opened a new school wing, I wrote about it,' Guy continued. 'I got chatting to Kevin and he told me about a sponsored walk he was organising. Then he called me up a few times to ask if I'd write about the club looking for more young players. One time, there was a fight between parents at an Under-13s game. It led to an assault charge, so I called him, because he'd been refereeing on the next pitch and broke things up. He gave me a quote. That was all. We didn't really know each other.'

Millie looked up to Guy, who had his lips pressed together. Ahead of them, the two men were continuing their assault on the ground. The hole was a good metre wide.

'He mentioned your wife...?' Millie said.

That got a shrug. 'We were never friends. I was as surprised as anyone. When he asked for me, I told the police I didn't know what was going on. He said he'd only lead them here if I was around to document it. Considering how long everyone's been waiting, I didn't think I could turn it down.'

Millie watched the digging for a few seconds. There was a steady *thunk-plonk* of the soil being lifted and dumped.

She still wasn't sure why, after nearly thirty years, Ashworth had decided it was Guy who should be here. Her own presence could have been up for debate but nobody had openly objected, even if she had received a series of curious looks from the bloke in charge. Everyone except Millie had a purpose in being on the moors.

Things had been a little like that in the year since a woman had apparently been pushed off a roof. There'd been no sign of her afterwards – and it had been left to Millie and Guy to figure out what had happened.

'Did he teach you?' Guy asked. He'd been silent for a good minute and Millie almost jumped. She needed a moment to remember what he was talking about.

'No. Ashworth joined the primary school the year I left. I didn't know that at the time. Only later, after he got arrested. Kids in our year would say how lucky we were.'

Guy thought on that for a second. 'He was very popular – both as a teacher and coach. People forget that. It's obvious why, of course. I know what he did...'

Millie almost whispered it to herself. *The Whitecliff Monster*. It was hard to square that with the limping, hunched man on the far side of the newly dug hole. This man, in the too-big coat and squelchy shoes, seemed so harmless. So pathetic, if she was honest.

And yet he'd directed them across the moor to the exact spot, to find... she wasn't sure what.

'I checked my archives,' Guy added. 'He raised almost eight grand for the football club with that sponsored walk. It makes everything afterwards so...'

Guy didn't finish the thought and Millie had no idea what word would have come. *Senseless*, perhaps? It had certainly been that. *Awful* was another possibility.

But, perhaps that was the point? Monsters could hide in plain sight and get access to their victims precisely because they *were* pillars of the community. Raising money for charities. Helping children.

Everything was quiet once more, except the steady *thunk-plonk*. One of the shovelers stopped to take off his coat. He swished his top, trying to cool himself, before getting back to the work at hand.

It was the afternoon, though closer to the end of December than the beginning. Light didn't last long at this time of year and, though it didn't feel as if the sun had been up for long, the murk was closing in.

'Are you saying you don't think it was him?' Millie asked. Something about Guy's final line had stuck.

'The opposite,' Guy replied. 'I always felt so sorry for his son and wife. The victims' families as well, of course. I'm not forgetting them but Kevin's son and wife were forgotten in it all.'

'Did you—?'

A nod. 'I spoke to them all at various times. Parents of the missing boys. Brothers, sisters, friends, teachers, other coaches. Some at the time – but there were always anniversaries. One year, five years. Ten. Twenty. It never went away...'

'Maybe *that's* why he wanted you?' Millie said. 'Because you know everyone?'

Guy didn't reply at first. When it came, his response was barely a whisper. 'Maybe...'

Millie thought on what Guy had said. About the anniversaries and the passing of time. That was the thing with big stories, like Kevin Ashworth. His shadow over the town wasn't only because of what had happened, it was everything since. It was the follow-up stories, the vague leads that didn't go anywhere, the documentaries and *Crimewatch* appeals. Millie had never forgotten his name and she doubted anyone who'd lived in the town would. His crimes were inescapable.

Ashworth was supposed to have been driving two boys to a football match, except they never made it. Before the advent of mobile phones, there was confusion. Most assumed there'd been some sort of crash and that his car would be in a ditch somewhere. Volunteers drove up and down the possible routes from Whitecliff to the ground, looking for any sign.

They were nowhere.

A day passed. Two. None of them came home.

A little over three days later, police found Ashworth hiding.

There was no sign of the boys or the car. He never told anyone what had happened. Despite the lack of bodies, he was convicted of double murder and sentenced to life.

And now, close to thirty years on, he was finally ready to reveal what had happened to those boys.

Or so he said.

Back on the moors, the two men with shovels were machines. Aside from each removing their coats, they hadn't stopped. The hole was around a metre-and-a-half square and deep enough to come up to Millie's ankle. The pile of dirt was up to her waist.

The *thunk-plonk* metronomed with almost disturbing regularity as Guy shuffled.

'Something's not right,' he said. He spoke so quietly that it was almost lost on the breeze. Millie edged even closer.

'What do you mean?' she replied.

'Look at them. They're fit, strong, relentless. They've been going for, what, ten minutes? Fifteen? They've barely got anywhere.'

As soon as he said it, Millie realised he was right. If they were taking such a time, then how long would it have taken one man by himself? How long would it have taken *Ashworth* by himself?

Millie glanced across to him. He was the shortest man of the group, barely taller than her. There was almost nothing to him and, though that didn't mean he was unable to dig, Millie knew what Guy was saying.

If they were *truly* here to look for graves, it would have taken an extraordinary amount of time for one person to dig one, let alone two.

Not only that, despite the length of time they'd walked, they had largely followed the road. In three directions, there was endless moorland but, in the other, at least three or four lone cars had passed since they'd stopped walking. It felt inconceivable someone could have been digging for so long and not been seen.

'Ashworth was missing for three days,' Millie said. It was an explanation she didn't believe but it was something. Perhaps there was a chance he'd only worked overnight, or in the dark? He could have dug the graves across all three days.

Guy didn't reply.

Another minute passed, and another. Someone was playing with the giant dimmer switch in the sky. Darker clouds were swarming as Millie rubbed away the damp from her cheeks. It was going to be one of those days where even the briefest of trips outside would leave someone soaked through, even though it wasn't raining.

Still the men continued digging. Another minute. And then... something happened that Millie didn't quite see. One of them stopped and then the other. The first man clunked his shovel into the ground but it didn't make the soft slurp of all the other attempts. There was something hard and solid underneath and, without a word, the police officers stepped forward as one. Guy was a pace behind and Millie another back from that. Ashworth was left between the prison guards as everyone else stared into the hole.

There was slimy water at the bottom, pooling between gloopy, slick banks of mud. But there, a metre or so below the surface, sat a small wooden box.

THREE

Guy had been correct – because something *wasn't* right. The box was rotting, with a brown mushy hole in one of the corners. It looked amateur, the sort of rickety thing an overconfident dad might knock together when trying to save a few quid on storage solutions.

Even that wasn't the problem.

If they'd been directed here to look for the bodies of two eight-year-old boys, then where were the bones? Why was there a box at all? And if it was some sort of makeshift coffin, then why was it so... *small?* It was a little bigger than a shoebox, although hard to know for certain because of all the silt and muck around it. It was much too tiny for a boy, no matter how old.

Guy was staring across to Ashworth, whose own gaze was firmly fixed on the hole in the ground. He took a step forward, then a second, still flanked by the guards. Nothing was spoken but the pair of police officers stepped aside, allowing Ashworth the opportunity to peer into the space.

Millie watched him gulp and let out a long, low breath that

spiralled into the murk. When he looked up, he caught Guy's stare.

'I made it,' Ashworth said, answering the unasked question.

'What's inside?' Guy replied.

Ashworth opened his mouth and, just for a moment, Millie thought he was going to reply. Then he bit his bottom lip and took a step away.

'You asked me here,' Guy added. 'Why do that if you're not going to say?'

Ashworth was avoiding the stare as he took two more steps away from the hole. He half-turned, staring out towards the part of the moor over which they had walked.

The men with the spades looked towards the police officers. 'Shall we get it out?' one of them asked.

The taller of the officers answered immediately with a brusque: 'Do it.'

The *thunk-plonk* was much more delicate second time around. The two men worked in unison, with smaller piles of dirt being removed. Eventually, one of them stepped carefully into the hole and began using his gloved hands to scoop away the mud.

Ashworth had slumped to the ground, sitting on the damp moss, knees to his chest, forehead on his knees. The two guards standing over him were exchanging bemused shrugs and wordless nods, unsure what to do.

Millie felt only confusion.

This man had disappeared with two boys. Almost three decades on, he had led them across a moor to uncover a small wooden box? All that was apparently under the guise of directing them to a pair of bodies. And he'd requested Guy be present.

Nobody appeared to know what was going on. The taller of the officers, the one seemingly in charge, had removed a glove and was busy jabbing something into his phone. He was like a holidaymaker abroad, angrily poking a menu as he tried to get a waiter to understand an order.

By the time his phone had disappeared back into an inside pocket, the scrabbling from the hole had stopped. The two men who'd been digging crouched in the dirt and then gently, carefully, lifted out the fragile box, which they placed on a springy patch of moss. They stood and stepped away as everyone stared at what they'd uncovered. It was a little bigger than a shoebox, but not by much. More like the sort of size that holds ankle boots.

The tall officer took a step towards it but Ashworth was watching once more, still from his sitting position on the sodden ground.

'Careful,' he said.

'What is it?' the officer asked.

'Something to be careful with.' Ashworth sounded solemn.

They eyed one another for a moment and something passed between them that Millie didn't quite catch.

'Is it dangerous?' the officer asked.

'No.'

Millie didn't know why – but she believed Ashworth as soon as he said it. Until that moment, the idea it could be something threatening hadn't occurred to her.

The officer didn't appear sure. His glove was back on his hand and he rubbed his chin as he looked between the box and Ashworth. He nodded to his mate, who'd magicked a camera out of thin air and began taking photos of the rock, the hole, and the box. When he was done, he stepped away, leaving the site clear once more.

It was one of the other officers who stepped forward: 'Guv, shall I—?'

The second officer didn't get a chance to complete his question as he was swiftly cut off with a 'no' by his superior. The taller man nodded towards one of those who'd been digging.

'Get the top off,' he said.

The beast who'd been digging so enthusiastically suddenly seemed wary. He approached the box slowly, before kneeling and resting a palm on top, as if trying to sense what might be inside. From nowhere, his companion had produced a crowbar, which he passed over.

And then it was done.

With a pop and a grunt, the top of the wooden box snapped, before crumbling into sodden splinters. For a moment, it felt as if the world had frozen. Nobody dared to step forward to see the potential horror but there was a smell. Millie had never known anything quite like it. Like stomach bile but fainter, almost as if it was a memory, as opposed to something actually there.

Ashworth was still sitting on the ground but his focus was fully on the box. The man who'd opened it was staring curiously at whatever he'd uncovered, as the two officers and Guy stepped towards it. Millie followed, a pace behind, inexorably drawn to whatever was inside.

She didn't want to see it and yet she did. This decades-long mystery, one that had partially defined the very soul of her hometown, had led them here.

All that and...

There were bones inside – if they could be called that. It was more the skull that Millie could identify, although she'd never seen one so small. She actually wondered if she'd ever seen one before, away from television or movies. This one was so tiny, she could have easily cupped it in her palm.

Was it a skull? The more she looked at it, the more Millie wasn't sure. It was like a golf ball, but with holes in the side.

It definitely wasn't the skeleton of a young boy, let alone two. Perhaps a baby?

She swallowed back a sudden lump in her throat.

'Who is it?' Guy asked.

Ashworth was still staring at the box as he held his knees

tight to his chest. With the state of his shoes and the ground, he had to be soaked.

'Kevin...?'

Guy's voice echoed around the vast expanse, the question unanswered.

One of the men who'd been digging had the shovel in his hands once more. 'Shall we keep digging?' he asked.

'No,' Ashworth replied, before anyone else could. 'No point.' He angled up towards the two men standing over him. 'You can take me back now.'

FOUR

Guy was holding an umbrella over himself and Millie as they huddled next to the cars. It had been a solemn walk back to the lay-by from which they'd set off. They were watching as Ashworth was ushered back towards the waiting, unmarked van.

On the walk back, Guy had told Millie that the taller officer who'd done all the talking was Chief Superintendent Baker. She didn't know much about police ranks but anything with 'chief' in the title sounded important.

Kevin Ashworth was about to be helped up onto the bottom step of the van as Baker called his name. The prisoner turned, a guard at each of his shoulders.

'Are you sure you don't want to say anything else?' Baker added.

Ashworth had been free of cuffs on the moors but he was back in them now. He glanced to Baker, then Guy, before lingering on Millie for a moment. She shivered under his stare. His eyes were dark, empty buttons.

'You brought us all the way out here for *this*...?' Baker said. There was disbelief in his voice. When no reply came, he added: 'What about the families? They've waited all these years.'

Ashworth was silent. He breathed in and then angled towards the inside of the van. A moment later and he got his wish as he was bundled inside, finally out of the squall.

Millie, Guy and Baker stood together as a trio. The other officers who'd been on the moor were still out there, presumably waiting for someone to come and take what had been found. Millie wondered how that would happen. Whether people in white suits would appear and tape off the area, or if someone would dig deeper in that spot. Someone would have to carry that rickety, rotten box off to a waiting car or van. More photographs would need to be taken.

Baker was eyeing Guy with a narrow steel. 'What went on back there?' he asked.

Guy had been watching the unmarked van disappear into the distance. He lifted the umbrella slightly.

'No idea,' he replied.

Whether it was the reply, or the lack of acknowledgement, Baker was instantly enraged. His nostrils flared and, not for the first time, he pushed himself up higher on his heels. He was already the tallest person in the lay-by but that apparently wasn't enough.

'I only allowed *you* to be here because I thought it might give some closure to the victims. I *assumed* there was a reason for all this.'

Millie had only known Guy for a year or so – but that was plenty enough for her to see he wasn't much for authority figures. He'd tolerate them when needed but that was about it. She knew what he was going to say before he opened his mouth.

'You know what they say about people who assume...'

Baker scowled as Guy returned to ignoring him. The officer pushed up on his heels once more and then dug into an inside pocket, before passing a card across. Guy slipped it into his coat pocket without looking at it.

'If you think of anything, that's my number,' Baker said. 'My mobile's on there and I don't give that out to just anyone.'

'I'll bear that in mind.'

There was a few seconds' stand-off as Guy ignored Baker and Baker ignored Millie. A triangle of unspoken resentment, for no apparent reason. Like a family at Christmas.

'Obviously, you can't tell anyone what happened up here,' Baker added, still talking to Guy. 'And that includes putting anything on that little website of yours.'

'I'll bear that in mind, too,' Guy replied.

'What about your friend?'

Guy nodded towards Millie. 'She has a name and you can ask her yourself. I'm pretty sure women are allowed to talk for themselves nowadays.'

Baker's eyes narrowed as he twisted towards Millie. 'This is all between us,' he said.

Millie allowed herself the smallest of smiles. 'I'll bear that in mind.'

The triangle of unspoken resentment continued silently for a few seconds until

Baker broke the impasse. He spun and strode away to his giant silver BMW, which had a wankery sort of look about it. The type of car whose natural habitat was parked crookedly across two spaces at the Big Tesco.

Moments later and he was gone, too.

'What time have you got to pick up Eric?' Guy asked.

Millie checked her phone screen. 'A few hours yet.'

'Fancy taking the long way back?'

The truthful answer was 'not really'. Millie wanted to get back to somewhere with central heating and a roof. Except that wasn't what Guy was asking. He had something he wanted her to see. She told him that was fine by her and they were soon in the relative warmth of Guy's battered Volvo. 'Relative' because the wind-up windows didn't seal properly and the heating was intermittent at best.

Guy stretched from the driver's seat and mopped the condensation from the inside of the windscreen with his sleeve. They waited as the engine chugged and the demisters made slow progress on clearing the glass.

'What happens next?' Millie asked.

'I presume they'll ask Kevin who or what was inside that box – and I'd guess he has no intention of telling them. After that, they'll probably send those remains off for some sort of analysis to find out exactly what they are.'

Millie considered that for a second. 'I thought it was a skeleton... A really small one.'

Guy made a *hrm* that sounded as if he agreed and they sat for a moment, watching the glass fail to clear. Millie flashed back to decades before, sitting in her parents' old car, waiting for the windows to clear. It felt like a relic of a different age. She didn't have a brand-new vehicle but even hers cleared within seconds.

'Did you know the chief inspector before today?' Millie asked.

'Only by name.'

'That sounds cryptic.'

'He was parachuted into the area. Promoted above other officers, so it's safe to say he isn't *that* popular locally. His dad's in the House of Lords.' A pause. 'Not that that means anything in particular, of course...'

Millie almost laughed because Guy wouldn't have said it if it had no meaning. The implication that Chief Inspector Baker had been promoted on name, not merit, was clear.

'He seems like a bit of a *you-know-what*,' Millie said.

'Not used to having his authority questioned,' Guy replied.

'Definitely not used to situations where he isn't in control. I suspect our paths will cross again soon...'

He left that hanging and there didn't seem much reason to labour the point.

'Where are we going?' Millie asked.

'Back to where this all started.'

FIVE

Guy had been driving for a little over ten minutes when he pulled onto the verge, next to a wide metal gate. In the time he had been on the road, they had only seen one other car. Millie wasn't sure where they were headed. They had spent minimal time on the main route back to Whitecliff, before disappearing into the web of narrow lanes and high hedges.

Guy had once told her there were a lot of secrets hidden in Whitecliff but she hadn't particularly believed him. And then, month after month since, it had somehow proved to be true. Sometimes, she had to remind herself that her *actual* job was the dog grooming and training business she owned and ran. It had taken a back seat over the previous few months.

'We're here,' Guy said, as he turned off the engine. The wipers screeched to a halt, halfway across the screen as the car juddered to a stop and he got out.

Guy was already waiting by the gate as Millie rounded the car, still fiddling with her coat. The gate was old and rusting, barely hanging from one hinge as the other lay shattered on the ground. A muddy track was on the other side, leading down to a dilapidated shack. A large once-white sign was on a pole at the side, with 'PRIVATE PROPERTY, KEEP OUT' printed in fading letters.

'This is where they found Kevin,' Guy said. 'When he disappeared with those boys, people assumed they'd crashed. I was on the paper and we sent a car up and down the side roads, checking the ditches. After about a day, and certainly after two, it was feeling a lot more sinister. The police eventually found him here, hiding in that building there.' He nodded towards the shack, which was barely visible through the low cloud.

'What is this place?'

'It used to be a farm a long time ago. Kevin grew up here. His dad owned the land and they ran a dairy farm for a few years.'

Guy angled around the gate post, pressing into the overgrown hedge and then bouncing out again. Millie followed as he led her along the track towards the old farmhouse. The building was a mix of crumbling brick and rotting wood. There was no glass in any of the window frames and two of the three drainpipes had fallen and lay broken on the ground. As they got nearer, Millie realised there were other buildings on the land. A sorry-looking pair of barns was off to the side, with a rusting tractor frame abandoned on an overgrown patch of weeds. It was a dystopian scene from a movie or video game. The sort of place someone might hole up after the zombie apocalypse.

Guy edged around another 'keep out' sign until they were close to what would have once been the front door. There was no door in place now, only a gaping hole, through which Millie could see a collapsed staircase.

'Kevin's dad sold the farm at some point,' Guy said. 'The small dairy farming industry fell apart once supermarkets started buying and selling in bulk. Places like this were all offloaded.'

'Doesn't look like anyone's lived here in a long time.'

'Whoever bought it off the Ashworths didn't last long. It's very hard to sell somewhere like this in the middle of nowhere. Developers don't want it, because they can't get planning permission. Most buyers couldn't afford the upkeep, or to rebuild. The only option left is if some builder themselves wanted to buy the place and do it up. But then you still need a buyer after that...'

The breeze whistled around the buildings as Guy tailed off. There was ivy, or some sort of other weed, growing around the window frames on the lower floor. It reminded Millie of a budget horror-movie set.

'There's a few of these places dotted around,' Guy added. 'They get repossessed but then the bank doesn't know what to do with them. They sell on the deed and then it ends up in limbo somewhere.'

Millie stayed quiet. The place invited silence. She followed Guy around yet another 'keep out' sign, as they traced the outside of the house. There were more bricks and more battered wood on the ground. At the side was an upside-down wheelbarrow which had rusted through. Millie wondered about the last time anyone had visited. It didn't feel like any time recently.

As they reached the far side of the farmhouse, Millie and Guy sheltered under the overhang of the angled roof and stared out towards the moors beyond. The cloud hung low. A swirling ceiling that Millie felt she could almost touch. It was as if the moor went on forever. An endless sea of greeny, brown nothingness until it reached the trees in the distance.

'How did Ashworth know the exact location of that box?' Millie asked. 'There was that rock but it was a good fifty or sixty metres from the road. Plus we walked for fifteen minutes or so from where we parked.'

Guy thought for a couple of seconds. 'Remember in the

woods last summer? The Kissing Tree? Other people would think it odd that you knew the route through the forest, away from the trails. You didn't use a map; you knew where to go.'

Millie was about to reply that they were different things – but perhaps Guy was right. The farmhouse was five or six miles from the site where that box had been discovered and, if Ashworth grew up here, it wasn't *that* odd he'd know places by sight alone. He'd have grown up before mobiles, before the internet. As she looked around, Millie couldn't see a telegraph pole, so there was a good chance the farm didn't have a landline. They were in the middle of nowhere, so of course a kid would get out and explore.

'Does Ashworth have any brothers or sisters?' Millie asked.

'I don't think so. I didn't know the family that well before everything happened. I met Kevin through the school and the football club – but even that was fleeting moments here and there. When those boys went missing, I was trying to play catch-up the same as everyone. I didn't know about this house until he'd already been found. There was a month or so where nobody could get near the place.'

'Because the police were searching for the boys...?'

'Exactly. I think his dad died not long after they lost the farm. His mum, too. I don't remember anyone saying there was another brother or sister... although, if there was, you can't blame them for keeping quiet.'

That was true enough. Kevin Ashworth's name still haunted the town decades on. Who would want that sort of attention?

The mist had dipped and turned into a clingy, sodden hug. Millie felt the chill through her jacket. Her feet were still wet but she couldn't bring herself to suggest leaving. She turned to take in the rear of the farmhouse, where there was a large hole in the wall, as if someone had punched their way out. There was glass in a couple of the windows, though both were shattered, with dangerous-looking shards lining the frame.

'Was he hiding here the whole time?' Millie asked.

'I have no idea,' Guy replied. 'I looked back through a few of my reports from the time but all it says is that he was found here. He could've been somewhere else in between times. His car was never found, neither were the boys. When it became clear he hadn't crashed, the police went to Kevin's house in Whitecliff. He had a place on that estate near the Asda. His wife and son were there but neither knew where he was. That's when it all hit the news. The police ended up here a day or two later.'

Millie was still struggling with the fact Ashworth had specifically asked for Guy to be part of whatever they'd just witnessed. Nothing Guy had said made it sound like they were friends, let alone that they still had a relationship so many years on.

But then Guy kept calling him 'Kevin', while Millie thought of him as 'Ashworth'. She supposed it was the difference between seeing him as a person and a monster. Even if it wasn't, she couldn't help but feel uncomfortable.

'Do you know where they searched?'

Being at the farm made everything feel different. More real, perhaps?

'I believe they dug under the barn,' Guy said. 'There was something with thermal scanners but I can't remember properly. Today happened so quickly that I couldn't find the papers in time.'

After working for so long for Whitecliff's local newspaper, Guy had a house full of old issues. He'd seemingly kept a copy of every paper produced since he had started work forty or fifty years before. It was as complete a library of the area's history as anyone could possess – except, given he was one man in a cottage, the archiving was erratic to say the least.

With enough time, Guy could find records of anything. But in the rush of Kevin Ashworth announcing he had something to show them on the moors, time was the one thing they hadn't had.

'Did they find anything under the barn?' Millie asked.

'Cow's remains, I believe. Neither of the boys.'

Millie found herself staring sideways towards one of the barns. It was tall, wide, and boxy. Like an abandoned warehouse. There were no doors at the front and she wasn't sure she wanted to see whatever was inside.

'Is his wife still around?' Millie asked.

'She died about fifteen years ago. She'd moved away by then but I can only imagine how hard it is to escape all this.'

'You said there was a son...?'

'Nicholas. He was sixteen, maybe seventeen, when everything happened. He changed his last name and moved away with his mum...'

There was something about the way he said it that made it sound as if there was more. If there was one thing Guy was good at, it was keeping information to himself until he wanted someone else to know it.

'What happened?' Millie asked.

For a moment, she didn't think she'd get a reply. Guy was staring off towards where the distant trees had disappeared behind the mist. His nose twitched, as if he could smell something that wasn't there.

'Kevin's son was back here about seven or eight years ago,' Guy replied. 'I was still on the paper then and someone came to our office asking if we had cuttings we could share with them. It was all a bit mysterious at first but it turned out they were working for a production company who was making a documentary about everything that happened. I didn't know Nicholas was back in town until they said. I don't know how they knew he was back but they were looking to do some sort of doorstep thing, where they'd confront him and film it. Some sort of "*son-of-a-monster*"-thing. Back at the scene of the crime.'

'What did you do?'

'Shut them down. I explained about the human right to privacy and how Nicholas wasn't anything to do with his dad. I said they'd be breaking the law by approaching him and that he'd be able to sue everyone involved on a personal level if they ever went through with what they were planning.'

It was rare that Guy sounded so forceful when he spoke. He usually underplayed his intelligence and knowledge – which Millie had seen first-hand would often lead to other people opening up to him. His guard was down a lot more often around her – but even Millie wasn't used to such fire.

'What happened?' she asked.

'The documentary never got made, so I assume they got scared off. I did play it up a bit, with the whole "*sue everyone on a personal level*"-thing. I thought they'd at least go and check with their own lawyers but I think they might've been a new company, looking to make a name for themselves.'

There was still a steel to his words.

'Why'd you scare them off?' Millie asked.

He turned to her and raised an eyebrow, as if she'd asked what two plus two made. 'Sins of the father, and all that. That's not how journalism is supposed to be. The story was *Kevin* Ashworth. Not his son. What his dad did is not his fault.'

Millie started to reply but stopped herself. She'd rarely seen this side of Guy – but there was something about it that made her feel safer with him. He was already her godfather – and someone who'd become something close to a father figure in the previous twelve months.

'What did Nicholas think?' Millie asked.

'I don't think he knew. We didn't approach him ourselves, so, unless the production company did, I suppose that was the end of it.'

'Is he still in town?'

Guy didn't reply instantly and, when Millie turned to him, his jaw was firm. Sometimes, she knew an answer wasn't going to come. Millie wondered if Nicholas was currently working in town. If he was someone behind a bar who'd served her, or, perhaps someone whom she could have known in her former life working at the council. They might have sat across from one another for years and she'd have been none the wiser.

Which was, presumably, Guy's point. It didn't matter if Nicholas was still in town, or what he was doing.

But, perhaps, that wasn't his *only* point.

It had been two-and-a-half years since Millie's own parents had died suddenly and unexpectedly. She'd inherited everything and, since then, had struggled to avoid the sideways glances and curious stares. The implication, sometimes silent, sometimes to her face, that she'd had something to do with her parents' deaths.

Even now, Millie struggled to escape those searching stares from people who thought she seemed familiar – and her parents had nothing of the legacy that Nicholas's father did. Millie had somehow missed it before but the day's events felt a little *too* close for comfort.

She shivered.

'Why now?' she asked. 'It's been so long. Why did Ashworth bring us here now?'

Guy shuffled as he cleared his throat. It was impossible to escape the sense that he knew more than he was letting on. 'I have the same questions as you,' he replied.

The mist was settling deeper and the trees on the furthest side of the moor were now a memory. Even the barn was only an outline as Millie bobbed from foot to foot, looking for warmth. Her feet squelched again as she stepped out from the overhang and angled back towards the car.

'Shall we go?'

. . .

The heat was working properly in the Volvo as Guy set off second time around. Millie kicked off her shoes and socks, stretching her toes towards the vents under the glovebox and trying to get some sort of feeling back into them.

They didn't talk much on the journey back to Whitecliff. That was one of the things Millie liked about Guy. He didn't fill silences for the sake of it.

Millie couldn't figure out whether the strangest of lunchtimes on the moors was a beginning or an end. Whether they'd never hear from Kevin Ashworth again, or if what they'd uncovered would set something larger in motion.

Guy's Volvo bumped its way around the winding country roads as they edged towards civilisation. The mist thinned as they headed further away from the moor. Before they reached the long descent towards Whitecliff itself, Guy turned onto the narrow track that led to his own house. It was a cottage on the cliffs, close to the woods and far from humanity. The sort of place that would put fear into a poor delivery driver, trying to follow Google Maps instructions.

Millie's car was parked on the trail outside Guy's cottage but, as they got closer, she realised that wasn't the only thing in sight. A little further along, a man was sitting on the low wall that separated Guy's property from the track.

In the year that Millie had been visiting the cottage regularly, she couldn't remember a time when anyone else had been around. Guy had no neighbours and didn't live close to any official hiking trails. In the summer, there might be the odd rambler trying to follow the line of the cliffs – but this was something new.

The man turned as Guy's car bobbled closer. He was in a hoody, hands in his pockets, as he slowly stood and faced them.

Millie had no idea who he was. He was perhaps in his late

thirties, somewhere close to her age, although it was difficult to know for sure. His hood was up and his clothes baggy.

Guy parked in front of Millie's car and crunched the handbrake into place. It was as if he'd not noticed the stranger sitting on his wall.

Or, perhaps, it wasn't a stranger.

'Who's that?' Millie asked.

Guy opened the driver's door and clambered out with a grunt. By the time Millie was out of the car, he was already a few paces away, heading towards the gate. She caught him as he was about to wrestle it open.

'Thanks for coming,' Guy said. 'I know we wound up our chief inspector friend a bit, but it's probably better if we don't say too much about what we saw out there.'

'I get it.'

Millie made a point of glancing to the man, who was still standing and staring. He was perhaps fifteen metres away, unmoving.

'Who's that?' Millie asked again.

'No idea,' Guy replied, too quickly. It was an obvious lie and perhaps not his first of the day. 'I need to get inside and check on Barry. I'll let you know if I hear anything from Chief Inspector Baker. Otherwise, we can regroup tomorrow, assuming you're still up for that...?'

Millie had forgotten that they had a second appointment. Somehow, this had become her life. Without meaning to, Guy's website – which was primarily for reporting news – had become known as a place where low-level local mysteries could be investigated. People came to Guy with problems to be solved. He was selective because they couldn't track down every missing cat, or find every dropped earbud. But it did mean Millie's days were rarely boring.

'I'll meet you there,' she said.

The man was still hovering as Millie got into her own car.

She started the engine and switched on the heaters, watching as he stood and watched Guy disappear into the house.

As she started to pull away, they locked eyes for a moment. A second or less, yet, as she turned back to the track, Millie had the strangest sense that he was someone she had once known.

SIX

The bell hadn't finished chiming before the front door was wrenched open. A string of white Christmas lights had been pinned around the doorframe, though the bulbs were currently off. Eric scuttled underneath the arm of the person who'd opened the door, before mumbling something that might've been, 'Hi, Mum.'

Millie nodded across to the vehicle that was parked across the front of the driveway she used to own. 'Uncle Jack's in the car,' she said. 'He's looking forward to seeing you. Isaac's there, too – so make sure you're nice to him.'

'Isaac...' Millie's son rolled the name around his lips. It was as if he'd not heard it before, even though they'd spoken about him on the phone at least twice that week. He finished with a chirpy 'OK' and then bounded towards the car. He was growing and growing, and ran like he had three sets of knees. Millie watched him launch himself into the front seat of the car – and then she finally acknowledged the woman who was glaring at her from the step.

'You're late,' Rachel said.

'It was four minutes,' Millie replied. 'And I would've been early except there's a water main burst down by the—'

'We don't *have* four minutes,' Rachel snapped.

It was fair to say there wasn't an awful lot of love lost between the two women. Millie's ex-husband was on the brink of marrying Rachel and, if it wasn't for joint custody of Eric, they'd have zero contact with one another.

Rachel was in a floor-length green dress, plus some sort of shawl that was much too small and perhaps closer to a bondage collar.

'You look nice,' Millie said, with a hint of passive aggressiveness that came naturally. It was met with a dismissive *pfft*.

There was movement from the hall beyond and then, as Rachel stepped onto the drive, Alex emerged behind her.

Millie's former husband was in a suit and tie as he passed Rachel the car keys. 'I'll be there in a sec,' he said. There was a hint of rolled eyes as his fiancée click-clacked towards the Range Rover.

'I thought you were running late,' Millie said.

'We are but I was wondering if you can have Eric overnight?' Alex crouched and picked up a small bag that had been left next to the door. He offered it to Millie, who didn't take it.

'I've got plans for tomorrow morning,' Millie replied.

'What plans?'

'None of your business.' A sigh. 'If you'd asked before, even this morning, I could've moved things around.'

'I told you she'd be difficult!' Rachel called over. She had stopped just short of the car and was standing with a hand on her hip. She shook her head dramatically and then opened the Range Rover's door, before clambering inside and slamming it.

'You're always hinting about access,' Alex said, quieter. 'Here it is – and you're saying no.'

He was such a dick.

'I didn't *say* "no",' Millie replied.

When the custody hearing had happened, her solicitor had strongly advised her to keep things as civil as possible with her ex-husband. A new arrangement would only happen if she could prove she was trustworthy and willing to stick to the rules. That meant she'd frequently found herself replying to him through gritted teeth.

'It's just very late notice,' Millie added. '*No* notice, in fact. This isn't even my night for access and I'm doing *you* a favour having him.' A pause. 'Not that I mind.'

She didn't mind, not really. A part of her was already planning how they'd spend the evening. Not that she wanted Alex to see that.

This time, there wasn't a hint of a rolled eye. Alex actually did it to make sure she'd see. He lowered the bag. 'Look, if you don't—'

'I'll take him,' Millie said. 'I'm just saying it would have been nice if you'd texted earlier.'

Alex offered her the bag again and, this time, Millie took it. She often felt as if her ex-husband was deliberately needling her when it came to access issues. It was her infidelity that had led to the separation and divorce. She'd never wanted the affair to become public. It wasn't as if she didn't have her reasons, but the very public revelations had led to this. Alex seemingly felt as if he could talk to, and treat her, however he wanted.

'Enjoy the rehearsal,' Millie said.

This time, there was no roll of the eyes but, as Alex closed the door behind him, there was something of a grimace. They might not be married any longer but Millie had known him long enough to see the discomfort. It was the look he'd had after they'd brought home Eric from hospital. The deer in the headlights mini-panic when she'd first asked him to change a nappy. It was there and gone, more of a reflex than anything deliberate.

'Are you still all right to pick him up from school the day

after tomorrow?' he asked. 'You're on the safe list with the office.'

Millie already knew that – but it still felt like a punch to the gut that she needed to be on a list to collect her own son from school.

'I've already got that in the calendar,' she said.

'Good. We've made plans that night, too.'

Alex stepped around her, towards the car. It was a somewhat familiar story that Alex and Rachel had plans in the evenings, or on weekends. He'd made such a big deal of getting custody but, as his second wedding day approached, Millie had found herself being asked to look after their son more and more.

It was rarely, if ever, a problem, though Millie often wondered how Eric felt about it all. Did he feel kicked out? *Left* out? It was something she should probably discuss with him, except their time together was still limited and she wanted him to enjoy being at her house.

'I need to get going,' Alex said, taking another step towards the car. For a moment, it felt as if he might tag on some sort of thanks – but of course he didn't. Instead, he got into his Range Rover and Millie took her time in restarting her own car. She was blocking them in and enjoyed the few moments that she knew her ex would be fuming as he waited. She adjusted the mirror, fiddled with the gearstick, turned down the Carplay volume. They always played by his rules, so her occasional – and minor – acts of rebellion were relished.

'Everyone got their seat belts on?' she asked, turning towards the back seat.

Millie's old friend, Jack, gave a grin and patted the belt across his chest as his four-year-old son, Isaac, showed off his.

'Away we go!' Millie declared, which got a small cheer from the back seat. Eric, despite being strapped into his car seat in the front, was already too old for such embarrassment from his mum.

Barely a second passed until Alex roared around them and disappeared along the road.

Nobody spoke for a short while until Isaac chirped from the back, 'Was that your dad?' As a four-year-old, he was a lot chattier and more confident around adults than Millie ever remembered Eric being.

Millie felt Eric looking to her, silently asking if he was the one being questioned. She glanced away from the road momentarily, nodding to say it was fine to answer.

'Yeah,' Eric replied.

'You have two mums...?'

'No. This is my mum. Rachel's not my mum.'

It was impossible for Millie not to feel a sense of happiness at how forceful her son sounded.

'I have two dads,' Isaac said, speaking so matter-of-factly that Millie had to remind herself this would have been anything but the norm when she was growing up. She caught Jack's eye in the mirror and he was beaming at the recognition.

'Is your dad coming to see the lights?' Isaac asked.

'He's got a practice dinner,' Eric replied.

There must have been some sort of curious look between father and son on the back seat because Jack was the next to speak. 'It's a *rehearsal* dinner,' he said. 'Eric's dad is getting married next week and they're having a special dinner tonight to get ready.'

Millie could sense Isaac thinking that over. Having a meal to practise for a different meal was a strange concept for a child to understand.

'Will they have chips?' he asked.

Jack laughed at that. 'Probably not.'

As Millie drove, the other three continued to discuss the options Alex and Rachel might be having at their rehearsal dinner. Millie doubted any of fish fingers, sausages, red sauce, or toast would be on the menu... although any of those would have almost certainly been a better choice than whatever they were being served.

It wasn't long until Millie pulled onto a local street to be met by a wall of light. Cars were crawling along both sides of the road as the occupants craned through the windows, taking in the long rows of lit-up houses.

For some reason, the residents of this particular road had decided to start some sort of unofficial competition of who could go bigger and better with their Christmas decorations. Each year would see grander inflatables and hundreds or thousands more lights, with each resident apparently trying to outdo their neighbours. That had led to something of an annual tradition as people descended on the single street with their children to absorb the spectacle.

As cars edged along slowly, other families were braving the cold to walk along the pavements. Some were posing for photos, others filming, or live-streaming.

The first property on the row had an enormous, dancing inflatable snowman that was bigger than the house. Long strings of lights lined the walls and the roof, with a lone reindeer cut-out in one of the windows.

The traffic was moving so slowly that Millie had almost stopped. She turned to see a wonder-struck Isaac pressed to the window, taking in the sight.

Eric was shielding his eyes from the glare. 'Dad said their 'lectric bills would be stupid,' he said.

'You're too young to know about bills,' Millie replied.

Eric twisted away from the window. 'Rachel says she'll make me pay the bill if I keep leaving on the bathroom light.'

'You probably should turn off the light if you're not in the room,' she replied diplomatically.

'She leaves her straighteners on all the time...'

Jack caught Millie's eye in the mirror. She'd felt him

drawing the gaze before he raised a single eyebrow. This was an argument to not get drawn into.

Millie had a moment of being back on the moors, where there were no lights, no radiators. Where it had been cold and wet, and...

She blinked it away. It wasn't the time to think about all that.

'Look at all those reindeer,' Jack said, changing the subject.

The next house had seven inflatable reindeer, stretching from the roof towards the front of the garden. It was enough to get the children's attention, as the traffic continued crawling.

It took close to half an hour to reach the end of the road, which wasn't a problem for anything other than general climate emissions. The boys had been getting steadily giddier as they'd lurched into fantasies of how they wanted to live in a house with giant *Star Wars* characters at the front.

The final house on the corner provided the biggest confusion – and also the biggest crowd. There was a large Santa on the front lawn, plus the usual amount of lights. It wasn't much in comparison to some of the other houses, except a queue of people were lining up to take pictures.

Millie didn't spot the reason at first. It was Jack who started with: 'Does that say—?' before Eric finished the sentence for him: 'Tits!'

It took Millie a couple of seconds before she realised what they were talking about. There were large letters spread across the various panes of glass at the front of the house. The message was large, clear, and utterly confusing: 'LE TITS NOW'.

'What are tits?' Isaac asked from the back seat.

Jack giggled, which wasn't exactly ideal parenting.

Millie simply stared, unsure why such a bewildering notice was on display. It was no wonder so many people were taking photos.

'I think it actually says "let it snow",' Jack replied. It was only as he said it that Millie realised he was right. The letters were spread out in such an uneven way across the frames that the innocent message was lost to smuttier minds like hers.

'Tits,' Isaac said, which made Jack laugh again, even if he did stifle it with, 'You shouldn't say that.'

They were off the main street of lights and on the road home – but it was too late for any sort of control. As Isaac continued to say 'tits', Eric decided to tell him that they were also called 'boobs'.

The boys sniggered – all three of them – as Millie decided there wasn't much point in trying to stop it. It had been a similar story years before when Eric decided the word 'poo' was the funniest thing he could ever possibly say.

As they wound their way through the various estates towards the centre of Whitecliff, the amusement began to ebb away until there was only the gentle hum of the engine.

Millie pulled into a parking space at the back of Jack's flat and then spoke over her shoulder. 'Did you enjoy that, Isaac?'

Jack's gentle whisper was the reply. 'He's asleep. Past his bedtime. Thanks for the drive. You made his day.'

'Are you OK getting him upstairs?'

'I didn't realise having a son would involve so much carrying.'

Jack reached forward and squeezed Eric's shoulder, before telling him to 'be good for your mum'. After that, he got out and rounded the car, before carefully lifting a lifeless Isaac from the seat. He cradled the boy on his shoulder, then headed for the steps up to his flat.

Millie watched for a moment, remembering the moments when Eric used to be small enough for her to carry. Not any longer. He was eight but it felt like he was a blink away from being a teenager. Then another blink away from him being bigger and taller than her. It was all moving so fast.

'Does Isaac know he's adopted?' Eric asked.

Jack was on the second step, with his sleeping son's face flopped onto his shoulder.

'Yes,' Millie replied.

'Does he have a real mum and dad?'

'He has a mum who gave birth to him, and a dad who helped make him – but they're not around. Jack and Rishi are his real dads.'

Jack was at the top of the stairs and rounded the banister onto the balcony. He waved with his free hand and then started fishing for the key in his pocket.

'I wish Alex wasn't my dad.'

Millie took a breath. Thought about how part of her wanted to punch the air, then squeeze her son and tell him he was hers, all hers. Then she thought about what she *must* say.

'You shouldn't say that,' she replied. 'And you should call him "dad". I've told you that.'

Eric was smirking, knowing exactly what he was doing. 'Do you mind Alex and Rachel getting married?'

It was the first time he'd ever asked such a thing. The answer was yes and no. 'No' in the sense that she didn't really care what they got up to. 'Yes' because Eric was always going to be a part of their collective lives – and she hated the idea of Rachel trying to take over as his mum. Millie didn't go out of her way to lie to her son.

'I want them to be happy,' she replied, which didn't exactly answer the question.

'Do you think they'll *actually* get married?'

Jack was at his front door. He had a knee raised, balancing Isaac as he fumbled with his key.

'Why would you ask that?' Millie said.

Eric turned to face the window. He didn't reply at first but when he did, she knew her son had been anticipating the question.

'No reason,' he said.

SEVEN

DAY TWO

Millie was waiting next to her car as Guy's Volvo chugged its way into the space behind. She wanted to ask about the mysterious man who'd been hanging around his cottage the night before – but Guy was ahead of her, setting the subject.

'How were the lights?' he asked. 'Did Eric enjoy them?'

'It was busy,' Millie replied. 'Last time I was there, it was only about half the houses taking part. It's everyone now.'

'Word's obviously gone around.'

'I blame Instagram.' Millie paused, then added: 'Eric stayed over last night. I just dropped him back with his dad – who seemed *very* hungover.'

That got a *hrm*. 'Things like rehearsal dinners make me feel so old. Carol and I got married in a register office. Most people did back then. More or less everyone we knew. Sometimes just parents as witnesses, then you'd have a party down the social in the evening...' Guy tailed off.

It was an out-of-character bit of colour. He had never particularly been one for an 'in my day' interlude, unless there was some point to it. He rubbed his eyes and blinked.

'Have you heard anything from the police?' Millie asked.

'Not a peep. That might be the end of it, if Kevin doesn't want to talk again.' He rubbed his eyes again but continued speaking before Millie could ask if he was all right. 'The mother of one of the boys still lives in Whitecliff. I was considering visiting her later. We've been in contact off and on since... well, since everything happened.'

That particular piece of information wasn't a surprise to Millie. Not only did Guy seem to know everyone, he'd maintained a degree of a relationship with them, too. 'Does she know we were on the moors with Ashworth?'

'She knows something might have happened – but not what, when, or where. *We* didn't know that until yesterday.'

That was true. It sometimes felt as if Guy knew everyone who'd ever had anything of a passing connection to Whitecliff.

That was why they were standing outside a pair of twelve-foot metal gates, with a wide driveway on the other side.

They were on the outskirts of Whitecliff, up on the hill near the big houses and the bigger redevelopments. This was where rich people had holiday homes, or even richer people bought a place for the value of the land. The previous summer, Millie had spent a lot of time trying to figure out what was going on in a squat a little down the hill. It was barely two minutes' drive away.

Guy pressed a buzzer next to the gate and then they waited under the watching gaze of the camera on a pole above. Thirty seconds passed. Forty. Guy checked his watch and then glanced back towards his car. He wasn't the sort to allow himself to be messed around – and it was Millie who'd been keen on visiting in the first place.

They tended to come as a duo nowadays – but requests for help, or tips about stories, usually came through Guy's news website. He'd forward her emails and ask her opinion. It was rare they disagreed – but this particular request was something she had found far more interesting than him.

Mainly because of the person involved.

Guy had taken a half step away when the box buzzed and the gate clinked open. They'd barely crossed the threshold when Millie stopped to take in the sight beyond. Life-sized plastic pink flamingos dotted the pristine lawn and there was a rainbow slide looping over a pond. Fake swans were drifting on the water, with a horse-sized unicorn in the far corner. A child's drawing of a garden was somehow an *actual* garden.

'Whenever I think I've seen everything...' Guy said.

Millie laughed as they headed along the long drive to the house itself. It was not quite as massive as Millie would have guessed, given the size of the garden. There was a big double front door in the middle, with a couple of windows on either side. Perhaps five or six bedrooms – which was still big but not up there with some of the mansions on the same street.

The doors opened as they approached and a woman a few years younger than Millie emerged. She was as recognisable as ever, even if her features were a little *too* tight. Her forehead a little *too* smooth.

She headed to Guy, stretching out her hand. 'You must be Glen,' she said.

'Guy,' he replied, shaking her hand.

If her forehead was capable of creasing, it would have. 'Right, yeah, sorry... I'm Zoe.' She glanced sideways to Millie. 'Is this your wife, or...?'

'Colleague,' Guy said. 'This is Millie. We've worked together for a while now.'

'Right... I thought it'd only be you. It's just... this is... sort of... um... a private matter.'

'Millie's as discreet as me,' Guy said. 'But if you're unsure, we can happily leave you to it...?'

Zoe baulked at the suggestion. 'No, it's fine. If Molly wants to—'

'Millie,' Guy corrected. 'With an "I".'

'Sorry... I've always been awful with names. No offence.'

They stood awkwardly for a moment, before Zoe apparently remembered that she was the one who'd asked them to come.

'Is it right you went to school with Dad?' she asked.

'A long time ago,' Guy replied. 'He was a couple of years younger than me but we got to know each other in our twenties. He worked behind the bar at The Pig And Duck, so we'd get chatting quite a bit.' A pause. 'That was before he met your mum. We kept in contact after he moved on – especially when it turned out his daughter was so talented...'

Zoe flipped her hair over her shoulder as she beamed at the compliment. 'Did he say that to you?'

'Repeatedly. He was always sending me photos of your various talent shows – and that was before mobiles. He'd drop them into the newspaper office and ask if we'd print them. He used to call me up to say there was an event on the coming weekend and ask if I wanted to cover it. You won't remember but I went to the odd few.'

Zoe gasped with what seemed like actual surprise. She touched her heart. 'I didn't know that. You're so sweet.'

It could've sounded sarcastic, especially with the hand on chest. Millie would have usually been sceptical but, perhaps because of who Zoe was, it felt real.

'I was sorry to hear what happened with your dad,' Guy added. 'I did send my regards.'

Zoe glanced off towards the unicorn, her head dipping a little. 'I couldn't reply to everyone,' she said, sadly.

'I understand. I didn't write because I expected a reply.'

'Do you want to come in?' Zoe asked. 'I can put the kettle on...?'

She didn't sound quite sure but led them inside anyway. They barely got through the doors as Millie stopped to take in the wonder of the hallway.

If she had been a few years younger, the hall would have been Millie's fantasy bedroom. Huge posters dominated the space, along with framed records and a shelf with a slim silver statue.

'Is that a BRIT Award?' Millie asked.

She realised she was reaching for it before she stopped herself.

'It's a replica,' Zoe replied. 'We won best band but the record company kept the actual award and gave us all copies. You can pick it up if you want. It's heavy.'

Millie couldn't stop herself. She lifted the award from the shelf and almost dropped it immediately. She struggled it up to chest height and, for a second, only a second, Millie pictured herself on a stage somewhere, accepting it.

This really was a fantasy.

Millie knew better than to offer it to Guy, so she returned it to the shelf. She took a few moments to take in the photos of Zoe in action. Girlstar had been big in the mid-2000s. The sort of band that had been everywhere for two or three years – and then disappeared almost as quickly as they'd arrived.

That sort of music hadn't quite been Millie's thing when she was in her early and mid-twenties – but she *had* been interested in Zoe, mainly because she was from Whitecliff. In the way every small community latched onto someone local with even the smallest amount of fame, the papers and news shows had been full of whatever Zoe was up to. It had been everywhere to the point that Millie could picture the short silver dress Zoe had been wearing on the evening Girlstar had won the BRIT award. That was close to twenty years before.

Millie shuddered at how long had passed.

'I didn't know you'd moved back,' Millie found herself saying.

Zoe was standing next to a huge framed photo of the band

picking up the award Millie had been holding. Or the original award.

'A few years ago,' she said. 'Dad kept trying to get me to invest in property. He reckoned it was the only thing that never went down in price.' She nodded to Guy. 'He asked you about places around here and you put us onto the seller. That's why I had your card.'

Millie hadn't known any of that – and Guy blinked in surprise at the chain of events. Not that it was uncommon. The six degrees of separation theory was more like two degrees at most with him.

'Dad said I could trust you if anything ever came up. I found that card and then googled you. That's how I got onto your website.'

'That was very nice of your father to say...'

'He was always talking about Whitecliff. About home. How he wanted to get back here one day. He wanted me to buy him one of those colourful houses on the hill. D'you know the ones?'

Millie and Guy both did. Whitecliff was at the bottom of a dip and, on the way out on one side, a string of B&Bs and restaurants were flanked by a row of terraced houses that alternated red, white and blue window frames. It was one of the things that ended up on postcards, or the tourist board's Instagram account.

Zoe had been lost in the memory for a moment, before remembering why they were there. She nodded towards the wide, spiralling staircase. 'It's up here.'

It was as Guy and Millie followed that Millie realised the house wasn't in as good shape as she first thought. There were scratches on the banister and a couple of the railings were missing. The carpet at the top was patchy and a vase in the window sat broken into two pieces.

At the top of the stairs, they continued along a wide hall, until Zoe stopped outside a plain wooden door.

'This is my room,' she said, as she rested one hand on the door. It was unclear what she wanted to happen, as if she was making a big announcement. Either way, it got no reaction from either Millie or Guy.

Inside and there had been an explosion of pink. The walls were pink, the bedding was pink, even the carpet was pink. As if they'd somehow walked into a candyfloss factory. Perhaps that was why Zoe had mentioned it was her bedroom?

A four-poster bed sat in the middle of the room, while, on the other side, rows of dolls stared creepily down from shelves.

As they moved further inside, Millie began to feel her arms itching. It was as oppressive as it was disturbing. If the farmhouse the day before was the set of a zombie movie, this was somewhere the evil dolls would come to.

Luckily, Zoe directed them towards the opposite wall, where there was a large, blank space with vague, faded lines in the shape of a rectangle.

'There,' she said. 'That's why I emailed you.'

Millie peered closer, wondering what she was missing.

'What are we looking at?' Guy asked.

'That's where the print was,' Zoe replied. 'It was framed on the wall and now it's gone. That's why I contacted you.'

Millie was struggling to hide her confusion.

Even Guy, who was usually unflappable, had a bewildered stare about him. 'Are you saying something was stolen?' he asked.

'Exactly.'

'It's just... if something was taken, we're not the right people. You should talk to the police. You never mentioned a theft in your email.'

Zoe was shaking her head. 'I looked at your site. Dad always said you knew loads of people, which is why I thought you could help. I can't tell the police. You know what they're like. It'll be straight in the papers.'

Millie had no idea what was going on as Zoe dug her phone out of a back pocket, flipped through the screen and passed it to Guy.

He blinked. Coughed. Blinked again. He was rarely, if ever, rattled – and Millie had never seen anything quite like it as he let out a quiet 'Oh…'

She was almost laughing as he handed her the phone, except…

'Oh…' Millie found herself saying.

She looked from the phone to the wall to the phone to the wall.

'Oh,' she repeated, as she handed back the phone.

Nobody spoke for a few seconds.

'It was stolen…?' Millie added, mainly because no one else seemed capable of words. Guy looked as if he needed a sit-down.

'Two days ago,' Zoe said. 'I was at an event and the kids were at Mum's. I went out and it was on the wall, got back and it was gone.' She stopped as she swiped away from the photo on her phone and then locked the screen. 'You can see why I can't involve the police…?'

That part was clear enough. Millie found herself staring at the space on the wall once again. The space where, two days before, a life-sized print of Zoe had been hanging.

A life-sized print of a very *naked* Zoe had been hanging.

EIGHT

It was hard to look at Zoe in quite the same way. She was in loose jogging bottoms and a matching top – but Millie had now seen far more of her than she'd ever wanted to see.

'I got the original picture blown up by a specialist my agent knows,' Zoe said, unprompted. 'He sorted out a lot of the pictures in the hall, too.'

Millie was struggling to understand why anyone wanted a naked photo of themselves on their own bedroom wall – let alone something life-sized. All those small faults that could be seen in the mirror would be bigger and bolder. Something that could be ignored would be impossible.

Zoe was still talking: 'If I go to the police, someone will leak it and I don't want to end up in the papers again. I had enough of all that. When the boys were young, the paps used to follow us to their nursery. I thought for ages one of my friends was selling stories about me – but I had my phone hacked. I didn't know until a lawyer said there was evidence. I wanted to go to court but the paper paid about sixty grand...' She breathed the thought away, before adding: 'That paid for the boys' school.'

Millie had known almost none of what Zoe had said. She

vaguely remembered the phone hacking cases and celebrities being named as victims. She hadn't thought much about it at the time.

Guy was back in the room. 'It must've been heavy,' he said, nodding to the empty wall. 'The frame, I mean.'

Zoe was nodding along. 'Harvey got it up on the wall when we moved in. My ex. The photos were all his idea...'

That came with a gentle eye roll, although it didn't feel quite true. If he was Zoe's *ex*, she didn't have to keep the photos up after they had split up.

Guy was already ahead of her: 'Could he...?'

A shake of the head. 'He's in Bali for *Celebrity Love Island*.'

Millie didn't follow celebrity news but some things were absorbed through a sort of osmosis. Stories were everywhere to the point that it was impossible to avoid – and Millie knew Zoe was divorced. She vaguely remembered something about her marrying a dancer, or something like that. She assumed that was Harvey, but maybe there was another bloke at some point? Perhaps Zoe's boys had a different dad, or...?

It felt rude to ask.

'How do you nick something that big?' Zoe asked, talking more to herself. 'That's what I said when I noticed.'

'Have you got security cameras?' Guy asked.

'They've not been working for ages. Nobody ever comes up here, so I didn't think it was worth getting someone out to do them. I've been busy anyway. I was on tour at the start of the year and I suppose I just... forgot.'

Millie remembered the camera on a pole at the gate. She'd assumed it had been filming them, as would most people. The presence was probably enough – and Zoe was right about one thing. Very few people visited this area of Whitecliff. There was no through road and, apart from the unadvertised, unmarketed, view over Whitecliff Bay itself, no reason to drive in this direction.

'I was hoping you could do your thing...?'

Zoe was talking to Guy, with the gentlest hint of a girlish flirtation. It was almost laughable, and borderline creepy, considering he was twice her age. Millie suspected Zoe was used to this sort of thing working.

After the momentary shock of seeing Zoe naked, Guy was back to his unflappable self. 'Were there any broken windows? Any spare key that's missing?'

Zoe's eyebrows almost dipped with confusion, as they fought against whatever had been injected above them. 'Nothing was broken – but the front door was unlocked,' she said. 'I suppose I don't tend to, er... lock up. Don't like carrying keys.' She waved towards the front of the house. 'I figured the gates would be good enough.'

At first, it sounded absurd – except it was still true that nobody had much of a reason to visit this part of town. Not only that, if Zoe was at some sort of event relating to her work, the idea of a pop star spending an evening looking after a set of keys did sound odd. Millie suddenly found herself wondering what famous people did at places like awards dinners when it came to holding onto keys, phones, credit cards, and the like. The very famous would presumably have someone to handle all that for them. But what about the others? Did TV actresses stitch a key pocket to the inside of their dresses? At least the men had pockets on their suits.

'What about your neighbours?' Guy asked, which brought Millie back into the room. 'Did you ask whether they have any cameras?'

'I didn't want to involve anyone else. The only people who know are me, my sister, Mum, and now you two. Oh – and the cleaner. She was in the next morning. I don't know my neighbours anyway – but if I went round and said I was looking for footage because of a theft, it would freak them out.'

There was a mini stand-off. Millie wasn't sure she could add anything and Guy had his thinking face on.

'You're overestimating what we can do,' he said. 'We're not police, or private investigators. We don't have access to traffic cameras or number plate recognition archives. We can't take fingerprints, or anything like that...'

'I'm pretty sure I know who took it,' Zoe said. As if she'd been waiting for the big reveal. 'I had a guy refitting the kitchen last month. He knew who I was and all that. He's the only person who's been in the house recently that's not family.'

'Did he see the bedroom?' Guy asked.

'No. Well... maybe. I wasn't watching him the whole time. Who knows?' Zoe reached into a back pocket and then offered Guy a business card. 'This is his. I dug it out. Thought you might want to talk to him and say you know what he did. That sort of thing...?'

The mood had shifted, although Zoe didn't appear to notice. Guy was outwardly a kindly old man – but there was steel underneath and he didn't like being taken for a fool.

'That's not what we do,' he replied firmly. He took a step towards the door. 'I'm a reporter. I report things and it feels like you want the opposite. I tell stories and you want something covered up.'

Guy was in the door frame, having seen and asked enough.

'Oh...' Zoe replied. The mood shift was impossible for her to miss any longer and she'd slumped slightly. 'It's just... I don't have anyone else to ask. I don't know what to do.'

Millie could feel Guy watching her and, probably for the first time since they'd started working together, she felt a tug of resistance against him. Despite the worlds between them, Zoe and Millie were of a similar enough age and from the same place.

'Has anyone been in contact?' Millie asked. 'Maybe it's

some sort of blackmail thing and they want you to pay to get it back...?'

Zoe stared at her, as if the thought had never occurred. 'I've got eighteen-thousand unread emails,' she said. 'Someone posted my address on a fan forum a while back. There might be something in there. Then I'm in so many WhatsApp groups that I don't use that anymore. It never ends.'

She retrieved her phone from her other back pocket and started swiping and scrolling. A few seconds passed before she looked up.

'I don't *think* anyone's been in contact. My mum wasn't surprised. She's always saying I need to sort myself out. Dad used to manage me and it's not been the same since he, well... *died.*' She whispered the final word, as if saying it quietly might make it less true. 'We were on tour at the start of the year,' she added. 'Did you see us?'

Millie stared blankly for a second. 'No.'

'Oh... I guess you weren't the only one.' She laughed humourlessly at her own joke. 'It was supposed to be a bit of a comeback but it wasn't what we thought. Mum says I should get a new agent. She thinks there's a load of them lining up but...'

The way she tailed off made it sound like a play for sympathy or help. Millie could feel the attempt at manipulation – she had an eight-year-old, after all – but she also realised she didn't really mind. Zoe was a few years younger than Millie and would have been in her late teens or early twenties when she got famous. Millie hadn't known fame herself – but she'd known infamy. After her parents died, leaving Millie to inherit everything, she'd had those sideways looks in a town that ran on rumours. That was after her affair with the local MP had been exposed.

The two women looked at each other and, for Millie at least, it felt as if there was an acknowledgement there. Some sort of kinship.

'Did you say your name was Millie?' Zoe asked.

'Yes.'

'Millie Westlake?'

'Yes.'

There was a hint of an attempted frown. 'Your dad was that newsreader guy? The one who killed himself?'

'Yes.'

'And your mum, too?'

'Something like that.'

'It was an overdose, wasn't it? Vicodin?'

They stood looking to each other for a moment and it was only as Guy shifted his weight that Millie remembered he was in the doorway.

'I read about what happened to you,' Zoe added. 'I thought it was awful that people were saying you killed your mum and dad. I thought about reaching out. The papers were always writing stuff about me back in the day. They reckoned I was pregnant with some footballer's baby – and it was someone I'd never met. I wanted to ask how you were but didn't know how to contact you. Then I guess I forgot...'

It felt like the truth, even though it might have been more gentle manipulation. Millie wasn't sure she cared.

Guy moved again in the doorway, keen to get away. Wanting to get back to what he'd consider a real story.

'I'll help you,' Millie said. 'I'll talk to your kitchen bloke and see what he has to say.'

Zoe touched her chest, flashing a set of sparkling silver nails that Millie had failed to spot before. 'You're so kind,' she said. 'I don't know how I'll ever thank you.'

Millie finally allowed herself to look in Guy's direction. He was watching her with something that might have been gentle amusement. It was hard to tell for sure, though Millie was certain of one thing. Regardless of what he thought, she was going to do her best to help Zoe.

NINE

Guy and Millie didn't speak of Zoe as they left her house. Millie resisted the urge to ask him what he thought, or whether he approved of her decision to help. A large part of her *wanted* his blessing, even though it felt slightly childish. She wasn't sure she liked the part of herself that still craved the approval of others.

They drove away and regrouped outside a different house, in an area of Whitecliff that couldn't have been more at odds with the mansions on the hill. Beyond the promenade and the shops, the lights and the chippies, there were rows of red-brick terraces, built when there was industry in Whitecliff and a factory that needed workers.

As Millie rounded her car, Guy was pointing towards one of the houses at the end of the row.

'That's where I grew up,' he said. 'Number eleven. I was born in an upstairs bedroom because we didn't have a car and Mum was only in labour for about forty minutes. She reckoned she'd never heard of a baby so keen to get out.'

Millie laughed as she stared off towards the house. The entire terrace looked more or less the same as the others, with flaking, chipped windowsills and dark front doors. Some had wreaths on their front doors, others had stringed tinsel in the windows, or glimpses of trees in living rooms. There was a narrow pavement and then nose-to-tail parked cars wedged together like Lego bricks.

'How long 'til you get a blue plaque?' Millie asked.

'You have to be dead for twenty years, so hopefully no time soon.' There was a twinkle in Guy's eye. 'Besides, you actually have to *do* something to get one of those.'

'When was the last time you were inside?' Millie asked.

Guy puffed out a long breath. 'Close to fifty years. It went up for sale a while back and I looked at the listing and the photos. You wouldn't know it was the same place. We didn't have central heating when I was growing up – and the toilet was outside.'

Millie grinned. 'And I bet you walked ten miles to school, uphill in *both* directions.'

That got a laugh and it felt as if any tension that might have existed at Zoe's had lifted.

Guy turned and nodded towards number thirty, on the other side of the street. 'Wesley's mother lives there,' he said.

The levity of the moment disappeared as if it had never been there. Wesley and Shaun were the two boys who'd gone missing when they were supposed to be heading to a football match with Kevin Ashworth. Millie didn't remember their last names but she'd never forget their first. They felt inexorably linked: always Wesley and Shaun, never the other way around. She could never hear one name without thinking of the other. The pair had been ingrained into the memory of anyone who lived in Whitecliff at the time.

'Is it just his mum?' Millie asked.

'His dad died a few years back and Wesley was an only child. I don't know if she has a new partner, or...' Guy tailed off and then answered Millie's other question without her having to ask. 'Shaun's mum and dad moved away and died a few years ago. As far as I know, Victoria is the only remaining direct relative for either of the boys.'

On the moor, there had been talk about 'victim's families' and Millie had assumed there was a long line of brothers, sisters, and parents wanting the truth. There might well still be uncles, aunties, nephews, nieces and cousins out there but, of everyone directly involved, there was seemingly only one person left.

'Does she know we're coming?' Millie asked.

A nod. 'I spoke to her before I ever agreed to do anything with Kevin. I wouldn't have gone near those moors if she'd said no. I told her last night we hadn't found Wesley's remains. Said I'd visit today to update her.'

Millie was watching the house, wondering if there'd be a twitch of the curtain. It was such a mood shift from Zoe's place, with the award and the photos.

'You don't have to come in if you don't want,' Guy added. 'It'll be hard. She's been through a lot.'

'Will she mind if I'm there?'

Guy shook his head. 'I did tell her I was working with someone. She's a kind soul. She'll welcome you the same as she welcomes anyone.'

It wasn't a surprise that Guy was proven correct almost instantly. The woman who opened the door had long, greying hair with the gentlest hint that it once used to be chestnut. She smiled and pulled in Guy for a hug, saying that it had been too long, before asking after Barry. Guy introduced Millie and there was recognition in the other woman's eyes.

'I used to love your dad on the telly,' she said. 'It's awful what happened to him and your mum. You poor thing. I never believed any of the rubbish people said about you.'

Millie was momentarily speechless, mainly because – even though she was often recognised – people rarely brought up her parents' deaths in anything other than a negative way. The directness was unexpected, yet welcome.

She mumbled a 'thank you' and then they were ushered into a living room that had been frozen in time. There was floral wallpaper and a speckled white border, with rows of pictures dominating one corner.

There was no need to get closer for Millie to recognise the boy in a school uniform who was featured in the pictures. She had worn the same grey trousers and dark blazer when she'd been at primary school. There were photos of Wesley on the pier and him on a bicycle on the terraced street outside. The pictures were old and faded, yet the frames and glass were free of dust and grime.

Wesley suddenly felt very close. Not simply one of two boys who disappeared – but someone that could've been in her class. Someone who lived a house or two down.

Millie realised she was staring at the shrine and was about to apologise when Victoria asked if they wanted tea. 'The kettle's just boiled,' she added.

Millie rarely drank tea but it felt rude to decline.

Victoria disappeared through to the kitchen, humming to herself, which left Millie and Guy alone in the living room. They didn't speak, because there was nothing to say. Millie was feeling the weight of the room and the house. The fact that a boy had once lived in this house. He'd left to go to a football match – and that was the last anyone had ever seen of him.

It was impossible not to picture Eric as Millie continued to eye the photos. He was the same age Wesley and Shaun had been when they'd disappeared. Millie suddenly had the urge to call the school and double-check Eric was actually there. The yearning she had for him to live with her all the time instead of his dad never left, not really, but it burned stronger as she stood in Victoria's living room.

She *had* to get custody. It wouldn't be easy, but it was

unfathomable he could continue to grow up with Rachel acting as his mum.

It felt like a blink but must've been longer. Victoria was back with mugs of milky tea. She talked about how a box of Yorkshire teabags were two-for-one at the Big Tesco that week, so she'd stocked up. 'You can never have enough, can you?' she said. She talked about how someone had started doing a milk round again 'like the old days', and how she got her milk from there, rather than the supermarket.

Anything that wasn't the reason for their visit.

Guy went along with it all as Millie desperately tried to stop herself staring at the corner. They talked about everything but, really, they talked about nothing. And then there was nothing else left to say, except for the thing nobody wanted to.

'I wish it was better news,' Guy said.

They were sitting by this point. Victoria in a battered armchair, with a hole in the material by her head; Guy and Millie on the sofa that sagged at the back.

'We found a makeshift coffin,' he added. 'It was buried on the moors, in the middle of nowhere. Ashworth led us there. He knew where he was going and said where to dig. I say "coffin" but it was more like a box.' He held up his hands, indicating the size, and it seemed so small.

'What do you mean?' Victoria asked.

'I'm not sure. Nobody is, yet. It looked like there might have been bones inside – and a skull – but it was hard to know. If they *were* bones, they didn't belong to an eight-year-old.' A pause. 'I'm sorry.'

Victoria accepted the explanation with a gulp and a nod. She licked her lips but her eyes said more than words. She was looking at Guy but not really. It was almost like she was asleep.

'Tell me everything,' she said, quietly.

And so Guy did. He explained how they'd parked in a lay-by, next to a stile. How the prison van had turned up not long after – and then their procession of police officers, prison officers, professional shovelers, plus Guy and Millie themselves, had walked out onto the moor. He called him 'Ashworth', not 'Kevin', and told how they'd followed his directions until they were close to some sort of big stone.

Victoria listened as she sipped her tea.

When the story was over, she pressed back in her chair. 'You said there were bones...?'

'I can't say for sure,' Guy replied, 'but if I had to guess, I'd say it was the remains of a baby.'

A pause. A long pause. Millie tried to think of something to say but the room suddenly felt so bleak.

'Does that mean he killed someone else?' Victoria asked.

'Maybe. He wouldn't say. The police are doing tests but there's no reason for them to tell me. We might never know.'

There was more quiet. More sipping of tea.

'He got football from his dad,' Victoria said after a while. It took Millie a moment to realise she was talking about Wesley. 'His dad was a big Leyton Orient fan because *his* dad had been. I was like, "You can't make him support Leyton Orient" – but his dad took him to a game and Wesley was hooked after that. His mates were all into Man United and Liverpool. The big teams. But Wesley was only ever bothered about Orient and whatever division they were in.'

She paused to sip her tea and flash a glance towards the picture shrine in the corner.

'His dad would take him all around. They'd be off to Plymouth one week, then up to Darlington the next. They'd leave at five in the morning and get back at ten at night. Orient would've lost but Wesley was already talking about the next week and the next trip. And that was just watching.' She prodded a thumb towards the street. 'He'd be over the fields with his mates and a ball. Or booting it up against the house at the end. We'd have the neighbours over, saying it was *thud-thud-thud* for hours. It was always football with him.'

Millie shuddered, thinking of Eric. She'd dropped him off with Alex that morning and assumed he'd got to school OK. He'd be there. She knew that... but she wished she *really* knew that.

'His dad took it bad,' Victoria added. 'Jonathan wasn't one to talk much. But he figured he was the one who got Wesley into football – if it wasn't for that, he'd have never been in a car with Ashworth. I kept telling him it wasn't his fault. Wasn't anyone's fault but Ashworth's. He wouldn't have it, though. He'd disappear some weekends and I'd assume he was up on the moors, walking around. Maybe looking for Wesley.' She nodded at Guy. 'When he got his diagnosis, I told you he wasn't going to fight. I think it was a relief to him, more than anything. A way out. He wanted to be ill.'

They drifted into silence again and the bleakness settled. Millie wondered how many times Victoria had told people about the day Wesley disappeared. About who her son truly was. She didn't know if Victoria was saying this for her benefit, or simply to get it out.

'Ashworth had taken Wesley to matches before,' Victoria continued. 'That's the thing I could never understand. It's not like this was some one-off. He'd been giving lifts to the boys all year, and the one before. Two or three lads at a time. Sometimes Wesley, sometimes not. I've never been able to stop wondering what was different *that* day. Why then? Why not the week before, or the one before that? Why our Wesley and Shaun? Was it something about *them*? Something about that week?'

Millie had no idea how to reply, or whether it was expected. It had somehow never occurred to her that Ashworth had been taking boys to football matches for a long time before anything happened. It was the same when she used to have dance classes. They'd sometimes visit other rec centres or dance studios, and parents and teachers would end up driving two or three girls in each car.

And that made things all the odder. Victoria wasn't only stuck with the question of what had happened to her son, she'd spent so many years with no idea of why it had been that particular journey.

The poor woman.

'His son's ill, you know...'

Victoria had spoken again but Millie had almost missed it among her own thoughts. Guy seemed surprised, too. He sat up straighter. 'Whose son?'

'Ashworth's. He's in the hospice out by the rugby pitches on the way out of town. He's got leukaemia.'

It was rare that someone seemed to know something before Guy. Even when they did, he was one of those people whose expression remained blank.

Not now.

He gripped his knees and pressed forward. 'Kevin's son has leukaemia?'

Millie didn't miss that Guy had slipped and said 'Kevin', instead of 'Ashworth'.

Victoria didn't appear to notice. 'A friend of a friend works at the prison,' she replied. 'It's not like I'm checking up on Ashworth. Not really. I never asked, or ask. But it's a small town. People talk.'

Guy was unlike Millie had ever seen him. He fidgeted in the seat, pulled up his trouser legs a centimetre or two, then pushed them down again.

'*Nicholas* has leukaemia?'

'I figured you already knew. You seem to be ahead of me on everything. Ahead of everyone. I found out about a month ago.' She stopped and sighed. 'I always felt sorry for him. It's not his fault who his dad is. I heard he was back in town ages ago and wondered if I'd ever see him around. I thought about what I might say, or what he might.'

She stopped for a second, as if she was there in the moment.

'I think, for a long time, I *wanted* to run into him. Every time I was in Tesco, or wherever, I'd picture walking around the aisle and seeing Nicholas there. I think he changed his name but someone told me he looks like his dad. I guess you can't change some things...'

It had already been a day of connection for Millie. She'd felt a small part of Zoe's frustration when it came to media coverage and, now, she knew precisely what Victoria was talking about.

When Millie's affair had been exposed and her life had fallen apart, she would walk the supermarket aisles, her hood up, and fantasise about the phantom conversations she'd have with anyone who dared challenge her. Things got worse after her parents died and the accusations went around town about what Millie's role could have been.

'We stopped at the farm on our way back.'

Guy was speaking again, bringing Millie back into the room.

'I always told you that's where Wesley's buried,' Victoria replied. 'He's somewhere up there. I've always known.'

'Didn't the police search everywhere?'

Millie realised she was the one who'd spoken. It was close to the first thing she'd said since Victoria had come back into the room. She was the third person and very aware of it.

Not that Victoria seemed to mind. She nodded along. 'They dug around the farm and in the barn. They had someone up there with those thermal camera things but never found our Wesley.' She looked to Guy. 'The police never tell me anything. Whenever I see your name on the phone, I think it's finally happened. They've finally found him.'

'I'd like to think they'd tell you before me.'

That got a shrug. 'When they found that body near the

train tracks a few years back, the first I heard was when someone from the *Mirror* knocked on the door. It wasn't Wesley but they thought it might be. When the *Crimewatch* thing got repeated, nobody told me. When they did that top ten cold cases programme on Channel 5, the first I heard was when next door came round and asked if I'd seen it.'

She was getting louder, the sadness becoming fury and then... it slipped once more. Victoria breathed. Pressed back into her seat. Breathed again.

'I drive past the farm every now and then. All those signs have been up forever about trespassing and all that. I've pulled in at the gates and sat in the car. I can't make myself go past but I can feel it when I'm there. Wesley. I know he's somewhere there.'

Millie knew what was coming a moment before it did.

'Would you go with me?' Victoria asked the question and looked to Guy, then Millie. She wouldn't turn away. 'Sometimes I think that, if I'm up there, I'll be able to feel him calling.'

Millie shivered.

'I've never been able to go past the gates by myself but I think, now, maybe...'

Millie could feel Guy watching but it was Victoria's stare that held her. She couldn't move and definitely couldn't look away.

'How about tomorrow morning?' Guy said and, mercifully, his words dragged Victoria's stare away. 'It gets dark so early,' Guy added. 'If we went up today, it wouldn't be long before the sun started setting. There are no street lights. We wouldn't be able to see.'

Victoria's attention was now with the corner of the room and the photos of her son. It took her a short while to reply but then: 'Tomorrow,' she said. 'We'll go tomorrow.'

TEN

Millie leaned on the kitchen counter, waiting for the kettle to boil. A part of her wanted to be back on the moors, on the farm, with Victoria. She wanted to believe that, somehow, Wesley's mother *would* hear her son calling to her.

She knew it couldn't happen like that. Except...

Eric was safe.

She'd called the school under the guise of checking when the next teacher training day would be. After getting an answer, she had asked casually if Eric had been on time that morning – and was told that he had.

She'd thought about going to visit Zoe's kitchen fitter and asking about the giant naked picture that was missing, except that felt so trivial after the visit with Victoria. Not only that, she did have a real job, even if, sometimes, like now, her heart wasn't in it.

The kettle boiled and Millie filled the Pot Noodle cup, before giving the soupy mess a swirl with a fork. Her mum had hated this sort of food, which was largely why Millie chose to eat such things now. In her mother's kitchen, with her mother's cutlery. It was even her mother's kettle.

Millie started eating as she drifted to the back of the house and the shed she had converted into a dog grooming station. As well as the hose and shampoos, there were the treat jars, some chew toys, various blankets and mats, plus a wobble board and some hurdles that she used for agility training. She always left the area clean and there wasn't much to set up.

When the doorbell sounded, she assumed her client was early. Millie hurried back through the house, storing her half-eaten food in a cupboard, before wiping her hands on a tea towel and answering the door.

It wasn't the client with the dog, it was Millie's friend, Nicola.

'Oh!' Nicola said. 'You're home. I was in the area and wondered if you fancied a catch-up...?'

It was obviously a bit put on. Nicola lived on the other side of town from Millie and wouldn't have simply been in the area. Not only that, the lights would have given away that someone was home.

Millie didn't really mind. They'd been friends since they were children and, despite years apart, had come back together a few months previous. Everything about them was hung on a Big Lie – and that meant the small lies, like this, were a part of what they did to each other. In the moment, the friendship felt worth it to Millie.

Before Millie could say anything, there was a grunt of an engine and then a Jeep rumbled onto the driveway. A woman bustled out of the driver's seat and then opened the back door to reveal a fawn pug, with a black face and a lolloping tongue.

She lifted up the dog from the seat and then crossed to where Millie and Nicola were standing. 'Lucky was so excited when I told him he was coming here,' the woman told Millie. 'I didn't tell him about getting a B-A-T-H but he loves the T-R-E-A-T-S.'

Millie lifted the dog from the owner's arms and cradled the

chunky little potato under her arm as Lucky started sniffing Millie's boob.

The woman was a repeat customer but would have had no idea who Nicola was. That didn't stop her talking to both women. 'We've got a family photo shoot for Christmas in the morning,' she said. 'It's up at the Marriott on the ring road. You book a slot and they take you around the gardens. Lucky's got to look his best. He's the guest of honour.'

Lucky was definitely more interested in Millie's boob than the idea of any photo shoot. He was also quite the chunk for a little fella. Millie passed him from one arm to the other. She said she'd have Lucky looking his best, made a bit of small talk about the Christmas lights in town, and then headed into the house with the dog and Nicola. As soon as the front door was closed, she plopped the pup onto the floor.

'You are quite the little pudding,' she said.

'Me?' Nicola replied.

Lucky had put on a spurt of speed and darted through Millie's legs towards the kitchen. She caught him as he was busy licking the floor next to the oven.

'*This* little pudding,' Millie replied, as she picked up the pug again. She carried him through to the back of the house, Nicola a couple of paces behind.

As soon as Lucky saw the hose in the shed, he started wriggling. Except he then saw the treat jar, and began lurching towards that. Torn between not wanting to get wet, but definitely wanting the beef liver, an uneasy truce was formed between woman and hungry beast.

Lucky sat on the step as Millie set the water running to get it warm.

'Can I ask you something?' Nicola said. She didn't wait for a reply. 'I want to go speed dating. I've tried Tinder but it's all kids on there. Someone called me a "GILF". I'd heard of a MILF but it apparently means Grandmother I'd Like To—'

Millie laughed: '*Grandmother?!*'

'I know. The cheeky sod. I'm not even forty. That's what I mean. All the guys on there are either fifty, desperate, and divorced; obvious cheaters; or eighteen- and nineteen-year-olds who think I'm ancient.'

Millie didn't point out that *she* herself was divorced, and that Nicola was sounding a little desperate.

'I didn't realise you were moving on so quickly,' she replied.

It had only been a few months since Nicola and her husband, Charlie, had separated.

'It's not *that* quick,' Nicola replied. 'It's not like I'm looking to get married again. Just to meet someone fun.'

Lucky was shuffling his pudgy bum on the step, eyeing the treats, as Millie gently lathered shampoo into his back.

'So... are you up for it?' Nicola asked.

Millie was trying to think of the most diplomatic way to say she would rather lose a toe than go speed dating. The number of people who gave her sideways stares had started to diminish in the two-and-a-half years since her parents had died – but she still got recognised. The last thing she wanted was to sit in the back room of a pub somewhere, playing musical chairs with a bunch of thirty-something losers. And she included herself in that description.

'I don't think so. I've got a lot on at the moment.'

'With Guy?' Nicola replied, failing to hide – probably deliberately – the bemusement in her tone.

'Yeah...'

Millie got it. She was almost forty and Guy was in his late sixties. It *was* strange to an outsider, even if they knew he was her godparent. She couldn't quite explain it herself. Things happened around him – and Millie enjoyed the thrill. It gave her a purpose after her divorce, her parents' deaths, and the respective fallouts.

Nicola was leaning on the wall of the shed and said nothing.

In the meantime, Lucky was turning in a circle, trying to avoid the soapy water being rubbed into his belly.

'I met Zoe from Girlstar today,' Millie said.

It took Nicola a moment to cotton onto what had been said. 'Zoe? Are you joking?'

'No. She lives just out of town.'

Nicola's mouth was hanging open. 'Are you...? You said...? I mean...?' Nicola stopped and composed herself. 'I went to the reunion tour in February. Me and a girl from work drove to Manchester for the Friday gig – and then we saw them again in Nottingham the next night.'

That was before she and Millie had reconciled, and Millie had the sense that she'd have probably been roped into going to those gigs had they been friends at the time. She hadn't had that sort of thing in her life any time recently.

Nicola was still talking: 'I still can't believe they got the original line-up back together. You remember when they all fell out? They reckoned Jonny the road manager got Leanne pregnant – but she was already engaged to someone different called Jonny? Then Chrissie started seeing the Jonny that Leanne had cheated on and...' She tailed off, realising Millie wasn't following. 'Anyway, we had a couple of good nights. The arenas were half-empty, though. They tarped off all the seats at the top and let everyone stay downstairs.' Nicola paused, breathless, then added: 'What was Zoe like? Everyone reckoned she was the quiet one.'

In the time Nicola had been talking, Millie had moved Lucky from the wet stage to the towel fight stage. She rubbed the pup's belly as he squirmed, gnawed and nipped playfully at her fingers. Once the worst of the water had been wiped away, Millie fed him a treat and then plugged in the blow-dryer.

'She seemed nice enough,' Millie replied.

'Why did you see her?'

'I can't really say...'

Nicola's eyes narrowed. She knew Millie didn't tend to talk about the stories she covered with Guy – certainly not while they were in the middle of something.

'Do you reckon you might be able to take me along to meet her?' Nicola asked. 'I'll be normal. Honest...'

In Millie's experience, anyone who was going to act normally in a situation didn't need to pre-announce it. She couldn't stop herself from giggling at the absurdity of it all.

'I don't know,' she said.

'Can you ask? We waited at the stage door in Nottingham but it was really cold and no one was coming out. We ended up having to get in a taxi and asking the driver to turn the heat up. I thought I was going to lose a finger.'

Millie smiled again. 'I'll ask. If she says yes, maybe keep the finger story to yourself. Sounds a bit... *stalkery*.'

She meant it as a joke and Nicola grinned along. 'I wonder if she goes out in town?'

'*We* don't go out in town. Everyone in the pub looks about thirteen nowadays.'

Nicola *hrmmmed* in agreement, before Millie started the dryer. Lucky leant into the warm air as Millie ran a comb through his fur. It was good to work with a small dog for a change and it wasn't long until Millie was feeding Lucky another treat.

Once the dryer had stopped, Nicola started talking again. 'I heard Isaac and Eric had a good night looking at the lights,' she said.

Millie didn't need to ask how Nicola knew. Jack was her friend originally – but he and Nicola had seemingly started messaging back and forth at some point since the summer. Millie was never quite sure if she minded. She told herself she didn't but there was a part of her that bristled every time she realised they'd shared something either *about* her, or *aside* from her.

She said something about the lights getting bigger every year. The usual sort of small talk. And then they were off and into the realm of *actual* small talk. Nicola asked if Millie had seen the state of the main Whitecliff Christmas tree. Then they talked about the weather, the market, the road being dug up... and all the usual things people spoke of when they didn't have much to say.

Millie helped Lucky through a simple agility course, then gave him a final brush down before his owner arrived to pick him up. It had been a small job but the owner was delighted with the results as she jammed the poor little thing up into her nose and sniffed him. 'He's so *clean*!'

After she'd gone, Millie and Nicola settled in the kitchen, where Millie remembered she'd left a partially eaten Pot Noodle on the side. She reheated that and then they sat and talked about nothing and everything. Millie wanted to be alone but she wanted that friendly voice, too. They talked in circles about old times and old Christmases. They gossiped about Alex and Rachel's upcoming wedding, the sheer audacity of them booking it for Christmas Eve, and how tacky it would all be. Millie didn't particularly believe it but sometimes slagging off someone behind their back gave a pleasure like no other. That was the truth, whether or not people wanted to admit it to themselves. Everyone secretly enjoyed sticking the boot into friends and foes alike.

Millie didn't want to talk about the big stuff. About what happened with her parents and how she desperately wanted custody of Eric. How it hurt to say goodbye to her son every time she had to. Nicola didn't want to talk about her big stuff, either. Her divorce. The Big Lie they both pretended wasn't between them.

It was hard to know if this was what friendship was. People would say that friends were honest with friends – but perhaps that was a lie in itself? Perhaps friends were friends precisely because they allowed themselves to believe each other's lies?

And so they talked and they laughed.

And they pretended everything was fine.

And Millie tried to stop seeing Eric's face every time she thought of Victoria's missing son.

ELEVEN

DAY THREE

Millie could hardly allow herself to look at Victoria. She knew they were awful feelings to have but seeing the stricken woman left Millie with a sinking sense of vulnerability.

She'd driven past the school that morning, watching the kids head inside. She'd looked for Eric, of course. Rachel had dropped him off and then zipped away in her urban tractor of a 4x4 before Eric had reached the gates. He'd waved to someone Millie couldn't see and then disappeared into the school without looking back.

Millie had been over the road, half hiding behind a grubby white van, having parked three streets away. It felt like a moment of madness as she drove away. It *was* madness. She'd spent most of the time trying to think of a cover story in case Rachel spotted her. It was a good job she wasn't seen, because she hadn't come up with much that felt plausible. She *was* picking up Eric from school that evening and wondered if she could get away with claiming some sort of mix-up.

After that, Millie had driven up and out of town. She stopped at the large gates to the farm where Kevin Ashworth had grown up, and she'd waited. Guy had arrived not long after, with his labradoodle, Barry, in tow – and then Victoria herself.

As soon as Victoria had clambered out of her car, Millie had to turn away. The haunted, desperate look of the other woman made Millie shiver in a way that was nothing to do with the wind.

Guy pressed himself into the bush at the side of the gate, flattening out a wide enough space that Victoria could step around without impaling herself on a branch. Millie followed and the three of them crept slowly towards the rotting corpse of a building. Barry charged ahead, nose to the ground, tail wagging ferociously.

'I came out here not long after it happened,' Victoria said. 'Maybe a week or so after the police ended their search. There were already signs up by then, telling people to keep out. I know I said I hadn't gone past the gates – but I did that one time.'

Victoria reached for Guy's gloved hand and he took it and squeezed. Millie was a pace behind and only realised Victoria was offering her other hand when it was a moment too late. Victoria lowered her arm and then slipped away from Guy before leading them towards the farmhouse.

'I stood here,' she said, from a spot around ten metres away from the front door. 'I thought about breaking in. There was a door then and glass in the windows. It looked more like a proper house. I thought the police couldn't have looked properly, else they would've found our Wesley. But I couldn't go in. I felt sure he was inside but didn't want to be the one to find him...'

Millie felt Guy twitch at her side. He wanted to say that Wesley *wasn't* in the house. Of everywhere around the farm, it was the place the police had looked the most. Floorboards had been taken up and walls had been pulled apart. Dogs would've gone in. Those thermal scanning things.

Barry was off towards the side of the house, looking back expectantly for permission to continue on.

Victoria took a step towards the house and then stopped and waited for Millie and Guy to get closer. It was another winter's day on the moors. The cloud was low, the wind fierce. Tiny stones skittled around the floor and Millie focused on them. On anything that wasn't Victoria.

Barry was sitting on the cold ground, eyes wide and hopeful. All it took was a gentle permissive flick of Guy's hand and the dog was bounding off towards the rusting, broken tractor.

'I'm not one of those mothers who carries on believing,' Victoria said. 'I knew Wesley was gone. Shaun's mum always thought they'd reappear somehow. As if Ashworth had hidden them somewhere and they'd stroll back through our doors one day. We were opposites like that. Jonathan and Shaun's dad would go down the Legion and spend their nights there. They'd try not to talk or think about it. Shaun's mum always hoped for the best, but I... I knew.'

Millie turned her back and pretended she was looking at the barn. She wanted to get away because Wesley was Eric but there was no way she could say that.

'Shaun's parents moved away after about a year,' Victoria said. 'We didn't have any contact for a while. I didn't know they'd died until you told me.'

Millie allowed herself to turn back towards Guy, who had his arms folded. He seemed so old in the moment. A man soon to enter his seventh decade, huddling from the wind.

'When Jonathan got his diagnosis, I knew he wouldn't get through it. I know people can't really fight cancer. People talk about it like it's a battle, as if you have any say. I know that's not true. The doctors catch it early, or they don't. It takes you, or it doesn't. But Jonathan really *did* give in to it. He wanted it to all be over – and then it was.'

They stood for a few moments, vaguely eyeing the battered,

collapsing farmhouse. For a while, Millie thought Victoria was going to suggest looking inside but, instead, she headed off along the path that skirted the side.

Barry darted ahead, nose still to the ground. Guy called his name and he stopped near the collapsed wire fence that separated the farm from the moor.

Victoria paused at the corner of the farmhouse and twisted one way, then the other.

'He isn't here,' she said quietly.

Millie almost asked who she was talking about – but just about stopped herself. She meant her missing, presumed dead, son wasn't there.

Victoria continued a few paces and then stopped to stare across the same moors that Millie and Guy had looked over two days before. The browny-green furry moss of the moors had a reddish tinge, while the trees in the distance were skeletal. Their dark trunks were silhouetted against the wispish white of the mist beyond.

'Was it you who told me about the land?' Victoria asked. She turned to Guy, who frowned a silent reply. 'Ashworth's family didn't just own the farm,' she added, before waving an arm in the general direction of the trees. 'The plot stretches for a mile or two in each direction but the land is pretty much useless. There's no access because it's all marshland and there are some low-lying ponds that way. Back when it happened, I'd ask the police why they couldn't just search the whole area. I used to think it would be easy to just walk around but then... look at it.'

Millie followed Victoria's gaze off towards the trees. The moors seemed to go on forever and it all looked the same. Ashworth had led them to that box but it would never have been found otherwise. Even a square mile of plot would take a team of people weeks to thoroughly search. Multiply that many times over and it would be an impossible job.

'I went to a psychic two or three years after it happened,' Victoria continued. 'She had this little booth in town, over the road from the pier, and said he was nearby. I asked how near and she said she could sense him. I kept asking where she was talking about but we went in circles. She'd say he was close and I'd ask where. Then she said he was dead but that she might be able to talk to him. I thought about it...' She held out both her arms, palms up, and breathed in the air. There was a sense that she was summoning something. As if the clouds might open and a beam of sunlight would stream down upon her.

Nothing happened.

Victoria lowered her arms and turned slowly, head bowed. She'd moved on from the psychic story. 'I don't know why I came...'

As if she'd called him, Barry trotted across to Victoria and gently butted her leg with his head. She crouched and nuzzled his fur until Guy edged across and helped her up.

'Do you want to head back...?' he asked. 'I can drive if you want and then we can come back for my car later...?'

Victoria said she was fine, even though she suddenly seemed rattled. She had spoken so freely and honestly, yet – as she shrugged off Guy and hurried back towards the vehicles – the grief had overwhelmed her.

Guy, Millie and Barry followed to the lay-by but Victoria was already fumbling with her keys as they caught her. She kept repeating that she shouldn't have come and wouldn't accept Guy's offer of driving her back to town. Before they could intervene any further, she'd started her engine and was reversing onto the mercifully empty road without looking.

Seconds later and she was gone.

'Do you think she'll be all right?' Millie asked.

'I hope so.'

'What do you think happened?'

Guy took a few moments to reply. 'I think... maybe she

really *did* think she'd feel something up here.' He took a breath and then added: 'Perhaps I shouldn't have told her what was happening with Kevin and the search. I thought it was for the best but...'

Millie blinked and saw Eric on the inside of her eyelids. That poor woman had been left without answers for decades – and she was still waiting.

'Was she right about the Ashworths owning all this land?' Millie asked.

'Probably. There are private property signs all over the moors. I come up with Barry sometimes and there are stone walls and stiles – but you rarely see anyone. In fact, aside from other walkers, I don't think I've *ever* seen anyone. I couldn't tell you who owns what. If you trace it back far enough, you'd probably find out the Crown owns most of it.'

It felt like an end of sorts. Ashworth had dragged them up to the moors for a reason that might never be revealed.

Millie stared past Guy, out towards the vastness of the land. It was barely a year ago she'd entertained the chance there was a big cat roaming the woods and the moors. It still felt like a possibility, as if this stretch was an entirely different world. There were no obvious power lines, or telegraph poles. No sewers or plumbing. There was so much open space. So much... nothing. There could be a secret government bunker in the middle and nobody would know. An alien crash site left in the open for decades, across which nobody had stumbled.

'I always wondered about the car,' Guy said.

'Huh?'

'When Kevin disappeared with the boys, they were in a car. At the time, everyone was focused on finding the boys. There's an obvious reason for that – but nobody ever talked about the car. If you think about it, it wouldn't be *that* difficult to hide two eight-year-olds away. But where would you hide an entire car? It never seemed to occur to anyone then but if they'd spent more time looking for the car, perhaps that would have led to the boys...?'

'Maybe he took it to a scrapyard?' Millie replied.

Guy waited until Millie turned to look at him and then he gave a gentle shrug.

'Maybe.'

TWELVE

Millie felt watched as she stepped onto the cul-de-sac. It seemed like the sort of place where retired blokes with too much time on their hands would spend their mornings calling up radio phone-ins to shout about bike lanes. Where a woman who'd never been on a boat in her life would have stringent views on fishing rights in the Channel.

If Millie was unsure she had the right address, then the large white van in the driveway was something of a giveaway. 'Luke Who's Caulking' was stencilled in big black letters on the side, above a phone number and a website address.

Despite her initial thoughts, it was a younger man who opened the door of the house next to the van. He was roughly her age with dark hair and the sort of *just-got-out-of-bed* stubble that needed some serious manscaping. He blinked at her and then broke into a curious smile.

'I thought you were gonna be Dennis from next door,' he said.

'Do I look like a Dennis?'

He laughed: 'I don't reckon you could pull off a flat cap the way he does.'

'You've not seen the cover of December's Flat Cap Monthly, have you?'

Another laugh: 'True. I guess my subscription is late this month.'

He glanced sideways, towards the hedge and, presumably, the house on the other side.

'Are you Luke?' Millie asked.

He nodded at the van. 'What gave me away? Dennis is always going on about me parking my van on the drive and blocking his light. That's why I thought you'd be him. Anyway, whatever you're selling, I'm not interested.'

Luke started to close the door, so Millie spoke quickly. 'I'm here about the job you did at Zoe Miller's house.'

That stopped the door moving as Luke's features slipped into a frown. 'Is there a problem? I checked everything before I left...'

'Sort of,' Millie said. 'It's kind of... *delicate.*' She nodded towards the hedge, where Luke had looked before, wondering if there was someone on the other side. 'Can I come in?'

Luke considered it for a moment. The friendly start to the conversation felt as if it had involved somebody else. For a couple of seconds, it seemed as if he was going to say no – but then he nudged the front door wider and stepped inside.

Millie followed him along a hall into a kitchen that was so surprising, she was temporarily speechless. She wasn't a connoisseur of in-home décor – but she knew what she liked. There was a large, sparkling chrome oven, with a matching microwave built into the cupboard space above. The doors and handles were a satisfying blend of speckled black and white, with an elegant array of glimmering appliances on the thick granite tops. It looked like something from an advert.

'Did you fit this yourself...?' Millie regretted speaking the moment the words were out. Luke was over by the gleaming sink, with a half-smile on his face.

'I wouldn't be much of a kitchen fitter if I hadn't,' he replied.

Millie ran a hand across the worktop, without particularly meaning to. It was cool and smooth and she found herself wondering why she was so impressed. Everyday things like this never excited her... except maybe that was the point. The quality of the work wasn't something she saw every day.

Luke was still by the sink, watching Millie with something close to a curious smile. 'Is everything all right with Zoe's kitchen?'

Millie suddenly remembered why she was there. 'She's missing something.'

'Like... what? I checked it all.'

'Something was stolen from her house...'

Millie was trying to say it without saying it. She wanted to see if there was any sort of recognition in Luke's face. If he knew about the giant naked print, he'd surely not be able to conceal his knowledge?

All she saw was a look of curious bewilderment. 'Hang on,' he replied. 'She thinks I *nicked* something? She's sent you round to ask if I did?'

Millie wasn't sure how to reply. That was, essentially, it. After all, he had the giant van that would've fitted the frame inside – plus he had the sort of build that made it look like he could have carried it down the stairs.

'Who are you again?' Luke asked.

'Millie Westlake. I'm a friend of Zoe's.'

They eyed each other for a few moments. Millie was looking for any sense of recognition, worry, or even annoyance. All she saw was confusion – and then a shrug.

'Look, "Millie"' – he did the bunny ears thing – 'I don't need to go round nicking stuff. I finished a job yesterday and I start another tomorrow. I've got jobs lined up for three months minimum. If I wanted, I could've booked far past that. I've got clients and recommendations coming out of my arse. Whatever she's lost is nothing to do with me.'

Millie sucked in her cheeks and then couldn't hold it any longer. 'You've got clients coming... *out of your arse?*'

Luke had folded his arms in indignation but he broke almost instantly into a snort. 'OK, maybe not the best turn of phrase – but I'm not a thief and I don't need to steal from clients.'

Millie believed him. She probably had from the moment she'd seen his van. Whoever had come up with 'Luke Who's Caulking' didn't sound like the sort of person who was getting by with a bit of theft on the side.

'What's she missing?' Luke asked.

'I can't say.'

That got a shake of the head. 'Whatever. You wanna look around? Go for it.'

Millie assumed it wasn't a serious offer – but Luke waved a hand towards the floor above.

'Go ahead, look wherever you want. Check the van if you need to. If you're desperate enough to come here in person and make vague insinuations, it must be something important. If it'll make you feel better, if it'll make Zoe happy, look around.'

It wasn't particularly what Millie wanted to do, except there was that part of her she assumed everyone had. The part that enjoyed a good nosey around someone else's house.

'You could've stored it somewhere else,' she said.

That got a roll of the eyes. 'Do you really want to retrace everything I've done for the last week. Mum and Dad live on the other side of town, but I reckon Dad'll let you look in the shed if you ask. I was at the pub on Monday, so you can try there. I do a couple of runs to the tip every week, so there are a few skips you can check.' He shrugged again. 'What do you want from me?'

Millie realised she didn't know. She hadn't exactly approached him subtly. Visiting had been a distraction from the gloom of the moors and the way she kept thinking of Eric every time those missing boys came up.

'It's fine,' Millie said. 'I believe you but I needed to ask.'

Luke craned backwards to look through the window beyond the sink, towards his neighbour's house. 'I kinda wish it had been Dennis at the door. At least he doesn't accuse me of stealing.' A pause and then he tried again. 'What's missing?'

'I really can't say.'

'Is it something expensive? I saw her award near the front. Is it that?'

'It's not that – but I still can't say.'

Luke pouted a lip. He was interested now – who wouldn't be? 'I didn't know who she was when she booked the job,' he said. 'Turned up and there was all those pictures in the hall – plus the award. She asked if I remembered her, so I said I did. I googled her later and it turned out she was in that band that did that song.' He clicked his fingers, trying to trigger the memory. 'You know the one.'

Millie told him and he nodded his head.

'That's it. D'you remember the summer it came out? It was everywhere. I must've heard it a thousand times.'

'Had it on CD in the car, did you?'

Luke took the joke and laughed. 'Bought the single *and* album. Anyway, Zoe seemed fine to me. Kinda normal, considering. It was her sister who was the whack job.' He stopped. 'You're not friends with her sister, are you?'

'Never met her.'

'Sharon, I think her name was. She was there almost the whole time I was working. Kept trying to offer bits of advice. Asking if I'd thought of using nails instead of screws. She asked if I could install the sink without turning off the water. That sort of thing. I thought she lived there at first.'

Millie realised she didn't know Zoe's set-up at the house. She was used to working with Guy, where he'd know the right people and the right questions. Millie hadn't even checked who lived at the house – let alone who had access to Zoe's room. Zoe had spoken about her 'boys' and that she had an ex. She said her mum and sister knew the print had been stolen – but that was only part of it.

The sister had clearly stuck in Luke's mind. 'That Sharon kept trying to get me to do extra jobs,' he added. 'Wanted me to give her a lift to some salon, then asked if I could check a dripping shower at her flat. I thought she lived at the house until she said that. I told her I wasn't really a plumber. I can connect hoses and taps, that sort of thing, but she should get a professional in. That's when she said she'd have to *pay* a plumber and I realised she wanted me to do it for free. She said her sister was paying for the kitchen I was fitting, so I could tag it onto her bill. I asked Zoe, and she didn't know anything about it. They ended up having this row about it as I was standing there.'

She was now fairly sure it was nothing to do with Luke and took a step towards the kitchen door. 'I'm sorry for bothering you. I didn't mean to imply anything. Your kitchen's lovely, by the way.'

Two more steps and Millie had one foot in the hallway. She stopped as Luke said her name. 'Do you fancy a coffee, or something?' he asked.

When she turned back, he was standing next to an espresso machine that was gleaming in the same way everything else in the kitchen was. She wondered if he was a clean freak.

'I've got to get off,' Millie lied. 'I have to pick up my son from school – and then we're going to the Winter Wonderland with a friend...'

She didn't know why she'd told him so much.

Luke tilted his head a fraction. It was barely a movement but enough to let her know the schools wouldn't be kicking out for hours.

'How about another time?' he asked. 'We can go somewhere

that isn't here. Maybe a café, or somewhere else if coffee isn't your thing? Some place during the day, nice and open in case I choose to nick your purse...'

Luke grinned and Millie realised she was doing the same.

Millie wondered if he knew about her. He probably did. There weren't many Millies around – and her affair and subsequent divorce had been fairly public, especially in a town like Whitecliff. News travelled fast and wide – and rumours stretched further than that.

Did it matter?

Millie thought of Nicola and her speed dating, or being a GILF on Tinder. She didn't want that for herself – and yet she was almost forty and divorced. Did she want *anyone* in her life?

Was that even what he was asking?

As if to emphasise the point, and almost like he'd read her mind, he added: 'It's just coffee. Maybe a croissant? Or a muffin, if that's your thing? I know this farm shop where they do a Bakewell tart like you wouldn't believe.'

'Sounds like you have a sweet tooth...?'

He laughed. 'I reckon they'll heat you up a sausage roll if you ask.'

Millie's mum used to say that you could tell a lot of things about a person by their smile and, though she was wrong about a lot of things, Millie often thought she might be right about that. And, besides, it *was* just coffee and maybe a slice of Bakewell tart.

'Let me think about it,' Millie replied. 'I don't want to say "yes" but then change my mind. Or the other way around.'

'Fair enough.' He reached for his phone on the counter. 'Do you want my number, or...?'

'I reckon I can probably figure it out from the side of your van.'

'That does get me into trouble,' he said. 'I should probably have sorted out a separate number for work. Sometimes I'll be parked in town, then I'll have a bunch of lads texting me photos of their dicks.'

'Set yourself up on Instagram as a woman, and you get the same...'

Luke smiled and then didn't. 'Sorry, I didn't mean...'

'I know. I'll text you.'

He moved quickly towards her and Millie reacted a second too late, stepping further into the hall as she thought he was lunging. Instead, he stopped short and apologised, before handing across... her phone.

Millie eyed it curiously, wondering how he had it.

'You left it on the counter,' he said, nodding towards the place where she'd rubbed the surface for no apparent reason. Then a wink: 'I didn't nick it.'

Millie accepted her phone back and tapped the screen to check it was hers, still wondering how she'd forgotten it.

'I'll see you soon,' Luke said, as he led her towards the front door.

'Maybe,' Millie replied.

THIRTEEN

Guy picked up the landline phone at his cottage just as Millie was about to give up calling. She'd tried his mobile – but his house had little to no reception – and there had been no answer. No answer on his mobile *usually* meant he was at home, although that was no guarantee he'd answer the landline.

Millie asked if he'd heard anything from the police about Kevin Ashworth and the box they'd uncovered – but he said hers was the first call he'd had all day. He asked how things had gone with 'the kitchen fitter' and she replied that she had a lead – which was a stretch, to say the least. After that, there was the sound of something falling over in the background, an annoyed cry of 'Barry!' and then Guy said he had to go.

A little after lunchtime, a client arrived with her dog – and Millie spent ninety minutes doing her *actual* job, while thinking almost non-stop about Victoria and those moors.

By the time she got to the school for the second time that day, the sun was beginning to dip. It had been largely hidden by cloud anyway – and the street lights were starting to flicker.

It was rare that Millie picked up Eric from school, even when she was going to have him for the weekend. It always felt like some sort of power play in that Alex would make her wait until later in the evening to get him, when it was close to Eric's bedtime.

That meant there were a lot of sideways looks from the other parents as Millie waited a short distance from the school gates. It hadn't been *that* long ago that Millie had been the mother who'd meet her son every day. He was nearing the end of his first year at school when her affair had been exposed and Alex had thrown her out.

There had been those chaotic weeks in which she hadn't known where her life would go. She'd been back living with her parents, while Alex's mum was doing the school run. Millie had rarely been to these gates since – and yet, now Alex was on the brink of remarrying, suddenly he and Rachel had other things to do for the wedding.

Millie nodded to a couple of the mums and dads who'd noticed her. She then took out her phone and vaguely scrolled through articles she wasn't actually reading. She was used to ignoring glances and stares from people who weren't brave enough to actually say something.

Except, one of the mothers was.

Millie felt someone nearby and looked up to see a woman standing a couple of paces away. The woman gave a little wave. 'It's Andie,' she said. 'I'm Jennifer's mum. I don't know if you remember me but—'

'I remember.'

Jennifer was a girl who'd been in Eric's class when they'd started school and, presumably, she still was.

'We've missed you round here,' Andie said, nodding towards a small gathering of women a little further along the kerb. Millie remembered the faces but not the names.

'It's been a while,' Millie replied, not knowing what else to say.

The woman gulped, which gave an indication of what was

to come. 'I know everything that happened and all that. I know what people were saying about you and your mum and dad. I was hoping I'd run into you one day just to say that I never believed it. I saw you once at the petrol station but you were leaving as I was arriving and I didn't want to shout and...' She left it there, with a hint of a shrug. 'How's Eric doing?' she added. 'His stepmum doesn't wait with us. She's usually off in the car, so I don't think I've ever spoken to her.'

Millie needed a moment to think. It was nice to talk about her son in a way that didn't relate to custody, or her ex-husband – though she couldn't quite get on board with Rachel officially being Eric's stepmum.

'He's doing great,' Millie replied. 'His spelling's probably better than mine.'

Andie laughed. 'Have you tried the phonics stuff with their homework? I don't have a clue.'

'Same for me. It's so different to what we were taught. It feels like he's teaching me half the time.'

'That's exactly what we say!'

Andie half turned, to indicate the group of women once more. The invitation was implied and Millie felt the pull. The urge of normality and the life that she'd thrown away. When she didn't move, Andie seemed to understand.

'We have a WhatsApp group,' she said. 'It's just the mums... well, there's a couple of dads in there, too – but you know what I mean. I can maybe add you? We go out every now and then. Have a few drinks and compare notes. We share bits and pieces we've heard from our kids as well. It's all very friendly...'

There was something in Millie's stomach that felt like hunger but gnawed stronger than any food urges she'd ever had. Why had she made the decisions she had? Why couldn't she have put up with everything Alex had been pulling and kept going for Eric's sake? Why? Why? Why?

She *so* wanted to be part of the group. To see the awful drawings stuck to other people's fridges, or the spelling attempts that accidentally threw up naughty words. She wanted to know what the kids in Eric's class were up to – and those promised 'few drinks' was a glimmer of something she was gradually realising she missed.

Except...

No matter how friendly the group, there would always be someone in it looking out for some slip she might make. Someone ready to screenshot a reply and spread it without context.

Millie's solicitor for Eric's custody hearings had told her she had to be whiter than white if she ever wanted things to be reassessed. She couldn't risk it.

'Maybe another time,' Millie said, trying to hide her own regret. 'Thanks for the offer, though. It's really kind.

Andie nodded slowly along, perhaps understanding, perhaps not. It felt as if she was about to ask something else when there was the sound of a bell from behind. It wasn't long until the sound of screaming singed the air around them. Millie had forgotten how loud it was at home time. Kids didn't simply *leave* the school, they screamed their way out of it.

Millie and Andie said goodbye and make vague commitments to see each other soon. It likely wouldn't happen but Millie was grateful someone had spoken to her like the mother she was.

When Eric came through the school gates, he was with Chloe. He'd told Millie months before that they were best friends and, from what Millie could tell, they sat together at every opportunity. Chloe had the level-headed politeness of a well-raised youngster who wasn't afraid of adults. She said 'Hi, Mrs Westlake,' before heading off towards her own mum a little further along the pavement.

The street was bustling, with parents hurrying their children off towards cars. The lollipop man knew every child's name as he greeted them, before dipping his pole into the road and then striding into traffic with more confidence than Millie would ever have. A bright fluorescent yellow jacket and a large reflective pole wasn't enough to stop the drivers in this town ploughing into someone while they were busy looking at their phones.

Millie and Eric crossed as she told him she was parked near the charity shop. They were barely across the road when he asked if she'd remembered what she'd promised. Millie was instantly suspicious because he'd specifically said 'promise', which sounded very unlike something she'd actually say.

'What did I promise?' she asked.

'You *promised* we'd have McDonald's for tea the next time you picked me up from school,' he replied.

'I'm pretty sure I'd have remembered saying that.'

'You did, though.'

'When did I say that?'

'Ages ago.'

Millie almost laughed. Her son was nowhere near the master manipulator he sometimes seemed to think he was.

'Where were we?' she asked.

'Um... at your house.'

'Was there anyone else there?'

'Uncle Jack was there.'

'We're going to meet him now – so we can ask him.'

Eric went quiet at that. He hadn't known they were picking up Jack and Isaac after school. She could almost hear him thinking as they continued along the street. The noise of the cars had dimmed, leaving a gentle hum.

'What if he doesn't remember?' Eric said.

'Then I guess that means I never said it...?'

Eric was still considering that as they reached the car, probably wishing he'd gone for a different name, other than Jack.

Once they were in the vehicle, and he was in his child's seat, Millie set off. She asked about his day and he gave her the usual 'not much'. If she listened to him and only him, the entire curriculum involved 'not much'. Instead, he told a lengthy story about how one of the boys in his class was visiting Lapland for Christmas and that the boy was going to ride a reindeer and possibly help Santa with the wrapping. Millie let him speak, enjoying his voice, even as the story rambled away from fantasy into the outright absurd. Apparently, the boy was going to arrange for Santa to deliver whatever any of his classmates wanted. It sounded like it might cause problems for plenty of other parents when the promise was inevitably broken. It was probably the sort of thing someone should flag on a WhatsApp group. Millie realised somebody had probably already done exactly that – except she wasn't a part of it.

When they got to the flats, Jack and Isaac were already waiting in the car park. They were bundled up in hats and gloves and coats with so much padding, they could probably take a bullet if things really got out of hand.

Millie drove and the journey was much like it had been two days before, when they'd been at the Christmas lights. Jack talked about the gloomy afternoons and the dark mornings. How the shortest day was two days off and that it would start getting lighter after that. It was a mistake, of course, because that started the questions from Eric and mainly Isaac. Millie kept quiet, figuring Jack could learn the hard way about things it was sensible to say in front of children. His explanations about the earth's orbit not being circular, then the sun, then the moon, then tides, then leap years, all ended up being quite the mess for a four-year-old to understand. More than once he threw in a 'what do you think about that, Mill?' to which she replied that she was concentrating on the road.

By the time Jack started talking about days, hours, minutes and seconds, which got the inevitable 'Who invented time?' and then 'Why are there sixty minutes in an hour?' and 'Why are hours so long?' and 'How many hours old are you?' Millie was struggling not to laugh. One time she'd accidentally mentioned primary colours and then spent half an hour trying to answer Eric's questions of where colour came from, and who'd invented it. Kids were obsessed with someone inventing things.

They were soon at the point where Jack had somehow introduced Stephen Hawking into the conversation. He attempted an unfortunate impression that left more questions than answers, then had the brainwave of pointing to the large billboard they were passing on the way out of town.

'Are you going to the Bay Burning?' he asked, talking to Millie.

She decided to bail him out. 'I told Eric I'd take him,' she said. 'What about you?'

'I think it's a bit scary up close for the younger ones. I told Isaac we could watch from the pier.'

Millie rolled her eyes. Had Jack really learned so little about parenting? Nothing made a child more interested in something than calling it scary.

'Is it *really* scary up close?' Eric asked.

'Not for someone who's eight,' Millie replied, thinking on her feet.

'Can I go?' Isaac asked from the back, which was quickly followed by: 'What's burning?'

Millie could sense the panic in Jack's voice as he stumbled over a reply that would have definitely put his son off going, albeit at the expense of traumatising him for life.

'It's a tradition in the town,' Millie said, taking over. 'It's been happening for hundreds of years. Everyone goes up to the cliffs that overlook the town. People get to write down all the things they're worried about. There's a giant marionette – a puppet – and it gets filled with all those bits of paper that everyone's written on. Then it's set on fire and all the worries are burned away...'

Millie immediately wished she hadn't tried to explain. It sounded better in her head, mainly because she'd grown up with the tradition. For a long time, she'd assumed every town had their own version of the Bay Burning on the shortest day. She'd been in her twenties and on holiday when she'd casually mentioned it to a lad, who had looked at her as if she had three heads.

'It dates back to when the town was a fishing community,' Millie found herself saying.

Isaac was still thinking on the last thing. 'What's a marion— a maria— a—'

'It's like a really big puppet,' Millie replied, though instantly realised her mistake as he repeated the word 'puppet'.

'Like The Fraggles?' Isaac added. There was a definite quiver to his voice. 'Dad said The Fraggles are puppets.'

It took Millie a moment to remember that The Fraggles were Muppet-like things from when she'd been growing up. They must have been brought back recently.

'Are they going to burn The Fraggles?' Isaac added, definitely panicked. 'Dad?'

'No—' Millie replied, quickly.

'But you said—'

'Not puppets like that,' she tried, desperately trying to think of a better explanation. How could she explain the concept of a giant marionette to a four-year-old? 'It's more like a giant *man* made out of sticks.'

That wasn't doing it – and Eric was involved now.

'They burn a giant man?'

'No, I mean... well, no. You saw it two years ago, remember? We watched from the beach when I said you were too young.'

There was a hint of panic in Eric's reply: 'I didn't know it was a man!'

'It's *not* a man. It's a sort of an... er, puppet. But not a puppet. They're *not* burning Fraggles. I cannot stress that enough.'

Jack was remaining annoyingly quiet, which felt like payback. The problem with mentioning burning Fraggles in the first place was that it inevitably put the image of burning Fraggles into the mind of a four-year-old. And an eight-year-old for that matter.

By the time they reached the large Whitecliff Winter Wonderland sign, it was a merciful relief to get the kids onto the subject of something that wasn't childhood icons being set on fire.

A bored-looking teenager in a fluorescent heavy coat was busy flagging cars onto a muddy field. There, a second teenager, who somehow looked more bored than the first, was taking ten-pound notes from drivers. Finally, a third teenager was directing drivers into filthy puddles that could only be described as a 'parking space' in the loosest possible terms.

The sound of opening and closing car doors was accompanied by a chorus of grumbles about the cost of parking, plus various slurps of people trying to walk through the gloop. Luckily, Eric had a pair of wellies that lived permanently in Millie's car boot – but Isaac wasn't so fortunate. He was in a pair of trainers and almost lost a shoe instantly, which led to Jack carrying him.

They followed the stream of people towards a set of lights next to a wide metal gate and then slotted into a queue.

From somewhere in the field beyond, there was the faint sound of Slade, or Wizzard, or one of those seventies Christmas songs that never seemed to go out of fashion.

If the ten quid to park wasn't enough of a shock, the twenty-pound entry fee for adults and fifteen for kids was enough to make even an oil company's CEO think twice.

'I've seen fairer muggings,' Jack mumbled to Millie, making sure it wasn't loud enough for Isaac to hear. They'd only just got past explaining burning puppets to the children, who definitely weren't ready to learn about muggings quite yet.

Through the gates of the wonderland and there wasn't much wonder going on. The mud of the field had given way to paths covered in wood chips and sand that were lit by strings of white lights just above head height. Despite Millie and Jack's scepticism about how fundamentally rubbish it all was, the boys were instantly interested in more or less everything.

There were yet more teenagers dressed as elves dotted around the paths. Some were doing basic magic tricks with string or cups, others were doing the sort of little thirty-second dances that were usually accompanied by thumping dance music in annoying internet videos. The whole operation appeared to be a front for the mass employment of Whitecliff's teenagers. Whether it was the lad serving the seven-quid hot chocolates, or the girl scooping nine-pound portions of chips into cones, nobody looked as if they were older than eighteen at the absolute most.

The four of them ambled slowly around the packed paths, as the huge speakers occasionally stopped playing Mariah Carey to give three minutes over to a different Christmas song. Isaac wanted to see Santa – but they quickly realised the queue for that wrapped a third of the way around the site. Jack had clearly learned one important thing about parenting as he told his son they 'might' come back to that. The 'might' was, of course, adult code for 'not in a million years'.

Still, the boys somehow enjoyed it. They weren't put off by the tractor covered in tinsel, because what's more Christmassy than that? Both had their photos taken in the driver's seat, and then Eric insisted he wanted to be a tractor driver when he grew up. The pair also had pictures taken next to the inadvertent Leaning Christmas Tree of Whitecliff, which looked as if a good gust of wind might take it down.

The whole thing was unquestionably a scam and utter rubbish – except it was *so* rubbish that there was almost a charm to it. Like watching a bad movie that was *so* bad, it became a cult classic.

They had been on site for around forty-five minutes when they finished the loop and ended up back near the beginning. The queue for Santa had two hours written all over it, but they were already eighty quid down on parking and admission alone. When Millie asked what the boys wanted to do, Eric said could they go round again – so off they set.

Millie and Jack walked side by side; hands in jacket pockets, scarves tight. Eric and Isaac were a little in front; Eric always half a step ahead and Isaac keen to keep pace. Mariah Carey seemed to be on a perpetual loop.

'They could be brothers,' Jack said.

Millie watched for a few seconds and, if she hadn't known better, she would have assumed they *were* brothers. They had the same stumbling inquisitiveness about them.

'Eric's never really been friends with boys,' Millie replied. 'His best friend is Chloe and, before that, there was a girl at nursery called Helen that he used to cling on to.'

'What did Alex think of that...?'

'I don't think *he* minded – but his new *mum* thought it was unhealthy. She's a proper old-school type who thinks girls should play with dolls and boys should play with cars. She bought him this transforming plane thing for Christmas one year and I think he only got it out of the box once. She was saying how it was expensive and I told her you can't force someone to be interested in something they're not.'

Up the path, Eric had drifted across to a stall where a man was throwing basketballs at a hoop, trying to win a giant soft elephant for his son. The game was either rigged, or he was an appalling shot – because he got zero points in six attempts. As the final shot hit the back wall, he punched a wooden post, shouted that the ball wasn't round enough, and then stormed off towards the toilets, his son a few steps behind.

Eric and Isaac had been waiting for Millie and Jack to catch up. As soon as they did, Eric turned with expectant eyes. He didn't get a word out before Millie answered: 'I'm not throwing basketballs for you.'

'But—'

'There's a darts game on the other side. Maybe we can do that?'

That was enough of an explanation, and compromise, with the boys setting off up the trail once more.

'Isaac's gonna be tired when we finish,' Millie replied.

'I thought about bringing the buggy but—' Jack didn't finish the sentence. There was no need because he nodded across to a woman, who was wrestling to get a pushchair across the mix of sand and wet soil. Jack had already taken a few steps over to offer help when she wrenched it free and accidentally swung it in a semicircle, narrowly avoiding decapitating her own daughter.

Back on the path, Millie and Jack continued to walk around the site, making small talk about the usual things. She wanted to ask how he was *really* doing being a father. Before the adoption, he'd nearly broken up with his boyfriend over the issue – and now it seemed, at least on the surface, as if everything was fine. Millie was almost afraid to ask. Their friendship had drifted a little in recent months and she sometimes wondered if it was because *he* was worried she'd ask.

Up ahead, some of the elves were handing out snacks to the people waiting in line to see Santa. Eric approached one with his hand out and managed to get what looked like a single nacho chip with a small party sausage. He turned and handed the food to Isaac, before getting more for himself.

They walked a few more steps, heading towards the promised darts game, when time slowed. Isaac reached towards his face, froze with his hand halfway there, and then collapsed to the floor.

FOURTEEN

Millie was running but it felt as if she was stuck. Every step she took seemed to take her further away from Isaac. Jack was running, too. Somebody screamed. Somebody else dropped their phone, or a bag of chips, or... something. There was too much to take in.

Isaac was on the ground, one arm spread and lifeless; the other feebly reaching towards his face. He was gasping, eyes wide and pleading. Someone shouted 'he can't breathe' and it took Millie a moment to realise it was Jack. She was somehow next to the choking boy, not quite sure how she'd got there.

'What do we do?' Eric asked – and her son was wide-eyed at her side. Everything had happened so slowly and yet somehow all at the same time.

Millie was about to crouch and check the boy's airway – except somebody else got there first. There was a woman in a belted jacket on her knees at Isaac's side. She said, 'I'm a nurse' to Jack and then started hunting through a giant handbag that she'd dumped on the ground. There was a hairbrush and a purse; a Cadbury's Flake and a roll of raffle tickets. Millie didn't know what was going on – except the woman plucked out what looked like a syringe and slammed it into Isaac's thigh.

It happened so fast that Millie didn't have time to question what was going on. She looked to Jack, whose face was a mix of a horror and helplessness. He managed a 'What are you—?' before Isaac's gasps suddenly became deep, desperate breaths. His skin was a blue-purple as he inhaled long and loud. A crowd had gathered in a circle around them, blocking much of the light. The nurse bobbed on her heels and waved someone away, then shouted loudly for everyone to get back. She spoke with such authority that everyone did as they'd been told without another word.

Jack was hunched over his son, touching Isaac's forehead and asking if he was OK. The boy's panicked gaze had shrunk to a weary, confused set of rapid blinks as he nodded and tried to sit up.

'I didn't do anything,' Eric said to Millie. 'It wasn't me.' She had an arm around his shoulders, holding him to her hip.

'I know, love,' she replied.

The nurse was resting back on her heels now, batting a hand across her face. She was rosy-cheeked and pulled off her beanie hat to let her tangled hair loose. 'Is he allergic to peanuts?' she asked, talking to Jack.

Isaac was sitting up now, head resting on the nurse's knee. Jack seemed lost. He was blinking around the circle of people, looking to Millie, then to Isaac.

'This is your son, isn't it?' the nurse asked.

Jack blustered a yes and managed to say that his son was called Isaac.

'Does he have a nut allergy?' the woman asked again.

'I don't think so. I mean... maybe. We recently adopted him. He's never done this before. I think— I don't—'

The nurse momentarily rested a hand on Jack's shoulder, which seemed to calm him. Isaac was breathing normally, although still seemed somewhat out of it. She was talking to him, asking if he was OK, and if he could breathe. A man passed across a bottle of water and the nurse held it as Isaac sipped. Jack watched, not knowing what to say or do.

'He had an anaphylactic shock,' the nurse said. 'I used my son's EpiPen to help bring him round. If it wasn't for that...' She tailed off as she manoeuvred Isaac so that Jack was supporting him.

As she started to stand, she pointed off towards something on the edge of the circle of people. Millie only realised what it was when she spoke again.

'I noticed someone handing out peanuts earlier,' she said. 'There are shells all over the floor.'

She twisted until she found the man who was presumably her husband. He was clutching a small boy on his shoulder.

'Get him back to the car,' she said.

The man didn't need telling twice. He turned and edged through the crowd, before disappearing into the distance.

'I'm going to find out who's in charge,' the nurse said. She was on her feet now, a face of thunder. She took a step away and then turned back to Jack. 'You need to take him to A&E and make sure he's definitely all right. Then you need to get an appointment with your GP and get the allergy diagnosed. You can get your own EpiPens after that. Keep one on you at all times. Leave another in the car, and more around the house. If he's started school, make sure there's at least one in his classroom.'

She stopped herself, because Jack was taking in none of it. He was staring glassy-eyed towards Isaac in his arms.

'Are you here with anyone?' the nurse asked.

'Me,' Millie replied.

'Did you get all that? I need someone to remember all this – or the GP stuff at least.'

'I've got it,' Millie replied.

The circle of people had started to thin, the crowd drifting back to the various attractions. One of the elves was staring open-mouthed, with a handful of other couples and children watching while pretending they weren't.

The nurse knelt next to Isaac. She asked his name, even though she'd already been told, and he croaked the reply. He said his throat was sore and she smoothed his hair as she said she understood.

For a moment, Millie thought it was one of the carnival games but, from somewhere in the distance, there was the faintest sound of a siren. The nurse looked up and muttered that someone must've called for one.

'Probably for the best,' she added, before turning to Millie, probably assuming she was Jack's wife. 'Once you're home, you need to check everywhere for nuts. Make sure there's nothing in the cupboards, and no old tins of chocolate. That sort of thing. Check the Christmas presents and the selection boxes. Mince pies, Christmas puddings, anything like that. If it has nuts as a possible ingredient, you'll need to get rid of it.' She paused, looking between Millie and Jack. 'This is going to be your life now.'

It sounded ominous, and it was.

Eric was at Millie's side. He'd taken her hand at some point and was squeezing.

The sirens had stopped but there was movement in the crowd. Things had happened so slowly and yet... seemingly not. Paramedics had appeared as if from nowhere and were striding along the paths, the two of them weighed down by their equipment. The nurse was on her feet, beckoning across to the paramedics, as Millie realised for the first time that she didn't even know her name.

Millie whispered a quick 'you all right?' to Jack – but there was no answer.

She moved away after that, taking Eric with her and waiting

next to a burger stand, where the warmth of the grill within kept her teeth from chattering.

The paramedics did their thing. One of them focused on Isaac, checking his pulse and talking to him. The other spoke to Jack, as Millie realised he was probably in shock. He looked as if he'd just woken up, with blinking, sleepy eyes and a glazed, aimless stare. Isaac actually looked OK. He was on his feet, talking to the paramedic and perhaps counting to ten. It was hard to know from a distance.

A few minutes passed and then the paramedics turned to head back to the ambulance. The nurse had long since disappeared, presumably – and probably justifiably – to rip the organisers a new one.

Jack stumbled towards Millie and, when he looked at her, it didn't feel as if he was actually seeing her at all.

'They're taking us to the hospital,' he said.

'Shall I call Rish?'

A shake of the head. 'I'll do it. Sorry for, er...'

The sentence ended there as the blinking got the better of him. He rubbed his eyes and then turned and hurried back towards Isaac and the paramedics. Millie watched, still holding Eric's hand, unsure if they were supposed to be following. It was probably best to give them space.

She waited, feeling the prickling heat of the burger van on her cheeks, until Jack, Isaac and the paramedics were out of sight.

Eric squeezed her fingers and she took him in. He'd been very quiet.

'Will Isaac be all right?' Eric asked.

'I think so,' Millie replied.

Except, perhaps strangely, given what had happened, it was Jack whose haunted, vacant stare would stay with her the longest.

FIFTEEN

Millie waited on the doorstep as Eric headed past his dad into the house. The sound of the television echoed from a distant room as Alex leaned on the door frame, cradling a large wine glass between his thumb and index finger.

Usually, there would have been a straightforward drop and go when it came to Eric. Most of the time, Millie wouldn't have even got out of the car. The very fact she was waiting around was enough to let on that something was up.

'What happened?' Alex asked. He was looking at her curiously, as if it hadn't occurred to him something serious might have gone on.

Millie told him about Isaac collapsing. About the likely nut allergy and the miracle of the nurse being there. Then the paramedics taking Isaac and Jack off to the hospital – and her very quiet journey back with Eric.

'Keep an eye on him,' she said. 'It was really traumatic. He might have questions, or worries. I tried to get him to talk on the way back but he was very quiet. Maybe let the school know, just in case...?'

Alex nodded along, stopping only to swirl the wine around

his glass, before taking a sip. It didn't feel as if he'd been listening.

'Jack's got a *son*?' he said.

'I told you a while back. At least twice. That's not really the point...'

Alex was still nodding as Millie realised he was tipsy at the very least. Perhaps even full-on drunk.

'How was the Wonderland?' he asked. 'Was it Wonder... *ful?!*' Alex giggled to himself, as if he'd just killed it on *Live At The Apollo.*

'It was fine,' Millie replied. 'That's not why I stopped to talk to you. I—'

'I'm glad you did stop actually...'

Alex leaned in, perhaps trying to put a hand on her shoulder. He missed, pretended it hadn't happened and then pressed his hand to the opposite side of the door frame instead. Millie edged away, smelling the booze on his breath. Neither of them had ever been big or regular drinkers when they were together. They'd share the odd bottle of wine, or perhaps a couple of drinks at the pub, or at a restaurant. She could go weeks without any alcohol – and so could he. It felt so strange to see this man she once knew so well in such an unfamiliar state.

'Look,' he said, 'I've got something to ask you.'

'What?'

'I was wondering if you might, er... come to the reception...?'

He was avoiding her stare and focusing on somewhere close to his shoes. For a moment, Millie wondered *what* reception he meant... because he surely couldn't be talking about the one after *his* wedding.

'Are you joking?' she replied. 'You want your *ex-wife* at the reception after your second wedding?'

'It's for Eric. You know he's been a bit... *awkward* lately. We don't want him causing a scene...'

That at least made some sense, although Millie suspected he'd used the word 'we', instead of the name 'Rachel'.

'You mean he's been a bit awkward since you started trying to force him to call Rachel "Mum"...?'

Alex mumbled something Millie didn't catch. '...trying to make things simpler,' he added. 'I'm still trying to get him to call me "Dad" again.'

There was a pause as Millie knew he wanted her to give him an update. Instead, she stayed quiet.

'Have you asked him about that again?' Alex added after a couple of seconds.

Millie let her ex-husband squirm for a moment longer. He and Rachel had tried to get Eric to call Rachel 'Mum'. He didn't want to do it and, as some sort of retaliation, was calling Alex by his name, instead of "Dad". Rachel had accused Millie of putting him up to it, and perhaps still thought that.

'I said I would,' Millie replied. 'But I can't force him.'

Alex swirled the liquid around the glass and then finished it in one. The sound of the television from inside the house had gone off and there was a silence that Millie assumed had arrived because Rachel was listening in.

'We went back through the guest list and realised there aren't going to be many children at the reception,' Alex added, back on topic. 'That's why we wondered if you might...?'

'You want me to babysit for you. At your reception?'

'I wouldn't call it that. It's just... he'll have a better time if you're there.'

'So you're admitting he likes spending time with me?'

Alex squirmed. 'I never said differently.'

'Your solicitor did when we got onto custody. It's not as if he said anything you hadn't already approved.'

Alex scratched his head and mumbled something that might have been an apology. He swayed slightly as he tried to stand straighter.

'I'll think about it,' Millie said. It was like talking to Eric again, where that was barely concealed code for 'no'.

'We do need to know soon,' Alex replied. 'The wedding's in five days.'

As if Millie could forget they'd booked it for Christmas Eve. Talk about making things about yourself.

'I need to think about it. It's not like I'm going to have loads of friends there. Your family hate me – and I doubt Rachel's are much different.'

Millie waited for a moment and he didn't refute it.

'What does Rachel think?' she asked.

'It's her idea.'

'So why isn't *she* asking?'

That didn't get an answer, not that Millie expected one. On a good day, the relationship between Millie and Rachel was a frosty morning in the north of Scotland. On a bad day, it was North Pole in a blizzard. Their communication was carried out via a series of passing nods, or through Alex.

Millie was holding her phone and it started to buzz. She glanced at the screen and Guy's name was there. He was always more of a caller than a texter.

'I need to answer this,' Millie said.

Without waiting for a reply, she stepped away from the doorstep. Alex was talking behind her but she was almost back by the car as she pressed to answer.

'Can you come over?' Guy asked. 'I wouldn't usually ask, not this late, but it's urgent.'

Millie pictured the man she'd seen hanging around outside Guy's house and wondered if it was something to do with him. Guy didn't throw around words like 'urgent' very often. And yet, he'd called her not the police.

'I'll be right there,' Millie said.

'Good.'

The call had ended almost as soon as it had begun, which

was Guy's way when it came to these sorts of things. He could talk for hours if the situation required, otherwise it was short and to the point.

Millie looked back to Alex, who was still swaying in the door frame.

'I've got to go,' she called.

'Will you—?'

'I told you: I'll think about it.' Millie reopened the car door and then waited for a second. 'Keep an eye on Eric,' she added. 'And talk to the school.'

'OK.'

It didn't sound like the 'OK' of someone who'd been listening, or who was going to do any of those things. Not that Millie could do much about it.

She started the car and pulled away, heading across town to where Guy was apparently waiting.

Millie had taken the turn towards Guy's house when she suspected she was being followed. It was dark and there was a pair of headlights behind that had remained a steady distance back for at least a couple of miles. If she'd been in town, she wouldn't have noticed – but there wasn't a lot of traffic on the country lanes that linked Whitecliff to Guy's secluded cottage.

She turned off the double-lane road onto the single track that led up to Guy's place. There were no street lights on the approach, not much of anything except whispering, swishing trees on either side.

Millie slowed, mainly because there was little option. The track was unmarked and a patchy mix of gravelly compacted dirt. Small stones pinged and flicked as the vehicle behind continued to follow at a distance.

By the time Millie reached Guy's cottage, the car had fallen further back. It was out of sight but she could hear it idling somewhere further along the track. The white of its headlights was silhouetting the trees and extending into the distance.

Millie got out of her car quickly and raced along the path to Guy's cottage. She rang the bell and then knocked, before hearing the muffled call of 'come in' from the other side.

The cottage was, as so often, unlocked – so Millie let herself in, just as Guy was emerging from the far end of the hall. Both sides were stacked with towering, perilously heaped, piles of newspapers, leaving a narrow path along the centre.

'Someone followed me up here,' Millie said.

Guy was frozen for a second – but only that. He strode along the hall, edged around her, and then opened the front door. Millie hadn't noticed how cold it was before but ice flooded the hall as she shivered. Beyond, the headlights had disappeared, the woods were still, and there was only quiet.

They stood in the door for a few seconds, staring outside... but there was nothing.

'I am expecting visitors...' Guy said, as he closed the door.

That in itself was a surprise. There was an irony in that Guy appeared to know everyone – except Millie never saw anyone around the cottage. That was the other reason that appearance of the random man was so odd. Something was going on – but Millie had no time to ask what because Guy was off.

'I got a call,' he said. 'They *were* bones in that box on the moor. The police have examined them and they belonged to an infant boy. They said he was days old at the most, but it's hard to tell for sure because of decomposition. They're still running tests.'

It was a lot to take in, especially as Millie had been thinking about something else entirely until seconds before.

'Ashworth buried a baby up there...?' she asked.

'Maybe. They found out something else – the remains are from someone related to Kevin. They think it might be his son.'

Millie was open-mouthed, stunned. They'd gone from assuming they were on the moors to find the bodies of two missing eight-year-olds to discovering remains from Ashworth's own child. A second son nobody seemed to know he'd had.

'That's... a lot to take in,' Millie said.

There wasn't much chance for anything else because, beyond the door, there was the sound of footsteps. Guy opened it before the bell could sound and there, on the other side, stood Chief Superintendent Baker, along with an officer in a uniform.

Baker seemed confused by the door opening before he'd got there and it was only as he stood examining Guy's 'no soliciting' sign that Millie realised he must have been in the car behind her. In the distance, vaguely illuminated by the gloomy moonlight, a dark hatchback was sitting behind her car.

When Millie turned to look at him, he gave her an irritated glance. When he spoke, it was specifically to Guy.

'I thought I said the contents of the phone call were confidential.'

'And I told you almost a week ago that anything between you and I also involves Miss Westlake.'

Baker gritted his teeth and ground his jaw from side to side. The sort of thing Millie's dentist would tell her off for.

She wasn't sure how to feel. A part of her, probably the biggest part, was grateful that someone was standing up for her. Another part would have been happier not to know all these things. She told herself that Ashworth was behind bars and that Eric was safe.

There was a stand-off as Baker angled towards the cottage, wanting to be invited in. His breath swirled into the freezing air as the officer at his side rubbed her hands together.

Guy didn't move. 'I assumed it must be important if you're here in person...?'

Baker was bristling, not used to the lack of control.

'Can I guess?' Guy added. He didn't wait for the invitation.

'You asked Kevin about the remains and he won't talk to you. He wants to talk to me – and that's why you're here.'

The officer glanced sideways towards Baker – and Millie knew Guy was correct.

'Something like that,' Baker replied. His lips barely moved. 'Are you free tomorrow morning? Early. Eight a.m.'

Guy waited a beat and then turned to Millie. 'Are *you* free tomorrow morning?'

'I can be.'

Guy looked back to Baker and smiled. 'I guess we are.'

SIXTEEN

DAY FOUR

Millie had secured her phone, keys, bag, purse, hat, scarf and gloves in one of the lockers at the front of the prison. She felt a bit naked after all that – and had been scanned twice, before being given a mini talk by one of the security officers about what was allowed and what wasn't. Following that, she and Guy were taken to a private room, with a pair of sofas. If it wasn't for the security camera high in the corner, it could have been a badly designed micro living room. The walls were beige, there was a patchy rug on the floor – and that was it.

With the way rent was going, someone would probably be charging a grand a month for it before long.

Millie and Guy were waiting on one sofa, as Ashworth was led in by a prison guard. He was in what looked like plain grey pyjamas, with dark shoes. The clothes were massive on him, making it hard to tell how thin he was. There didn't seem to be much to him.

Ashworth was in handcuffs but the guard unlocked them and told him to sit.

It felt too informal. Millie had expected a big waiting room and Ashworth cuffed to the table. She'd thought there might be some massive guard to bellow 'no touching' if anyone moved. This was a Sunday chat at gran's house compared to that. If the officer had offered them tea and biscuits, she'd have only been half surprised.

Moments later and the door was closed, leaving the three of them alone – except for Baker and whoever else was watching the live video feed, of course.

Ashworth covered his mouth as he coughed gently. It was only then that Millie realised what was on his face. She'd not seen it in the gloom of the moors – but there was a bubbling, rippled swoosh of scar tissue across one cheek that looped under his mouth.

It was exactly the sort of thing she'd tell off Eric for doing – but Millie couldn't stop staring.

'Why will you only talk to me?' Guy asked.

It was something Millie wanted to know as well. She'd assumed Guy actually knew but was reluctant to say. It felt as if Baker thought the same thing.

'Someone's going to have to tell this story one day,' Ashworth replied. 'I want to make sure it's *my* story, not the one the police will tell.'

Guy thought on that for a second as Millie realised he hadn't actually answered the question. If it was Ashworth's goal to tell his story, it could have been any reporter. He hadn't said why Guy in particular.

He wasn't the sort to have missed the evasion – but Guy moved on anyway. 'When you say "one day", it makes it sound like that's not today...?'

Ashworth was quiet at that and it felt as if he wasn't going to say anything he didn't want to.

'Who was in the coffin?' Guy asked.

Ashworth had his knees curled underneath him and he was hugging his arms across his front. He was holding himself tight and staring towards a spot on the wall behind them.

'I don't understand why we're here,' Guy added. 'You took us to the moors. You obviously wanted us to find what was there. You called us back today... and you're still not talking. This is twice. They won't give you a third chance.'

Guy deliberately glanced up to the camera. Ashworth would've known everything was being recorded, though he seemingly didn't take the extra nudge.

Millie had little idea what was going on. It all felt so... pointless. If he had something to say, then say it.

'If you want your story told,' Guy added. 'We're right here.'

Ashworth shook his head a fraction. It was barely there and likely not caught on the camera.

'If not the coffin, what about the boys?' Guy asked. 'What about Wesley and Shaun? I saw Victoria the other day. She's still desperate to know what happened. All these years on and she wants to believe you'll do the right thing...'

That wasn't entirely true but Millie figured Guy knew the situation better than her.

This time, there was the mildest of nods – and Millie again doubted it had been caught on camera.

'Do you know about Nicholas?' Ashworth asked. His voice was croaky, as if he hadn't spoken much in a while.

'I know he moved back here,' Guy replied. 'That he changed his last name.'

That got a proper nod.

Ashworth released his arms from around himself and stretched his legs. 'Can't remember the last time I sat on a sofa,' he said, as he stretched again.

'Hardly a surprise that he changed his name...'

It took Millie a second to realise it was her voice that had spoken. She'd been thinking it and then the words had come out.

Guy stiffened at her side but only for a moment.

She felt Ashworth's gaze shift from the wall onto her.

Millie forced herself not to wilt under the stare. Made herself sit still and not shiver. His eyes were dark; brown or maybe even black. It felt as if he was trying to read her mind. She wondered if she'd blown whatever it was that was happening. That perhaps Ashworth would want to go back to his cell and Victoria would never get her answers.

Then he bowed his head a fraction. 'True,' Ashworth replied. 'Very true.'

Millie held his eye, not wanting to look away first.

'Do you have children?' he asked.

She pictured Eric. Had to force herself not to shiver again. 'I don't think you need to know that.'

Millie couldn't face him knowing Eric's name. She didn't want to hear him say it.

'I really wanted Nicholas to like football,' Ashworth said. 'I got into it because of my dad and it was this family thing growing up. Well, for the men, I suppose. I assumed Nicholas would like it too. That we'd go to games together, that I could coach his age group as he got older. All that.' A shrug. 'But it wasn't his thing. I'd try to have a kick around at the park but he didn't want to. He was always into engines, cars, that sort of thing. I don't know where he got it from. It wasn't me. When he turned eleven, Nicholas said he wanted to be a racing driver when he grew up. He was into rallying and he'd videotape it off the telly, then watch it back to try to remember the courses. He had pages of notes. He even built his own go-kart. He'd get parts from the scrap yard and would drive his mum and me crazy...' He tailed off and then: 'Pardon the pun.'

After that, he finally turned away from Millie as she realised she'd been holding her breath. She let out a low, long gasp.

'Will you visit him?' Ashworth was talking to Guy again, asking him the question. 'He's in the hospice. I can get you the

address. I'm not allowed any longer.' His eyes flashed to the
camera and away. 'I need you to pass on a message.'

Nicholas's leukaemia had been unspoken and, to a direct
extent, it still was.

Ashworth's question hung for a moment. It had come so
quickly that nobody knew what to say.

'What message?' Guy asked.

Ashworth risked another glance to the camera and then,
when he spoke again, his voice was barely there. Millie wasn't
sure if she heard it, or lip-read it. Just one sentence.

It was after he'd said it that Millie realised he hadn't wanted
Baker, or whoever else was watching, to hear it. She wondered
where the microphones were hidden and whether they caught
it anyway.

'I'll tell you everything after you've seen him,' Ashworth
said. He was speaking at a normal volume again, knowing what
he was doing.

'I can do that,' Guy said. 'Or I'll try.'

Ashworth eyed Guy for a few seconds, probably trying to
figure out if he meant it. And then, once convinced, he turned
to the camera and spoke to those on the other side. 'We're done,'
he announced.

Seconds later, there were bounding footsteps, then the loud,
thick door was opened. The same guard as before re-cuffed
Ashworth and led him out of the room. There was the sound of
more footsteps, more doors opening and closing – and then,
temporary silence.

'What happened to his face?' Millie asked.

Guy had been lost in thought. 'He was attacked by other
inmates. It was maybe a year ago? Something like that. I think it
was boiling water.'

Millie wished she'd never asked. She vaguely remembered
seeing something like that on a TV show in the distant past. It

was hard to separate Ashworth from what he'd done, impossible, and yet the way his skin drooped was awful to see.

Chief Superintendent Baker had appeared from nowhere. He filled the doorway, standing tall, with one of the prison guards not far behind.

'What did he ask you to tell his son?' Baker asked, talking to Guy.

'Not much.'

'What does that mean?'

'It means that if he wanted you to know, then he'd have asked you to do it.'

Guy pushed himself up from the sofa and, though he was shorter than Baker, there was less of a power imbalance now.

Millie also stood, although it felt unnoticed. She didn't like being the spare part.

'He killed two boys,' Baker said. 'Maybe three. Maybe more. You know that, don't you? He's held families hostage for more than twenty years – and you're here playing games.'

'I want what I assumed *you* want,' Guy replied. He was calm and unruffled. 'That's answers for the families.'

'He's messing us all around. This is all one big game to him. One final chance to make himself famous. That's the only reason we're not taking it to the *proper* media. The only reason we're trusting you to do the right thing.'

The 'proper' hadn't gone unnoticed. Millie saw the merest of flinches from Guy, although he didn't react more than that. 'It doesn't feel like a game,' Guy said. 'He led us straight to the coffin. He wanted us to find it.'

'He didn't say who was in it. He still hasn't.'

Guy made a motion to move, except Baker was still blocking the door.

'What did he ask you to do?' Baker repeated.

'It's not my place to say.'

Baker clamped his mouth closed and breathed heavily through his nose, before turning to Millie. 'What did he say?'

Millie almost laughed. She might have told him if he'd asked a minute before. If he'd asked her first. 'So now you know I exist,' she replied.

He glared at her and there was a time she would have wilted. Her father had that same long, direct stare. When she was younger, that stare could force her to tell the truth. She was scared of him as much as she was desperate to impress.

But that was then and she was a different person as an adult. Those sort of fiery glares did nothing except make her more determined to do her own thing.

'That man killed at least *two* boys and the pair of you are indulging his nonsense.'

Neither Guy nor Millie replied as Baker turned between them, presumably trying to get some sort of answer.

Eventually, he shook his head. 'I knew this was a waste of time!'

He turned and thundered along the corridor, before wrenching open a door at the other side.

'Waste of time!' he bellowed – and, quietly, without wanting to say that to Guy, Millie wondered if Baker was correct.

SEVENTEEN

They'd visited at the prison so early, that it was still before ten when Millie got to Zoe's house. She was buzzed through the gates and was getting out of her car when a small white Mini pulled up behind her. A woman with dark hair got out and started unpacking a crate of cleaning supplies from the boot.

She was heading to the front door when Millie asked if she'd been working on the day something had been stolen from the bedroom.

'I didn't take anything,' the woman replied quickly, while avoiding eye contact.

'Sorry... I didn't mean.' Millie stopped herself from digging any deeper. 'I'm helping Zoe. I was wondering if you saw anything?'

The cleaner lowered her head further. 'I don't know anything.'

'You know what's missing, though...?'

There was no proper reply but Millie could see from the other woman's gentle shrug that she knew all about the giant print from the bedroom. It wasn't the sort of thing someone would forget.

'I only do a few hours a week,' she replied.

'But were you here that day?'

A nod.

'Was there anyone else here that day?'

'No... I don't think so. Maybe Sharon. I'm sorry, I don't know anything.'

The cleaner hurried through the unlocked front door and left it open for Millie as she disappeared into the house. Millie didn't blame her – but there were times in which she felt exposed without Guy. He'd have known the cleaner's dad and, before anyone knew what was happening, it would have turned out he was at the woman's christening. They'd have had a lengthy conversation and the cleaner would have told Guy the names of everyone who was in the house on the day of the theft, plus the exact times they arrived and left.

Millie was about to head inside when there was the sound of the gates grinding at the far end of the drive. She stopped and watched as a small pink car accelerated along the tarmac and then screeched to a halt behind the cleaner's Mini. A woman in a pink tracksuit and matching slippers got out and stared at Millie. She had big hair and bright chunky jewellery. Her teeth were so bright, they reflected the sun like a child messing around with a watch in class. After a couple of seconds, she rounded the car and dragged two large shopping bags out of the back, before approaching Millie.

'Who are you?' she demanded.

Millie didn't need to ask who the woman was. Zoe's mother had the same eyes as her daughter – although it was likely the only part of her face that hadn't been altered. As well as the teeth, her brows were bloated with filler and her lips looked like someone had had a go at them with a bicycle pump.

'Zoe invited me over,' Millie replied.

The woman wrestled the bags higher. The name 'Wendy' was embroidered in gold sequins on the tracksuit. 'Oh, you're the super sleuth, are you? A right little Miss Marpole. Who's the other one? Inspector Cluedo?'

'I think it's—'

'Who did it then? Who's the perv?'

'I don't—'

'It'll be that kitchen fitter. I said that at the time. I told our Zoe—'

This time, it was Zoe's mother who was cut off. Zoe had appeared at the door, which was enough to end the conversation.

'I picked up your shopping,' Zoe's mum told her daughter. She hefted the bags slightly higher. 'The click and collect woman didn't ˋknow what she was doing. Thought I was someone called Janet. Then she wanted to talk about the weather for half an hour. I said—' She cut herself off again, then moved towards the door. 'I'll carry this lot, shall I? Put everything away as well, shall I?'

Zoe reached to take a bag but her mum angled it out of her daughter's grasp.

'Don't worry. I'll do it. Like always. You have a chat with your Columbine.'

Zoe's mum bumbled into the house, balancing both bags as she grumbled under her breath.

'I think she means Columbo,' Zoe said.

There was a bang from the inside and Millie didn't say anything because she knew that type of parent. From nowhere, she was ten or eleven and her mum was complaining that Millie never helped put the shopping away. Millie would offer but her mum would say she didn't know where things went... and so there was no way to win. She saw it in Zoe as she winced at the bang.

'I said I'd get everything delivered but Mum reckoned it cost too much, so said she'd pick it up,' Zoe said.

It felt like such a strange conversation for a pop star to be having. Obviously singers needed to eat and yet Millie couldn't quite picture someone like Zoe browsing the aisle for dishwasher tablets.

Millie was momentarily lost in that thought as Zoe continued: 'Did you find it?'

It took a second for Millie to remember she was there to say she'd spoken to the kitchen fitter. To Luke.

'No,' Millie replied. 'I needed to check a few more things with you.'

'Oh...' Zoe nodded towards the house. 'Let's go inside. It's cold out here.'

Millie followed the other woman inside. It was hard to move through the hall without stopping to take in the size of it all.

Millie's father had been something of a local celebrity when she'd been growing up. He'd been the main newsreader on the evening broadcast across the area. That meant he was invited to open or host all sorts of events. A young Millie got to meet lots of low-level soap stars, TV presenters and the like. Probably because of that, she'd never been massively impressed by celebrity – but Zoe was fascinating. Parts of her seemed so normal – and yet she'd won a BRIT award. She had life-sized nude prints of herself on her bedroom wall. She lived in a massive house, with huge gates, and apparently never locked the front door.

The mystery wasn't only who'd taken that photo, it was Zoe herself.

Millie was looking at a photo of Girlstar on a huge stage, with backing dancers, fireworks and lights.

'Wembley Arena,' Zoe said. 'That was our biggest tour. We did all the arenas in the UK, then went round Europe. We did a few dates in Japan, then had a week off before doing America. I was only home for nine days in seven months. When we got back, we did that final date at Wembley Arena – and then took about a year off. What we didn't realise is that everyone would forget about us in that year...'

Millie moved closer to the photo. The five women were standing arms up, with wide, relieved smiles. She could see it now she'd been told. They were exhausted and the grins were those of a group of people thankful it was over.

'My friend's a massive fan,' Millie said. 'She went to a couple of your shows earlier in the year. She saw you in Manchester, then Nottingham the next night.'

'Does that mean you're *not* a fan.' When Millie turned, Zoe was smiling. 'I'm teasing,' she added. 'If I'm honest, I'm not really a fan of the music. I liked the dancing and the shows. The work and rehearsals. But we always had to sing what they wrote for us. We wanted to do a rockier second album but they wanted that poppy-country stuff plus the covers...' She tailed off and then added: 'Who's your friend?'

'Nicola. We went to school together.'

Zoe nodded as if she knew, even though she couldn't. 'Most of the people at the gigs were our age,' she said. 'We knew there'd be fans from way back but our agent reckoned they'd bring their kids and we'd get a whole new fan base.' She stopped, then added: 'Didn't quite work out like that.' She pointed to a photo near the door that led into the rest of the house. 'That was this year,' she said. 'Our final night in Edinburgh. Might be our final night ever, I suppose.'

Millie looked at the picture and it was the same five people in the same pose as the Wembley photo. The faces were older, the fake tan darker, the clothes not quite as skimpy. The expressions were different. Not relief, not even smiles. Perhaps a collective resignation.

'I didn't know you'd split,' Millie said.

'We haven't... well, maybe we have. The arenas weren't as full as we thought. Our management said we'd sell out easily but then they said they were hoping for eighty per cent, then fifty. We've still not been paid properly. My agent said there was something in the contract about costs having to be covered. Then she stopped answering the phone, or replying to texts. It's the same with the other girls. We were told it'd be fixed by the end of the year, so I guess there's another ten days or so. Everything shuts down the week before Christmas and New Year. If it's not sorted this week, it won't be. Claire was talking about getting a lawyer but...'

Zoe blinked away the thought. It sounded like something she'd wanted to get out, even though she hadn't expected it to be Millie she told.

'Did you at least enjoy the tour?'

Zoe frowned momentarily, not that her features moved much. It was as if the thought had never occurred to her. 'I suppose. It was nice to see the girls again and the fans have always been lovely. It was good for the boys to finally see what their mum does. They weren't old enough the last time we were touring.'

None of that actually made it sound as if Zoe had enjoyed any of it. She spoke as if describing a job, not a passion.

'I hoped it might lead to *Dancing on Ice*, or *I'm A Celeb*. *Strictly*, if you're really lucky. Maybe even *Pointless Celebrities*. That sort of thing. I'd do anything to be a *Loose Woman*. Have you seen them on there? Hard to get any of that when your agent won't return your calls.'

'I think you'd do great on any of those shows,' Millie said. She knew what she was doing.

Zoe touched a grateful hand to her chest. 'Thank you *so* much. I just want people to see the real me.' She puffed out a sigh and then spoke quickly: 'People assume you're rich because you had a big song. Because you were on TV and in arenas. But we never wrote anything. That's where the money is. The writers get some, the record company gets some – and then we have to split whatever's left. And there are five of us. Plus, do you know they make us pay for all the stage stuff? The fireworks, the backing singers, all that. We didn't know that first time out. We assumed *they* were paying but it was all us. We scaled it back this time.'

Millie scanned the walls, where all the performance photos seemed to involve bright lights, packs of dancers, or some sort of indoor firework display. That was a lot of money on show.

'Obviously, I made *some* money.' Zoe held up a hand to indicate the house. 'I paid off Mum and Dad's place, too. Bought Mum's car. That sort of stuff. You know what it's like...'

She threw that in casually, as if Millie *did* know what it was like. The truth was, finance had only flowed in one direction for her. Her parents had died and she was the sole beneficiary. It wasn't the conversation she expected or wanted.

'Mum forgets all that,' Zoe added. She waved a hand in the vague direction of the rest of the house. 'I was only nineteen, twenty, and the biggest earner in my family. I went from talent shows to TV, then touring. Dad set me up as a company. He and Mum were my employees, so I was paying them. She goes on about how she does everything but she forgets she spent years on the payroll...'

There was a hint of spite to Zoe's tone, although she quickly cut herself off. It felt like the sort of thing that had been sitting on her mind for a while, without anyone to tell.

'What are you going to do next?' Millie asked.

A shrug. 'I'm not quite sure. I did a couple of cruise ships – but that was months away from the boys. I did a couple of summers in Ibiza. There's always work in the clubs out there. I had a show on local radio for a few months. Did you hear it?'

'Yes,' Millie replied, even though she hadn't. The lie had slipped out because she knew Zoe wanted to hear it.

'I loved doing it,' Zoe said. 'They let me play all the songs I wanted. Then there was this agony aunt thing. People would phone in with their problems and I'd try to help. One of my boys reckoned I should start a podcast. Everyone's got one nowadays, apparently. He reckoned one of his mates has one about trainers. Says he talks for an hour about shoes. I don't know how anyone listens to that...'

Millie had definitely heard of *worse* podcasts...

'Where are your boys?' Millie asked.

'They live at their dad's during term time. Their school is closer to him than here.'

'Didn't you say your ex is in Bali...?'

Millie knew she'd said the wrong thing instantly.

Zoe straightened, eyed Millie carefully to see if there'd been some sort of dig, and then decided there wasn't.

'That's a *different* ex,' she said, firmly.

'I have a boy,' Millie said. 'He's eight and his dad has custody.'

Zoe nodded along, not entirely placated by the sleight Millie hadn't meant. 'We're all going to do Christmas this year,' Zoe explained. 'Him, his girlfriend, her daughter, the boys, me. One big happy family.' She said that with a hint of a smirk. '*Maybe* happy,' she added. 'The boys don't finish school 'til the twenty-third. I dunno why it's so late this year, but I'm driving up that night. I'm going to be there Christmas Eve and Christmas Day, then I'm bringing them back down Boxing Day.'

She beamed and, for the first time since they'd begun talking, seemed genuinely happy about something. Millie knew that feeling. She craved those days with Eric: those moments in which it was only her and him.

'I'm taking Eric to the Bay Burning tomorrow,' Millie said. 'He's not been old enough to go up the hill before. We watched from the beach but it's not the same.'

Zoe started to nod. 'I remember the Bay Burning. Gosh, I've not been in years. Are they still doing it? It all seemed so scary when I was a kid. They set fire to this giant puppet thing and throw it off the cliff. I remember telling one of the girls in the band about it and she thought I'd had some sort of cheese dream.'

Millie laughed at that. Filling a giant marionette with the year's worries, setting it on fire, and then hurling it off a cliff really did sound like an over-the-top fever dream. Not only that, Millie's mum had always banned her from eating cheese in the evenings because she claimed it would cause nightmares. It sounded like the sort of nonsense parents made up.

As Millie was thinking of her mum telling her that she had to eat her vegetables if she wanted to stay thin, there was a bang from further in the house. The thump seemed to bring Zoe back to the moment because, when she next spoke, the wistful reminiscences were over.

'Sorry, you said you needed to talk to me...?'

It took Millie a moment to remember. 'I visited Luke,' she said.

'Who's Luke?'

'The guy who fitted your kitchen. I'm almost certain he's got nothing to do with your picture going missing.'

'Oh...' Zoe started tugging at her clothes, as if she had somewhere else to be. There was another bang from deeper into the house.

'Is that—?'

'Cupboard door,' Zoe said. She moved on instantly: 'I just don't want that picture getting out.'

'I suppose I don't understand why you had it on the wall if you didn't want it getting out. I'm not trying to victim blame – but if you had contractors in, visitors, that sort of thing. There was always a chance someone would see it. Even if they just took a picture on their phones...'

Zoe was nodding along, not disagreeing. 'I know you're right. Mum said the same but do you ever...' She let the sentence drift, before deciding to go for it: 'It was a reminder of what I *could* look like. I trained really hard for the arena shows. All the dancing and the costume changes. I hadn't done it in years and almost got back to what I was like the first time around. It's harder now, though. Sore knees. Sore bum. Stiff neck. I never used to get any of that and I suppose I left that picture up because I wanted to look like that again. I figured it was a goal.'

It was the first time Millie felt as if she understood. Not completely – the outward, unembarrassed nakedness was still alien to her – but she knew the appeal of youth. For craving what was lost and likely wouldn't return. She felt that – and she didn't have the fame and fortune in her past.

'If it wasn't Luke, who else might have been in the house?' Millie asked. 'I think you said something about your mum and sister being around...?'

It was a little lie, considering the cleaner had mentioned Zoe's sister being in the house – but Zoe didn't appear to notice.

'They're always here,' Zoe said. 'But I don't know if Mum was around that day. She might've been. Sharon definitely was.'

'Should I talk to either of them? Perhaps they saw something, even if it seemed innocent at the time?'

That got a gentle roll of the eyes. 'I doubt Mum will talk to you. She thinks this whole thing is my fault. Sharon will be over soon, so you can ask her.' A hint of a smile crept back onto Zoe's face. 'She wants us to start a group together. Just us.'

'A music group? A band? You don't sound convinced...?'

'No... I'm beginning to think I need something that's not music. Or not *performing* music. I always wanted to write something.'

'You should,' Millie said. 'You've sung enough songs.'

Zoe nodded in agreement but didn't answer because the

front door bumped open. There was a gust of chilled air and then another woman appeared. There was a definite similarity between Zoe and her sister. Sharon was a couple of years younger but it wasn't necessarily obvious. Between the sisters and their mother, Zoe had unquestionably got the looks in the family.

Sharon closed the door behind her and looked Millie up and down. 'I've been telling you to get a new cleaner,' she said.

'I'm not the cleaner,' Millie replied.

'This is Molly,' Zoe said. 'She's trying to find out who took the picture from upstairs.'

That got a roll of the eyes and Millie didn't bother to correct Zoe on her name this time. They'd been having a conversation for fifteen minutes and, the whole time, Zoe had thought she was called something else.

'I said you should forget about it,' Sharon said, with a dismissive wave of the hand. 'Who cares about some dumb picture?'

'*I* care,' Zoe replied. 'Besides, if someone walked in once and took it, they might get in another time. I don't want some weirdo walking around here, taking things.'

'Are you *sure* you didn't just... *lose* it?' Sharon asked.

'How can you lose something that big?'

'You lost those shoes I told you I wanted.'

'They were *shoes*. Not something six foot tall. And I told you – I think I left them in the dressing room in Cardiff. Someone was supposed to be picking them up.' A pause. 'Anyway, you were the last one here when the picture got taken.'

Sharon reeled back in what felt like mock horror. '*Me*? What are you on about?'

'I was out,' Zoe said. 'I got back and noticed it was gone that evening. You were the only one here in the morning. That was the day the kitchen guy finished.'

'Pfft.' Sharon batted a dismissive hand. 'It was probably

him. I told you he kept trying it on with me. If it wasn't him, it was the cleaner.'

She almost spat the word.

'Why would Ania steal that?' Zoe asked. 'She's worked here for years. If she wanted to take something, she could've done that at any time. Why that? Why now?'

A shrug: 'I don't know. It's not like *I'm* a cleaner. Ask her. She probably needs the money.'

On the walls around them, among the photos, the award, and other memorabilia, there was a silver crown that Zoe must have worn on stage at some point. In the glimmering reflection, there was a flicker of movement. Out of sight from Zoe and Sharon, the cleaner – Ania – was hovering around the corner. Millie didn't know if she'd just arrived, or if she'd been listening for a while.

Zoe stepped to the side, ready to move away. 'You two can talk,' she said, meaning Millie and Sharon. Millie instinctively touched Zoe's arm to stop her moving into a place in which she'd spot the cleaner.

'Before you go,' she said, talking loudly enough that Ania would hear, 'I was wondering if you would mind signing some of my friend's CDs? I can bring them over next time, if that's OK?'

In the corner of her eye, Millie saw Ania disappear from the reflection, presumably into a different room.

'Oh.' Zoe seemed genuinely surprised. 'Sure. Bring her over if you want. I'll do some selfies and sign her CDs – though I thought everyone used Spotify nowadays.' She looked back to Sharon. 'Mum's in the kitchen banging around. Molly wants to talk to you, so you can go in the conservatory if you want. I'm going to go back to bed for a bit.'

She yawned and batted it unsuccessfully away, before heading for the stairs. Sharon and Millie watched her go and then Sharon huffed dismissively under her breath.

'Molly, is it?'

'Millie.'

'Whatever.' She flipped back her hair. 'I guess it's time to confess.'

EIGHTEEN

Sharon started unlooping a long scarf, before kicking off a pair of rubber boots. 'This way,' she said, before striding across the echoing floor.

Millie followed as the other woman led her out of the hall, past a couple of closed doors, and then along another passage until they emerged into a bright sun room. There was glass on all sides, with a pair of sofas set apart from each other, and a massive television on a stand. It was somehow warmer in the conservatory than the rest of the house and, as Sharon plopped onto one of the sofas, Millie took the other.

'I can't believe my sister got someone in to figure all this out.' Sharon started to pick at a fingernail. 'It's such a waste of time. How much is she paying you?'

'Nothing. I'm doing it to help.'

Sharon stopped instantly, one fingernail resting on the other. 'You're doing this for *nothing*...?'

When she put it like that, it did sound odd. Millie and Zoe weren't friends... but then neither was she friends with Victoria. She hadn't given up her time to be on the moors, or visit the prison, because she was being paid. Guy shared the advertising revenue from his site – but that was inconsistent and not that much. Millie lived from the money her parents had left her, plus the income from her own dog grooming and training business.

Sharon didn't wait for an answer. 'She is ripping you off big time. *Big* time! I don't even know why she's making such a massive deal about it. Have you seen the dresses she used to wear? You could see more or less everything anyway. It's not as if nobody's seen it all before.'

Millie didn't know which dress Sharon was talking about – though there was a definite difference between wearing *something* and wearing *nothing*. Also a difference between willingly having photos published, and not.

'You said something about a confession...' Millie prompted.

Sharon appeared to have forgotten that interaction from the hall. 'Did I?' she replied. 'Are you sure?'

'That's what you said.'

A shrug: 'I suppose I'm confessing that I don't care. It'll be something to do with her ex anyway. Or the kitchen bloke. Or the cleaner.'

Millie remembered Luke telling her that Sharon had tried to get him to do some work for free. She believed his side of whatever story was being spun.

'What about the ex?' Millie asked.

'You know the sort. He was always into that stuff. He was the one who wanted those pictures. He's a right perv. I dread to think what's on his hard drive.'

Millie suspected she *did* know the type. 'I heard he's in Bali.'

'Course he is. He's a celebrity collector, isn't he? Went round all the girl groups, then ended up on *Celeb Big Brother* and got himself a column in the *Sun*. Tried it on with me once.'

Millie had never heard of a celebrity 'collector' – and given what she assumed it meant, she was glad she hadn't. He still didn't sound like a suspect, given he was on the other side of the planet. It was also beginning to sound like Sharon believed everyone had tried it on with her.

'You a fan then?' Sharon asked.

'Of Zoe?'

'Pfft. Obviously not. Of me.' Sharon flipped her hair back again, as if that would make it easier for Millie to place her. 'It happens all the time,' Sharon said, obliviously. 'Zoe hates it that her little sister's the famous one now. Can't handle it. She's been the centre of attention so long, she doesn't know how to deal with it.'

Millie had no idea what was going on. She didn't recognise Sharon and had no clue she was supposed to be famous. It was the first she'd heard of it.

'What's your favourite video of mine?' Sharon asked. 'I put one up last week where I was in the back of an Uber. The driver was pretending he didn't know who I was, so I was playing him videos on one phone, while filming it with the other.'

It sounded horrific. That poor driver.

'Are you some sort of YouTuber?' Millie asked.

Sharon's nose wrinkled. 'We don't like to be called that. It's an offensive term. Would you call someone a lesbian?'

'I mean... if they were...'

'God! You're so hateful. That's hate speech. You're not allowed to say that any more. What if *I* was some sort of lezzer? Would you say that to my face?'

'I think "lezzer" is more offensive than—'

Sharon wasn't paying attention. She'd pulled out a phone from somewhere and passed it over for Millie to see. 'That's one of the best ones,' she said.

From what Millie could tell, the video was Sharon trying on clothes. Even from the twenty or thirty seconds Millie watched, it was bewilderingly dull. It also had almost one-hundred-and-fifty-thousand views.

'I'm working on my brand,' Sharon said. 'Next step is to get my channel past twenty-thousand subs. I reckon I'm shadow-banned, though. I've heard about it from a few other girls. Them lot who run TikTok, Insta and YouTube pick their favourite girls and send all the subscribers their way.'

Millie glanced back to the video, in which Sharon was talking to the camera. She handed it back.

'I wanted to talk about your sister,' Millie said.

That got a roll of the eyes. 'What about her?'

'The picture from upstairs was taken at some point in the late morning or early afternoon. It sounds like you were the only person here, so I—'

'I only come over because the light's better here.' Sharon pointed upwards, as if Millie wouldn't understand the concept of light otherwise. 'It helps with my videos.'

Sharon held up her phone again and, this time, the video showed her spinning to show off an outfit in the conservatory where they were currently sitting.

'That vid's got forty-nine thousand views,' Sharon said.

Millie wasn't sure if that was good... but it didn't sound like *that* many. She figured she'd play along and see what happened.

'The light's perfect in here for you,' she said.

'I know! It really brings out my freckles.' She brushed her cheeks, where Millie could see zero freckles. 'Anyway, I didn't see anything, or anyone. And I definitely locked up when I left.' Sharon stopped and made a point to look in both directions, even though there was nobody there. 'If you ask me, Zoe hid it herself.'

'Why would she do that?'

'Publicity, innit? She can tell people something's been nicked and get loads of people talking about it. Then she says it's been returned and she's back in the magazines, or whatever. That's what you have to do when your little sister upstages you.'

Millie thought on that for a second. 'But Zoe doesn't want

publicity. As far as I can tell, she hasn't told anyone that something's been stolen. She specifically didn't want the police involved.'

That got another roll of the eyes. More dramatic this time. 'Don't you know *anything*? This is how they all do it. When her tour flopped, she didn't have any choice, did she?'

Zoe had hinted at the tour going poorly – but Sharon spoke with such venom that it genuinely seemed as if she was enjoying it. Millie wasn't sure how to respond. She didn't have any brothers or sisters, though, even if she did, she doubted she'd have this level of spite against them.

'Choice about what?' Millie asked, not sure she wanted to hear the answer.

'Her career's dead. That tour was her last chance – and she blew it. They all did. Nobody cares about some ancient band. I told her to come in with me. I'll get my peeps interested and we'll start our own band.' A shrug. 'She doesn't want it. I reckon that's what all this is about. Some lame-oh cry for attention.'

Millie still wasn't sure she understood. If Zoe was after publicity, she was doing the opposite. She didn't want the news to get out.

'Anyway,' Sharon continued, 'Zoe reckoned your dad was some sort of celeb.'

'He read the news,' Millie replied.

'Oh...' Sharon didn't bother to hide her disappointment. 'I thought she meant a *real* celeb.' She started picking her nail again, having dispatched her phone back into her bag. 'So what do you do?' she asked.

'I have a dog grooming business, plus I report a bit of local news on the side.' That got yet another eye roll, until Millie added: 'I used to plan events.'

Sharon looked up, suddenly interested. 'Like what?'

'Concerts, festivals. I ran a beach concert series every summer for a few years. Booked the bands, that sort of thing.'

Sharon was nodding along and the change was unmissable. From abject disinterest, she was suddenly staring at Millie like a dog at a bowl of food.

'Are you busy tomorrow?' she asked.

'I'm busy a lot.'

Sharon wasn't listening. 'Why don't you come over to mine? I've got a plan that might interest you.'

Millie held back the laugh. She was about to say no, when the thought occurred that it would give her a free look at Sharon's place. It might be a long shot but maybe there'd be some sort of clue about the missing picture.

'I can probably do tomorrow,' Millie replied.

'Great!' Sharon said. 'This is going to be massive. It's such an opportunity for you.' She clapped her hands together and then reached for her phone, before adding: 'What was your name again?'

Millie told her – and then spelled it out letter by letter.

Sharon tapped something into her phone and then squealed. 'That's such a lovely name. I wish *I* was called that.' She flipped her phone back into her bag. 'I think you and I are going to be best friends. Don't you agree?'

Millie managed the thinnest of smiles, while just about stopping herself replying that, of all the things that might happen, the pair of them becoming best friends ranked a little below aliens invading.

NINETEEN

Foam was spilling from the back of the seat as Millie shifted her weight in an attempt to get comfortable. They were the sort of waiting-room chairs that had seemingly existed since the invention of sitting. The type of scratchy, uncomfortable things that had irritated backsides for generations.

Millie wriggled again as Guy remained still at her side. She didn't know how he was managing it.

The waiting room was quiet and sombre. Tinsel had been strung across the ceiling, though a thread had come away from the tape and was dangling into the centre of the room. The bleakness was at complete odds with Sharon's manic energy from Zoe's house.

'Do you think Nicholas knows who was in that coffin?' Millie whispered.

For a moment, she wasn't sure Guy had heard. He didn't react but then, from nowhere, he whispered back. 'Maybe. He might not be... *well enough* for questions.'

Millie didn't reply. He was probably right.

She'd never been in a hospice before but it reminded her a little of the nursing home at which she volunteered. There was the reception desk at the front and then a separate waiting room, in which they were currently sitting. The corridors and room numbers she'd seen felt familiar – except the hospice had much more of a hospital feel to it. It was spotlessly clean and she'd seen one bloke at the other end of the reception hall wearing a white coat. It was very quiet. The sort of silence that almost felt loud.

This was the type of scenario that made Sharon's question about being paid sound ridiculous. Of course there was never going to be any sort of money for this. But even 'this' didn't feel quite right. Millie and Guy were there to pass on a message from a killer to his son. It was hard to escape the sense that they were betraying Victoria by doing what felt like a favour for the man who'd killed her son.

If Guy was thinking something similar, then he hadn't said it. Was this how the real world worked? Do something for a killer because he might then offer up information?

This was not Millie's world.

If it was Eric who'd gone missing, would she want someone else negotiating with the person who took him?

That thought was interrupted as the door sounded. A man in a jumper appeared. He had a tie knotted at the top of the V-neck and shook hands with the pair of them, while checking their names.

'Nicholas is awake and happy to see you both,' he said. 'It's all a bit late notice but we try to be flexible with visiting hours – and this is something of an unusual circumstance. I spoke to somebody from the police, who explained the situation...'

He looked between them, fishing for a little more informa-tion than he seemingly had. When neither of them filled him in, he clapped his hands gently, like a Sunday School teacher about to begin a singalong.

'I need to warn you that Nicholas is a very ill man. I don't know whether you've been to many hospices in the past – but it can be a bit of a shock for some.'

Guy said that he'd been to a couple but Millie could only shake her head. She'd been around people who were ill at the nursing home – but this was more than that. There were rooms were occupied by people who were actually dying. She wasn't sure she felt prepared for that. She wasn't sure how anyone could simply get ready for such a thing.

'There's no issue with you talking to Nicholas,' the man said. 'But our job here is to make sure his final days are as comfortable as they can be. I do need you to be respectful of what's happening.'

Guy replied that they understood – and then the man turned and said 'this way', before leading them along a series of hallways. They paused outside a room with the number thirteen on the door. Before anything more could happen, Guy asked the question that Millie had been too afraid to bring up.

He spoke in a whisper: 'How long has he got?'

'Hard to say. It could be a matter of days.'

Guy nodded shortly but didn't reply.

Millie *couldn't* say anything. She wasn't sure she wanted to head inside. She had seen death, with her parents, and she didn't want to see it again.

It was too late. The man knocked on the door and then headed inside without waiting for any sort of confirmation. Guy followed him in and Millie felt as if she had no choice.

The room was part bedroom, part clinic. There was a TV on a large dresser, with some sort of ambient radio playing in the background. There was a ventilator next to the bed and other medical machines dotted around the room, most of which Millie didn't recognise.

A man was sitting in a chair that was part of a small lounge, next to the patio door. His skin was grey, his face gaunt. Patches of his hair were missing and, when he tried to smile, it was as if his lips got stuck halfway there.

'This is Nicholas,' the man who'd led them into the room said. 'Nicholas: This is Guy and Millie.'

They each gave a 'hi', before the man told Nicholas he could press his button at any point if there was a problem. As Millie took in the room, she realised there were a series of panic buttons dotted around. Some were on the wall, others on the various tables and counter tops.

As well as Nicholas's chair, there were two more lounge seats by the large window. Millie and Guy slotted into them and there was an awkward moment as nobody appeared to know what to say.

Nicholas looked ill – but the idea he could be a day or two from the end felt absurd. He could move, he could talk... he was right there in front of them.

Millie realised she didn't properly understand what leukaemia was. It was a bit late to ask. She wondered how they could know he had so little time left.

'So... where are we going dancing?' Nicholas asked. His voice was croaky but he managed a smile.

'I think my dancing days are long gone,' Guy replied.

'Even I'm too old for that,' Millie added.

Guy started to introduce himself but Nicholas cut him off with a friendly 'I know'. He didn't expand on *how* he knew, which left Millie wondering when he'd last spoken to his father. He'd changed his last name to disassociate himself from his dad – but perhaps it was more about making his life easier?

She found herself considering whether this had all been planned by Ashworth. The trip to the moor and then this.

Nicholas looked towards Millie, eyes dwelling on her face for a moment.

'I couldn't do what I do without Millie,' Guy said, answering the unasked.

Nicholas nodded slowly and made a low gurgling sound. 'How are Dad's burns?'

'They don't look great,' Guy replied. 'He didn't seem to be in pain but the scarring is impossible to miss.'

'They put sugar in the boiling water,' Nicholas said. 'It makes it stick to the skin. Someone should've been prosecuted – but nobody was ever charged. Just because it happened in prison, they're acting as if it's fine. Then it's hard to get the grafts and surgery when you're inside...'

'Does that mean you've been visiting him?' Millie asked.

Nicholas didn't answer for a while but, when it came, it was almost a reluctant-sounding: 'Sometimes...' He waited a beat and then added: 'You're the first visitors *I've* had.'

'How long have you been here?' Millie asked.

'Almost two months.'

He tried to force another smile but there was no doubting the sadness. There wasn't a lot to show for a life when a person could be in a hospice for two months with no visitors. It felt like such a waste.

Millie stood and crossed to the dresser. She picked up one of the photo frames, which showed a man in his early twenties standing next to a bright red sports car.

'Is this your car?' Millie asked.

Nicholas laughed so hard that he started coughing. He patted his chest and there was a moment in which Millie was worried he might not be able to stop. When he did, the grin remained.

'That's a Ferrari F40,' he said. 'There was only about 1,300 made. You'd be lucky to get one for a million nowadays. That was at a track day at Brand's Hatch. There a bunch of super cars and you could pay to do a lap in one.' He sighed gently and then added: 'That was a good day but I never quite loved driving like I once did.'

Millie almost asked what he meant, but decided not to. She

returned the photo to the counter and scanned the others. There was a couple of him with an older woman, who Millie assumed was his mum. Another showed him grinning next a muddy rally car, with a helmet under his arm. The final photo was of Nicholas standing next to the ocean somewhere. He was topless, showing off a tanned, toned stomach. Millie couldn't help but compare the Nicholas of the photo to the one in front of her. He was so slender now that he was almost half the man.

'We can talk about Dad if that's why you're here...?' Nicholas waited a moment and then added: 'It's OK...'

Millie hadn't realised they'd been stalling. *She'd* been stalling.

'Is that what you want to talk about?' Guy asked.

Nicholas twisted a little until he was able to look out the window once more. The view beyond was a sculpted garden. There was frosty grass and a fountain that wasn't running. In the summer, it would be a beautiful respite but, here, now, it looked cold.

'Did you know him much when he was younger?' Nicholas asked.

Millie re-took her seat and she realised she wanted to know the answer too.

'Sort of,' Guy replied. 'We were never friends but I reported on his work with the football and school. He helped with a couple of stories and I helped promote a few things.'

Guy reached for his battered satchel and dug around until he pulled out a newspaper that had been folded open to a page somewhere in the middle.

'I found this,' he said, passing it across to Nicholas.

The younger man took the paper, wincing slightly as he stretched.

'It's about a charity walk he organised,' Guy said. 'I was looking for things I'd written about your dad and found it by accident. I brought it in case you wanted to read it...?'

Nicholas squinted at the page and then coughed for a good thirty seconds. He held a hand to his chest the entire time, before it finally passed. 'My eyes haven't been working well,' he said. 'Can you read it for me?'

Guy took back the paper and immediately started fumbling in his satchel for the reading glasses Millie knew were there. The problem was that his bag was a mini version of his house. It contained all sorts of useful things – but that didn't mean any of it was in order.

'I'll do it,' Millie said, reaching for the paper.

A primary school teacher has raised more than £30,000 for charity after organising a sponsored walk.

Kevin Ashworth, 41, who works at Whitecliff Primary School, arranged a 40-mile walk from Whitecliff Pier to Steeple's End. Forty-four people attempted the walk but only nine completed it.

The money will be donated to Whitecliff Football Club's youth division, where Ashworth is an assistant coach of the under-nines.

Ashworth said: 'After an easy beginning, the walk got tough when we reached the moors. There are lots of hidden rocks and tree roots and we had a few unfortunate injuries.

'It was a relief to reach Steeple's End before dark – and the boys at the club will put the money raised to such good use. Our training pitch has needed better drainage for years and we'll finally be able to renovate the changing rooms.'

Millie continued reading the rest of the article, which included quotes from some of the walkers who'd finished and a few who hadn't. There was a big photo of Kevin Ashworth looking much younger. He was standing somewhere on the moors, with what looked like a lake behind him. There were trees in the distance and then an awful lot of not very much. He was in small red shorts and a dark vest with 'adventure' printed in yellow letters on the front. There was a second photo showing a group of people at the finishing line. As well as that, a small rectangle of a map marking the route was next to the main photo.

When Millie finished, she looked up to realise Nicholas had his eyes closed. For a moment, she thought he was asleep – but then he started to speak.

'Thank you,' he said.

She wondered if there was more to come when he opened his eyes and looked to her.

'Do you love your dad?' he asked.

Millie realised her mouth was open. She wondered if he knew who she was, or who her dad had been. Whether this was something he was going to ask anyway.

Nicholas didn't wait for an answer. 'People don't understand why I visited him a few times. It's hard to explain. I was engaged for a while. She didn't want me to ever visit him. Said she didn't want to start a family with me if I still saw him. I had to choose...'

He didn't explicitly say who he'd chosen – but there were no photos of children or a wife on the dresser. Plus nobody had visited him in two months.

Millie couldn't reply. She didn't understand and wasn't sure she ever would. He'd chosen his father over his own life. His own happiness.

'Did you want to ask me something?' Nicholas said. He was looking to Guy. 'They didn't say why you were coming – just that you'd visited Dad and that you wanted to see me...'

Millie watched Guy, wondering if he'd ask about the coffin they'd found on the moors. Wondering if he'd ask Nicholas whether he knew he possibly had an infant brother. She wondered if he'd ask about Wesley and Shaun.

And then she realised that he couldn't – and neither

could she.

This poor man was days from death and he'd not had a visitor in two months. He was sitting in a small room with a handful of photographs and only memories. This moment shouldn't be about his father, it should be about him.

'If there anything you want to do?' Millie asked. 'I don't know the rules, or anything like that. But are you allowed out? Is there somewhere we can take you? Something we can do for you?'

She felt Guy watching her and wondered if he agreed. If he had a problem, then he didn't say anything.

Nicholas was biting his lip. 'There is one thing...'

It was forty-five minutes later that they were all back in more or less the same places. Millie had made a quick run to the closest supermarket and returned with what Nicholas had requested. The person behind reception had magicked them a dessert spoon from the kitchen – and now Nicholas was sitting in his chair, with the widest of smiles on his face. There was even a little more colour to his features.

'The nurse says this is a bad idea,' he said.

'We don't—'

Nicholas cut off Millie with a laugh. 'I don't think it matters now.'

He wielded his spoon like an ornamental sword – and then thrust it into the previously untouched side of the two-quid Iceland Chocolate Gateau that was sitting on a plate. He jammed a massive spoonful of cake into his mouth and swallowed it down.

'Remember when they used to be called Sara Lee Gateaux?' he asked. 'Mum used to buy them and I was allowed a slice every Sunday night. It was a treat because it was the end of the week. We'd watch *Bullseye* and I'd have a slice of gateau.'

He scooped himself a second spoonful, largely demolishing the side as he did so.

'I always wondered what it'd be like to have a whole one,' he said. 'Mum used to cut them into six. I once asked if I could have a whole one for my birthday but she said it'd make me sick. I was thinking about it in bed the other day. How, if I could have just one thing, it'd be this.'

Nicholas dug the spoon into the middle of the cake and fed himself a third mouthful. There was chocolate around his lips and it didn't feel right to talk to him while he was eating. There was something wonderfully serene and peaceful about watching someone do something they'd been thinking about for so long.

It wasn't only peaceful. Millie couldn't stop herself from thinking about how this might be the last thing he did for himself. She thought of what she might do if she knew she only had a few days left. Something with Eric.

Nicholas didn't eat all of the gateau. He didn't even get that close. The spoon started to seem heavier in his grasp, harder to lift. He'd managed barely a quarter of the cake when he put down the spoon and pressed back into his seat.

Guy shifted it into the mini fridge. Millie helped Nicholas wipe his lips clean and then he smiled to himself and allowed his eyes to close.

'That's what I wanted,' Nicholas said.

The light from the window brushed his pale, greying skin. He suddenly seemed so tired.

'Your dad asked us to pass on a message to you,' Guy said.

Nicholas didn't open his eyes but he was listening.

'He asked us to tell you that he loves you. He said it was a pleasure to be your dad.'

Nicholas nodded gently and his whispered reply was barely there. 'Thank you,' he said.

TWENTY

Guy and Millie were outside the hospice when she realised she had a missed call and a text from Alex.

> Did you think about what I asked last night?

Millie had almost forgotten that her ex-husband wanted her to go to his wedding reception. She wasn't in the mood to send a reply, so put the phone back in her bag.

Guy was rearranging his satchel on the bonnet of his car as Millie pulled on her hat and scarf.

'Was Carol ever in a hospice?' she asked.

Millie and Guy hadn't had many conversations about his wife. Carol had been Millie's godmother – not that she'd known that when it could have mattered. Guy rarely brought up his wife and, when he did, it was usually as a passing throwaway comment

'She didn't know she had cancer,' he said. 'She'd been having headaches and didn't think it was anything serious. It was always such a hassle to get into the doctor's. Not their fault, there's no money, but it was one of those places where you had to phone up at eight on the dot and hope you got through to someone. She didn't want to bother with all that, so was taking paracetamol during the day. She went to bed one night with a headache – and never woke up.'

Millie remembered he'd said something similar once before. 'Sorry,' she said.

A shake of the head. 'Best way to go, I think. Without the pain and worry of what's coming. I can't think of a better way.' Guy nodded towards the hospice. 'I can't think of anything worse than that. When you know what's happening but can't do anything about it. That poor boy. No visitors for two months.'

He opened his mouth as if about to add something – but then closed it. Millie knew why. There were so many unasked and unanswered questions. About Nicholas's father, about the coffin, his mother. Perhaps even more recent things. None of it felt right.

They had passed on Ashworth's message to his son, which was the reason they'd gone in the first place.

'Do you think he moved back to see his dad?' Millie asked.

'It feels like that might be the case.'

Guy finished repacking his bag and clipped the top into place. The buckle was so old and worn that it immediately unclasped itself.

'Relationships with parents can be difficult,' he said.

He was looking to her and Millie wondered if it was a question. She had never told him everything that happened with her parents. He'd asked once – but then told her not to answer. She often wondered what would have happened had he not changed his mind. Would she have told him? Would this have been her life if she had?

Guy's bag re-spilled onto the bonnet and he brushed everything back inside once more.

'Can I take the article about the charity walk?' Millie asked.

Guy didn't ask why. He passed across the paper, which Millie took.

'I've been looking for other pieces about him,' Guy said. 'Not the obvious stuff about the boys. There's loads of those but I know I wrote more. There was one from when the school opened a new wing but I can't find it. I feel like there might be others, too. I've been wondering if there's something throwaway that I wouldn't have noticed before. I even dug out some of my old notebooks but I didn't keep them all and I've not found the right one.'

'How many do you reckon you went through over the years?'

A laugh. 'Thousands. *Tens* of thousands.'

'How many did you keep?'

Another laugh. 'Thousands. Though maybe not tens. Carol wasn't happy with the papers, but at least I could say they'd prove useful one day.'

They hovered there for a moment until Guy said what Millie had been thinking. 'They might not let us talk to Kevin again.'

'He said he'll only talk to you.'

'True – but they won't like the stunt he pulled this morning. I don't blame them, really.'

'You could've told Baker what Ashworth asked us to tell Nicholas.'

'I could. So could you.' He might have winked at her. If he did, it happened so quickly that Millie wasn't sure she'd seen it. 'There didn't seem much point in risking anything getting back to Kevin. If he wanted Chief Superintendent Baker to have heard, he'd have spoken louder. It seems like a reasonable enough message for a father to pass on to his dying son.'

That was true – and partly why Millie hadn't told Baker what Ashworth had said. There was also the fact that he only acknowledged her when he wanted something.

'How's Zoe?' Guy asked.

Millie told Guy about Zoe's sister's theory that Zoe was behind everything herself as some way to reignite interest in her career.

'She sounded so sure,' Millie added. 'But really spiteful with it. Like she was enjoying Zoe's downfall.'

'I guess it's not only relationships with parents that are complicated...'

'I sort of get her point, though. If it was a *real* theft, why wouldn't they take the BRIT award? They don't know it's a replica. Why not go hunting for jewellery or cash? It doesn't *feel* like a proper burglary.'

'That's what I thought.'

'But if it's all a set-up, then where's the pay-off? Zoe doesn't *want* publicity. She didn't want you to write something. She doesn't want the police to investigate, because she thinks someone will leak it.'

Guy pressed back onto the side of his car. They'd been outside for too long and Millie was beginning to feel the chill through her jacket.

'I've been conned into writing things in the past,' he said.

Millie wondered if it was some sort of joke. He always seemed so unflappable and sceptical of what was in front of him.

As if reading her mind, Guy continued, 'I wasn't always like this. When I started out, I'd take everyone at face value. There was one time a councillor told me a piece of derelict land was going to be sold and turned into a casino. He said it was off the record, so I reported it without using his name. There was a big outcry in town. People didn't want a casino, let alone near to a school. There was a protest and weeks of letters. Then, about five months later, that same councillor bought the land himself at a knock-down price. The people who'd wanted to build a casino had backed out of the deal and the land went back up for sale. There were no other takers and he was the only bidder in the end.'

Millie scoffed at the cheek of it all. 'He can't have known it would work out like that?'

'True... but he'd have had a good idea that the locals would be against a casino. It worked out as he'd hoped – but, even if it hadn't, he wouldn't have lost anything. That was the point. I reported what he told me without bothering to think about *why* he was telling me what he did.'

Millie thought on that for a second. She tucked her hands underneath her armpits, trying to stay warm. 'Are you saying Zoe might be using me?'

A shrug. 'I'm saying you shouldn't discount that there will definitely be a "why" involved somewhere.'

'But why us? Why me? If she wants publicity, there are so many better ways.'

'Maybe it's not publicity? Or maybe it's not publicity *for her*?'

It felt so true, so obvious – except Millie still couldn't see what she was being used for. It was *something*.

'Do you think Ashworth is using you?' she asked. Millie had been thinking it for a while and, suddenly, it felt like the time to ask. It was a challenge to Guy, something she'd never properly done before. But, if they were truly equals, that's what people did.

Wasn't it?

Guy nodded. 'Unquestionably. I have no doubt whatsoever that Kevin is trying to use me. I just don't know for what.'

'For passing on a message to his son? Maybe that's what this was all about?'

'Maybe...' Guy yawned and stretched as he did so. 'Been a long day already,' he said. 'I should get back to feed Barry.' He paused for a moment and then added: 'Are you OK? Today was a lot...'

Millie said she was fine and, in a way, she was. She felt drained from the time they'd spent with Nicholas. It felt barely believable that his time left could apparently be counted in hours. Surely there must be a mistake?

Her phone buzzed with another message and Millie had no doubt who it would be. She and Guy said their goodbyes – and then she waited in her car with the fans blowing as she checked her phone.

> Did you think about what I asked last night?

Alex had sent the same message twice, with an hour in between. It was the sort of thing he'd do. He was a lawyer, after all. What was the point in rephrasing when he could simply ask the same question again.

Millie tapped out a reply, deleted it, did the same again. She knew she wanted to say 'no', that she *should* refuse to go. Except some things weren't about her. It probably *would* be better for Eric if he had someone to sit with that wasn't a stranger. If he ended up on the top table, he'd want attention and end up frustrated at the lack of it. He was eight. It wasn't easy to understand that not everything was about you at that age.

Which is what Millie told herself. It wasn't about her.

> I'll go – but I'm picking who I sit with. I'm NOT ending up somewhere with your parents. I want to bring Nicola.

Millie hadn't actually *asked* Nicola if she'd go – but it felt like she probably would.

The reply pinged back almost instantly.

> Great! We can talk about the tables.

Millie started a reply to say that she wasn't going to negotiate when it came to tables – but she deleted it without sending. It was something for another day.

The question of what she should wear to her ex-husband's wedding reception was also a question for another day, albeit one that would likely keep her up through the nights between now and then.

A spitefully gleeful thought that she should show up in white occurred – and, though she knew she'd never do it, it would *almost* be worth it, solely for the look on Rachel's face.

Instead, Millie sent a message to Nicola, asking if she wanted to go to Alex and Rachel's wedding reception as her plus-one. If Nicola had previous plans for Christmas Eve, then she hadn't mentioned them.

It wasn't long until Millie received back a stream of texts that involved many question marks, including a 'what?' and an 'are you serious?'

Millie said she'd explain later and then dropped her phone onto the passenger seat.

The mist was starting to clear from the windows of Millie's car and feeling was returning to her toes. As she waited for the fog to fully clear, she picked up the paper Guy had given her and re-read the article about Kevin Ashworth and his charity walk. It was such a strange read, given what had happened. He'd helped raise a significant amount of money for the youth section of the football club – and then, a couple of years later, he'd disappeared with two of the players.

It made even less sense.

As well as the photo of Ashworth on the moors, there was a map of the route that led from the centre of Whitecliff, up the hill out of town. The walkers had headed onto the moors and then crossed from one side to the other, ending up at a village forty miles from where they started. It was a long, long way.

Millie read it all but couldn't escape the sense that there was something she'd missed when reading it to Nicholas. It wasn't only that Ashworth's about-turn seemed so bizarre, it was something else. Something that felt it was in front of her, even though she couldn't see it.

The windows were clear and Millie knew she should go home. The clouds were rolling in again and the days were so short that it felt as though it never got light.

She put down the paper but, as soon as she did, her phone started to buzz. She expected it to be Alex – but Zoe's name was on the screen. It was hard to ignore the thrill that someone famous – *actually* famous – was calling. Nicola wouldn't believe such a thing was possible.

'Is that Molly?' Zoe asked when the phone was answered.

'Millie.'

'It's Zoe. Are you on Insta?'

Millie needed a moment to figure out Zoe was talking about Instagram. 'I have an account that I use for my business,' she said. 'It's mainly pictures of dogs.'

Zoe asked for the account handle and then, moments later, said: 'I've sent you a link.'

Millie checked the link to the account that had been forwarded. There was no biography and only one photo had been posted.

'They tagged me in,' Zoe said – and as Millie clicked through to see the photo, it was suddenly clear what it showed.

It was cropped tight and focused on someone's tanned, toned thigh. The caption was short and simple. Zoe's name was tagged, along with a simple 'Coming soon'.

TWENTY-ONE

DAY FIVE

Sharon lived in an apartment on the edge of the closet city to Whitecliff. It was twenty-five miles inland – and the narrow country roads and tight blind bends meant it took Millie more than an hour to get there.

For some reason, likely the size of Zoe's place, Millie had expected her sister to be living somewhere bigger. The apartment block where Sharon lived was the sort of place that people ended up buying because it was cheaper than a house. There was nothing wrong with that – but the way Sharon had talked herself up made it sound as if she was in her own massive house, like Zoe's.

Before she rang the bell for Sharon's flat, Millie took a moment to recheck the Instagram account Zoe had forwarded. She was following it with her dog grooming account – and there had still only been the one post. It wasn't just Zoe who'd been tagged in the single photo. Since it had first been posted, whoever had put it up had also alerted a long list of newspapers and magazines by linking them in. There was only one comment – 'Why is this on my feed?' – from someone whose profile said they worked as an correspondent for an entertainment website.

If the goal was publicity, then it wasn't working. Millie figured it was probably because it was so unclear what the photo actually showed. She knew it was a part of Zoe's body – but she wouldn't have guessed if she didn't already know.

Sharon had her phone in her hand when she answered the door. She was having a conversation on speakerphone and, as she held open the door for Millie, said: 'Gotta go, babe. The party planner's here.' She pressed to end the call and then closed the door. 'Good to see you're early.'

'I'm not a party planner,' Millie replied.

'Close enough. It's this way.'

Sharon headed along the short hall and took the second door. 'This is the boujee room,' she said, again holding open the door for Millie.

Inside, there were two racks of clothes against one wall, with a ring lamp and phone tripod facing the other. A small table was set up in a cramped corner, along with a fold-down table in front of a mirror.

'Gorge, innit?' Sharon said. 'I always wanted my own studio.'

Millie wasn't sure what to say. There were cables across the floor, shoes scattered in all directions and a bin overflowing with tissues.

'Did you see the Instagram post that tagged in Zoe last night?' Millie asked.

'She sent something over, but who cares? Someone's always screengrabbing my stuff and putting it up. They wait until I'm leaning forward to get the angle. You don't see me moaning about it.'

Sharon slotted herself onto an uncomfortable-looking stool at the side of the ring lamp and indicated for Millie to sit in the matching one across from her. It felt like they were about to do some sort of interview.

'You said something yesterday about a proposal...' Millie said.

'...And you're just the woman I've been looking for,' Sharon replied. 'I'm going to relaunch my brand in the new year. I've been thinking about a big event on the pier. Fancy dresses, smart suits. I might get Zoe to ask if her old band mates can come down. I figured with your old connections, you might be able to pull some strings....?'

Millie waited for a punchline that didn't come.

'I don't have any strings to pull,' Millie replied. 'I might know a few booking agents I can put you in contact with, depending on the budget...'

She knew almost immediately where things were headed. She'd probably known the day before.

Not that Sharon had any shame. 'I was thinking you could organise it all – and then I'd promote you on my channels. Tell all my followers that you're the best at organising stuff. It'll definitely get you some bookings.'

Millie almost laughed. It was what Luke had said about Sharon trying to get him to work for free.

She knew the visit would be a waste of time – but it would still be a chance to snoop around Sharon's place if she strung things along.

'Are you saying you don't have a budget?' Millie asked.

'People don't *need* a fee,' Sharon replied. 'They'll make ten times whatever their "fee" might be once I promote them.' She made bunny ears. 'People have to start seeing things as an opportunity. It's not always about money.'

Before Millie could reply, Sharon's phone began to ring. The volume was up and the ringtone some thumping electronic dance track. The sort of noise authorities would play on a loop to get protestors to move on.

'I've gotta get this,' Sharon said. She hurried out of the room with a 'Hi, babe' – and then there was the sound of footsteps along the hall and a door closing.

Millie didn't bother to wait. As well as tissues, the bin was full of ripped papers and crumpled envelopes – and she pulled out a handful, before flattening them on the floor.

She didn't have to dig far to see that Sharon owed a lot of money. The first credit card statement was across nine pages and the minimum payment was in the four figures. Sharon had spent thousands in various clothes shops and boutiques. She'd spent four grand at the Apple Store on one day and almost two more a week later. There was an eye-watering six-thousand that she'd spent at an online shoe store – and then, on the same day, fifteen-hundred on Facebook advertising. Among the massive purchases, there were Amazon orders, a gym subscription, four different payments to streaming services – and on and on it went.

That was only one credit card.

The interest from the previous bill was more than Millie would spend in a month. Even conservatively, Sharon was forty- to fifty-thousand pounds in the hole – and that was only her credit cards.

No wonder she didn't have a budget for her relaunch. Or the budget for anything else.

It was hard not to wonder whether Sharon could have taken the picture of her sister, thinking there might be money in selling it. She had been the last person at Zoe's house, after all.

Luke had warned Millie about Sharon – and he'd barely known her.

Luke...

Millie had forgotten that he'd asked her out. She had been swarmed and swamped with thoughts of Kevin Ashworth and those poor boys. Of his dying son.

She was still sitting on the floor, surrounded by ripped-up

credit card statements when Millie tapped out a message to Luke.

> Sorry for taking so long. RU free this aft? Know it's late notice

She wanted something lighter. Craved something less serious.

A door opened somewhere along the hall, so Millie shoved the papers back into the bin and was back on the stool as Sharon bundled her way back into the 'boujee room'.

'So did you think about it?' she asked, as if she'd never left.

Millie needed a second to remember what they'd been talking about. 'I can't plan your event,' she said. 'I don't do that now. It was my old job. I gave it up a while back. I did tell you that...'

Sharon raised a single, plucked eyebrow, as if she didn't recall any of that. 'What do you do now?'

'I run a dog grooming business and write a few pieces about local people and local stories.'

Sharon made a low humming noise. 'Don't take this the wrong way,' she said. 'But that sounds a bit... lame. Why not come work with me? We can relaunch my brand together. Obviously it'll be my name all over it – but I'll tell people you were there.' She stopped, looking Millie up and down, and then added: 'No offence, but nobody knows who you are.'

As usual when somebody casually threw in a 'no offence', there was clear and probably deliberate offence.

Millie bit her lip both metaphorically and actually. The truth was, people in Whitecliff *did* know who she was – and she'd have preferred it if that wasn't the case. Also, even if she did have the mildest interest in Sharon's proposal, if it could be called that, she wasn't entirely clear what the other woman's brand actually was.

'It'll give you the chance to get back into a real job,' Sharon continued. 'You must be missing all the famous people you used to work with?'

'Not really,' Millie replied. 'And they weren't *that* famous. I usually dealt with the agents and talent bookers.' As she was speaking, it suddenly occurred to Millie that Sharon was a couple of years younger than Zoe, who was already younger than Millie herself. She might be the right age... Before Sharon could utter any more nonsense, Millie continued: 'Did you grow up in Whitecliff?'

Sharon had started to say something about how many followers she had online but cut herself off when she realised she'd been asked a question.

'Haven't you seen the video?' she replied. 'I did a walk-around for my followers. Showed them a few places from where I grew up.'

'Did you go to Whitecliff Primary?'

'Everyone went there, didn't they?'

'Were you taught by Mr Ashworth...?'

Something changed at the mention of that name. Sharon had been playing with her hair but she let it fall and, for the first time since Millie had arrived, she put down her phone. And then, unexpectedly, a smile slipped across her face.

'He was my form tutor,' she said. 'He was *so* nice. There was this one boy who used to pick on me – but Mr Ashworth saw it happening once and made him sit at the front of the class. He told me I could go to him if I ever had a problem.' Sharon was swinging her legs back and forth through the legs of the stool. She stopped to think and then added: 'The boys would never let us play football with them. They used to say girls didn't know how to play properly. I told Mr Ashworth and he came out the next lunchtime and made sure we could join in. I didn't even like football – but I wanted to play because they said I couldn't. He was just really... *kind*.' She paused, lost in the moment, and then added: 'Was he your teacher?'

'I'd already left,' Millie replied.

'I didn't know what to think when all that other stuff happened with those boys... I reckon it's better to forget, isn't it? No point in going on about it all the time...'

'Maybe you'd feel differently if it was your brother or sister who'd never been found...?'

For a moment, it felt as if Sharon would ask why Millie was bothered – but she moved on instantly. She had stopped swinging her legs and leaned in a little. With a flutter of her glued eyelashes, she was herself again. 'Can I tell you a secret?' she said.

'Sure.'

'I'm seeing Dane Delaney. We had a couple of dates last month. That's who called me just now. We might go away for New Year.'

Sharon picked up her phone again and swiped, before holding it up for Millie to see to screen. There was a picture of her sitting on the lap of a guy who had dark hair, designer stubble, and a neck tattoo.

Millie couldn't think of a politer way to say it. 'I have no idea who that is.'

Sharon looked to her phone, then Millie, then her phone, as if checking she was showing the correct picture. 'He was on *Botox Boys*,' she said.

'I've never seen it.'

'*Ex Therapy?*'

'I don't watch that much TV.'

'*Always Look On The Brighton Side?*'

'What?'

'You've not seen *Ab-solutely Ab-ulous?*'

'With Jennifer Saunders?'

'Who? No. With Dane. There's all these guy with abs and they have to do these tasks. Someone gets voted off each week. Dane finished third.'

'Sorry...'

Sharon was scrolling on her phone again. She held up a series of photos of her with the mystery man. Most of them involved her pulling a duck face and him staring with the intensity of a serial killer, while wearing a top that apparently didn't fasten.

She continued flicking and scrolling past more pictures that all seemed to be the same. Millie almost looked away, except, as her thin level of interest was about to pass, Sharon flipped across a photo that was familiar. It was a large frame on a wall, containing the image of a naked young woman.

'Was that your sister?' Millie asked quickly.

Sharon stopped scrolling and thumbed her way back. She turned the phone around so Millie could no longer see it. 'It's an old photo,' she replied.

'Why's it on your phone?'

Sharon's nose wrinkled: 'That's none of your business.'

For someone who'd been open about everything, including many things Millie didn't *want* to know, Sharon was suddenly defensive. She put down her phone and stood.

'I'll let you know when I have more details about the relaunch,' she said. 'If you can start reaching out to your people—'

'I'm not going to do it,' Millie said. 'I'm sorry but I don't do that now. If you manage to come up with a budget, I can recommend an agent or two – but I can't do much more than that.'

Sharon scowled, or tried to. Her face didn't move much. She moved to the door and held it wide. 'I've got things to do,' she said. 'Dane said he might come over later, so...'

Millie didn't need telling twice. She thanked Sharon for the opportunity, figuring it was best not to burn bridges, and then she was back outside in the cold. It had already been a bewildering start to the morning – but at least one thing was going her way. Luke had replied while she'd been inside. He said he could be free that afternoon – and asked where Millie wanted to meet.

She sent him a reply and he fired right back to say he'd see her there.

It was only as Millie was getting back into her car that she realised it was going to be her first official date since before she'd married Alex. Her first official date in more than fifteen years.

TWENTY-TWO

The staff smoking area at the back of Whitecliff Nursing Home was officially used by zero smokers. Despite that, it was an area for members of staff and volunteers to have a bit of a skive – and conversations that couldn't be overheard.

That's why Millie still followed Jack outside when he was on a break. He'd given up smoking when the adoption was getting near, having fought against his boyfriend's wishes for years. Even the vaping had gone and, in its place, he'd taken up... Rubik's Cubes.

Millie and Jack slouched on the bench under the cover and stared across the sloped field towards the houses at the bottom. The lights on a Christmas tree were blinking through one of the windows, while, in the distance, the tide was in with the choppy sea blasting the shore.

It was impossible for Millie to stare at the scene below without focusing on the roof from which a resident had said she'd seen a young woman pushed, or fall, a year before. If it hadn't have been for that, Millie wouldn't have asked Guy for his help. Without that, she might not be friends with Nicola again.

Those little ripples.

Meanwhile, Jack was absentmindedly twisting and turning his Rubik's Cube. To an untrained, and *trained*, eye, it all seemed somewhat absurd. But it did give him something to do that wasn't smoking.

'I know you said Rish has been staying home with him – but how has Isaac been?' Millie asked.

'He's fine. He came into the living room last night holding a peanut and said he found it on the floor. I thought Rish was going to have a heart attack. Turned out it was a piece of wood chip Isaac had put in his pocket when they'd been at the playground earlier. Isaac finds the whole thing hilarious. Keeps coughing and saying he can't breathe – then he bursts out laughing.'

Jack was turning the sides of his Rubik's Cube in the frantic way he did. There was a gentle *click-click-click* as his thumbs sped across the toy.

'Where did he learn such savagery?' Millie asked.

'Not off me and definitely not off Rish. That kid's gonna be some sort of prankster when he grows up. We've been trying to tell him it's not funny.'

'How's Rish taking it?'

That got a raised eyebrow stare. 'How do you *think* he's taking it? He's turned cleaning into an Olympic sport. He gets up at half-five every morning so he can sweep the living room. I tell him nobody's snuck a peanut into the flat overnight but he says we can't be too careful.' A pause and a sigh. 'I think he feels guilty because he wasn't there when it happened...'

There wasn't a lot Millie could say to that.

'We've got EpiPens in every room,' Jack added.

'It's hard to blame Rish for that.'

'I know... it's just... exhausting. All of it.' He nodded back towards the nursing home. 'I used to take home leftovers for dinner some nights. I can't do that now because Rish is paranoid about outside food. He buys everything fresh and makes all our meals himself.'

'Can I come over?'

Another sideways look. 'I wouldn't mind but he's still full-time at the coffee shop. Or he would be if he hadn't taken sick leave. I don't know how it's all going to work after new year when he's definitely got to go back to work. I had to plead with him to take Isaac to the playground. He thinks there are nuts hiding everywhere.'

Millie rubbed his arm gently and Jack gave a soft small smile as he continued to work on the cube.

'Isaac's having night terrors,' he said. 'They started about three weeks ago, so I don't think they're related to what happened. He's himself during the day – but then he'll scream the flat down every couple of nights.'

Jack yawned and didn't bother to cover his mouth. He apologised and then immediately did it again.

'I just need a good night's sleep,' he said.

'Did you ask the doctor about the night terrors?'

'And the social worker. They both said it's something that can happen. That kids grow out of it. They talked about regular bedtimes, eating early, all that – but we already do it.'

Another yawn.

Jack put down the Rubik's Cube – and it didn't appear any more complete than it had been when he'd taken it from his bag.

'Are you coming to the Bay Burning tonight?' Millie asked.

Jack shook his head as he fought another yawn: 'No. We were thinking about watching it from the beach but we're not going to do that now. You're in Rish's bad books for making Isaac think the town are going to set fire to The Fraggles. Isaac won't even watch the show any more. Rish said he's surprised you didn't tell him Santa's not real.'

Millie reeled back. 'Santa's... *not real*?'

A snort. 'Sorry to break it to you.'

They sat quietly for a moment, watching the houses at the bottom of the valley. A light flickered on in one and then went off again. Moments later, a string of fairy lights around a window frame blinked to life.

'Can I tell you something?' Millie asked. 'You can't tell anyone. Not even Rish.'

'I told you before: you're not meant to stick it up there.'

Millie snorted this time – but it was only momentary amusement.

'Do you know the name Kevin Ashworth?' she asked.

'Of course. Who doesn't?'

'I've met him twice this week,' Millie replied. 'I was out on the moors with him – and then I saw him in prison yesterday morning.'

Jack had been about to blow into his hands but he stopped and turned to her. 'Are you joking?'

It was spilling out of her now. 'We thought he was going to show us what happened to those boys but he led us to some sort of coffin. There were bones inside – but not from Wesley and Shaun. We think they were from a baby. Maybe *his* baby...'

Jack was silent and staring. His mouth was open. 'This isn't funny, Mill.'

She took his hand and squeezed. His fingers were cold but so were hers. 'I'm not joking.'

Jack let go and picked up his Rubik's Cube. Without looking, he started rotating and turning. 'What? Why you?'

'Not me. Not really. He knows Guy from way back. He told the police he'd only talk to Guy – and Guy said he'd only speak with Ashworth if I was allowed to be there.' She waited a beat, re-running what she'd said. 'Guy did ask me if that was OK,' she added.

'And you said you wanted to be involved?' Jack sounded somewhat disbelieving.

'Sort of. Yes, I suppose. I didn't know what it would be like.'

'What *is* it like?'

Millie sank lower in the seat, allowing her head to droop. She rubbed her thumbs into her eyes and watched the greeny stars dance inside her eyelids.

'I can't stop thinking about it,' she said. 'I keep seeing Eric as one of the boys who went missing. I have to stop myself from calling Alex, or the school, to make sure Eric's safe.'

Jack let out a long, low breath which didn't feel too reassuring. 'Wow...'

Millie didn't speak for a while. She was already regretting telling someone about what was happening, even though she didn't think Jack would pass it on.

'What's he like?' Jack asked.

'Ashworth? Kinda pathetic,' Millie replied. 'He was attacked in prison and there are bad scars on his face. I think, maybe, he just wants attention. He's been locked up for so long and he knows he's never getting out.'

'Does that mean he's going to tell you what happened to those boys, or...?'

When she wasn't worrying about Eric's safety, it was the question that Millie was endlessly asking herself.

'I don't know,' Millie said. 'I'm not sure we'll see him again. The police probably don't want us to talk to him again – but if he'll only talk to Guy, then maybe they'll have no choice?'

She thought for a moment, wondering if she should hold back the rest, before deciding that she'd already told Jack things that should have been kept to herself.

'I was at the hospice yesterday, too,' she added. 'Ashworth's son is there. He's my age, more or less. A little older. He's dying of leukaemia. They don't think he'll make Christmas. His dad asked us to tell his son that he loved him.'

'*Christmas?* That's only' – Jack counted on his fingers – 'four days...'

He looked to Millie who nodded. 'I know...'

Jack started to ask 'Why couldn't—' but then stopped himself. Nicholas was too ill to go to the prison, while his dad wasn't allowed out. 'Is that why he asked for Guy? And you? Because he wanted that message passed on but he didn't trust the police?'

'Maybe. It feels like there's something I'm not getting.'

'Like what?'

'If I knew that, I wouldn't be missing it.'

Millie apologised because it had come out harsher than she'd meant. Jack was busy with his Rubik's Cube anyway. She could sense something coming – but it was still a surprise when it did.

'Mr Ashworth was one of my teachers,' he said.

Jack was younger than Millie – but she hadn't considered that Ashworth might have taught him.

'*Really?*'

A nod. 'It's weird how you always think of them as "Mrs" or "Mr", isn't it? I know his name's Kevin because of the court case and all the news reports. But I always think of him as "Mr Ashworth". I don't remember him that well. You know when you don't have a specific memory but it's more of a feeling? It's like that. I couldn't tell you anything he ever said, or did, but I remember liking him. I thought he was funny but I can't tell you why?' A pause: 'Did he teach you?'

'I'm too old.'

Jack laughed. 'I didn't want to be the one to say it...'

Millie rested her head on his shoulder. It had been good to unload on someone. The weight of Ashworth wasn't quite what it had been that morning.

'Can I tell you something else?' Millie whispered. She didn't wait for the answer. 'I sort of feel sorry for him.'

'Ashworth?'

'Yeah... His son's dying and he doesn't get a chance to say bye. He had to get strangers to do it instead. I'm not saying they should let him out, I just... I feel bad for feeling sorry for him. I think about the mother of one of those boys – and I think about Eric and I know I should hate him. I want to. I sort of do. I tell myself he's a monster, but then monsters don't want to pass on messages to their kids that they've been proud to be their dads. I can't quite fit it all together...'

Millie wasn't sure what she wanted to hear. Probably nothing, she'd simply wanted to speak. And that's what happened. That's why Jack was her friend. He put down the cube and slipped an arm around her. They sat, listening to the breeze, watching the blinking Christmas lights below.

It was a text message that brought Millie back to the bench. Her bag buzzed and she was stunned to see Guy's name on the screen. He didn't really *do* messaging. Texts were almost beyond him and anything like WhatsApp certainly was. He preferred calls and actual conversations, which is why it was a surprise to see 'Baker says he's done with games' as a message.

Jack wouldn't normally snoop – but he must have seen something in her face as she re-locked the screen. 'Problem?' he asked.

'I don't think the police are letting us see Ashworth any more. It's not really a surprise.'

'So you're not going to know what happened?'

A shrug: 'I guess not.'

As Millie was dropping her phone back into her bag, she noticed the time. She'd only popped in for a couple of hours.

'I have to get off,' she said. 'I'll be in for the Christmas party the day after tomorrow.'

They stood, hugged, and then stepped away.

'Where are you off to?' Jack asked.

'I have a date.'

Millie slipped it in quickly, as if telling him she was stopping off for a sandwich. She was a step or two away when Jack realised what she'd said.

'What?' Jack said. 'How is this the first I'm hearing of it? A date? With a guy? An *actual* guy?'

'What other sort of guys are there?'

'Where did you meet? What does he look like? Has he got dark hair? He's not bald is he? What's his name? Do I know him? He's not one of those blokes who lifts and talks about "gains", is he? I told you about that—'

'He's just a normal man,' Millie replied. She hoped it was true. 'I'll tell you about him another day. Maybe. If it goes well.'

She moved towards the door as Jack put an arm across her. 'You can't leave me hanging like this. At least tell me his name!'

'Say "hi" to Rish for me. And Isaac.' Millie stepped around his arm. 'I'll see you at the party if I don't see you before.'

TWENTY-THREE

Millie was early. She'd considered going home to get changed – except it wasn't quite lunch – and it also wasn't the sort of place where *anyone* got dressed up.

That's why Millie had chosen it.

That, and she felt safe there.

The grungy diner on the outskirts of Whitecliff was the place she'd been with Guy a little over a year ago when she'd realised she trusted him. There was foam spilling from the benches, the ceiling was coated with a thin sliver of oil, and the whole place smelled of fried food. The sign outside claimed the all-day breakfast was 'world-famous', which Millie doubted – although it was the sort of thing a person who ate it wouldn't forget in a hurry.

There were only two other women in the caff – and one of them was behind the counter. Other than that, there were a lot of drivers and workmen on a break. That was the crowd, after all.

Millie had a booth to herself as some sort of hair rock played quietly through the speakers. Luke wasn't late but she checked her phone anyway, wondering if he'd sent anything to say he was on his way... or that he wasn't coming.

There was nothing since they'd swapped messages that morning. Millie had suggested the diner almost as a joke. A joke that wasn't a joke. She wondered if he'd say no, almost dared him, but he'd simply replied that he knew the place and he'd see her at two.

With nothing from him, Millie checked her Instagram. There was a message from someone asking about her rates for grooming a long-haired dog – and Millie took the time to reply, even though the information was on her webpage.

She then re-read the forwarded message Zoe had sent her the day before, and clicked through to the profile that had uploaded a snippet of the stolen photo.

There were two pictures on the account now.

The newer one had been posted an hour before and was much like the first. It was a zoomed-in, cropped image of what looked like it might be a neck. The caption was the same as the first – 'coming soon' – but more media organisations had been tagged in.

There were no comments and, though Millie couldn't see how many likes the picture had received, she doubted it was many. The account itself only had two followers – Zoe and Millie – and Millie's wasn't even in her own name.

Millie forwarded the post to Zoe and asked if she'd seen it. The reply was instant. She'd been tagged in it but untagged herself as soon as it had appeared. Millie asked if Zoe had received any other messages but there had apparently been none. No demands, no threats, just a simple 'coming soon' offered to as many media organisations as the poster could seemingly think of.

It didn't look as if any of them had bitten.

Millie was beginning to have an idea as a shadow drifted

across her. A man dumped his coat on the bench opposite and slid onto the seat.

'Fancy seeing a woman like you in a place like this,' Luke said.

He was grinning as he said it, before pulling off a jumper that he put on top of his coat.

'What's wrong with seeing a woman like me in a place like this?' Millie asked.

'I suppose I didn't have you pegged as the fried egg, Bon Jovi type.'

'I figured it's a bit out of town. People who come here don't care who else is in the caff...'

Luke turned and took in the rest of the room, although it felt like he already knew. There were men in ones or twos, reading papers, or scanning their phones as they ate. For a public place, the diner was as anonymous as it came.

'Don't want to be seen with me, huh?' Luke replied.

'It's not that. It's just...'

Millie could see that he knew.

He bowed his head a fraction and then confirmed what she'd feared all along. 'I know who you are,' he said. 'It's not why I asked you out – but I live in Whitecliff. It's pretty much impossible to not know who you are.' He stopped and picked up a fork that he started to twiddle between his fingers. 'I did wonder why *you* turned up on my door asking about stolen goods...?'

Millie left that one open. The answer felt too complicated to explain when she was trying to give off the air of being somewhat normal.

Luke nodded to the counter. 'Did you order?'

'Not yet?'

'What do you want?'

'You don't have to pay for me. I think I'd prefer we pay for ourselves.'

That got a shrug. 'Suit yourself. I guess I'll see you there.' Luke took four steps across to the counter and grinned back at her. 'You snooze, you lose.'

Millie got in line behind him and, a minute or so later, they were back across from each other in the booth.

Luke removed another top and it looked as if he had at least two more underneath.

'Been working outside,' he said, by way of explanation.

'Do people fit kitchens *outside...*?'

He let her have the moment. 'I'm working at one of the big houses on the hill. They're splitting it into three and refitting it as an Airbnb. I spent all morning pulling stuff out. I'm back there tomorrow to start putting new stuff in.' He faked a yawn and patted his mouth for emphasis. 'Do you *really* want to talk about my work?'

'I like it when people who know what they're on about talk about things. Plus I've been doing a lot of talking recently and, sometimes, it's nice to listen.'

Luke tilted his head a fraction as Millie realised it was deeper than she meant it to be.

'I'm not usually this serious,' she said.

'It sounds like you have a lot on?'

Millie found herself sighing, which wasn't a great impression. 'I don't think I'm great company,' she said. 'Sorry... I didn't mean to waste your time. I'm not used to... *this*.' Millie waved an arm around, meaning the date, the meal out... everything.

'It's not a waste of my time.'

Luke sounded truthful, which was a kindness Millie wasn't sure she deserved.

'I suppose I've been wondering why you asked me out,' she said. 'I worried it was because you knew who I was – and now it turns out you do.'

'What's wrong with that?'

'Because people always want to ask the same thing. About

why I had an affair with that MP. About how my parents died and if I had anything to do with it...' Millie took a breath. She was blowing it as big as anyone had ever blown anything. Why on earth had she brought up the affair? Of all things. On a first date. 'Sorry...' she managed.

Luke smiled kindly. 'I don't really care about any of that stuff – unless you want to talk about it for some reason.'

'I don't. But I'm still wondering why you asked me out. If it's not about that...'

'You must have some clue.'

He was smiling in a knowing way, as if there was an obvious answer that Millie couldn't see. As she struggled to think of a reason, he came out with it.

'I asked you out because I fancied you. Is that what you wanted to hear? I thought you seemed interesting, despite you accusing me of theft the first time we spoke. I thought you might be a laugh.'

Millie wasn't sure how to reply. It was all a bit... teenagery. And yet many of the same things were true for her now as they would've been then. When she'd asked out Mark Reynolds in high school, it had been because she fancied him. Because she thought he was a laugh.

'I'm not sure I'm much of a laugh,' Millie found herself saying.

'But you're admitting you're fanciable...?'

'I didn't—'

Luke's grin stopped her mid-sentence – and then they were interrupted by the waitress appearing with two plates of food. Millie had gone for the same tomatoes on toast she'd had when she'd last visited. Luke was having the all-day breakfast – but it was something close to a portion that one person could finish, without needing a stomach pump. He squirted a blob of brown sauce into the corner and then set about cutting up a sausage.

'How about you?' Luke asked. 'Why did you agree to come out with me?'

Millie was chewing a mouthful of tomatoes, which gave her a few seconds to think. As disastrous as things felt like they were going, there was at least honesty between them.

'I suppose I thought it would be nice to be out with someone who I don't really know. Someone I'm not arguing with. Someone who's more or less my age. There's only so many times you can sit across from an eight-year-old boy in McDonald's and listen to them talk about stickers.'

Luke dipped a piece of sausage in his egg and swirled it around. 'I love stickers. I only need two more shinies to complete this year's Premier League book.'

He laughed, unable to keep up the pretence.

'I'm guessing that's *your* eight-year-old boy?' he added. 'You're not just rounding up random kids off the street and taking them to McDonald's?'

She laughed. 'Yes, my son. What about you? Divorced? Separated? Kids?'

'No, no and no.' There must have been something in Millie's face because he added: 'Is that really a surprise?'

Millie chewed a piece of toast, giving herself a moment to think. 'I suppose I don't know anyone roughly our age who's not one of those three things.'

Luke was swirling the egg yolk into the brown sauce, into the bean juice, which had encompassed the potato shreds. Everything was mixed together and there were no barriers on his plate. It was a demented way of eating.

'I travelled a lot in my twenties,' Luke said. 'I worked in resorts around the Med. A year or two in one place, then onto the next. I didn't have kids and I don't think it's my thing. Even if it was, I'm probably a bit old for it now.' A pause. 'Do you have just the one son?'

A nod. 'Eric. He turned eight last summer. I'm taking him to the Bay Burning later.'

Luke was still stirring his food into a giant beany casserole. 'I remember the first time I went,' he said. 'I would've been about seven or eight. I was terrified. It's a completely mad tradition when you think about it. I remember being in Faliraki and trying to explain it to a local girl out there. She thought we were all savages.'

Millie laughed again. 'Everyone from Whitecliff has a similar story. You assume it's normal, then you mention it to someone who's not from round here, and they think you're a maniac.'

Luke laughed at that and they sat contented for a short while. Each eating carefully, their mouths closed. Best behaviours and all that.

'Eric's dad has custody,' Millie added. 'He's getting remarried on Christmas Eve. I don't really want to talk about him but it felt relevant.'

A nod. 'It's fine.' Luke put down his fork and picked up a triangle of fried bread that he dipped in the soup he'd created. 'So, basically,' he said. 'We're two single people in our late thirties. It sounds like we have at least that in common...?'

Millie used a fork to mush the remainder of her tomatoes into a pile, away from the toast. Guns N' Roses were playing through the speakers and the man sitting alone in the booth directly in her line of sight was nodding away to the music.

'I'm not sure I'm after a relationship at the moment,' Millie said, while staring at her plate. 'I know it's a cliché. I probably shouldn't have said yes to all this. Maybe we can just... enjoy this? Maybe we can do it again next week and see what it's like?' She looked up. 'I don't know what I want. You're the first person to ask me out, probably since school.'

Luke didn't reply right away. 'I don't mind. I usually have

cheese and pickle sandwiches in the front seat of my van for lunch. This is a definite improvement.'

Millie finished her tomatoes and picked up the final piece of toast. Being around Luke felt close to normal. Comfortable. It really was true that Millie couldn't remember the last time she'd eaten out when there hadn't been a child there.

'Sorry for accusing you of theft,' Millie said.

That got a friendly looking roll of the eyes. 'It's not every day I get asked to install a kitchen for a pop star – and then have a local celeb turn up to accuse of nicking something.'

'I'm not a local celeb.'

'I'm teasing. Anyway, that's something awkward and odd that happened to me. What about you?'

Millie only needed a moment to think about it. 'I got a call last summer from the hospital. A man had been found unconscious. The nurses didn't know who *he* was but he had my details on him.'

'Who was he?'

'A hoarder who lives in Whitecliff. I was at his house the week before that happened. It's a long story why but I sort of *borrowed* some photos from him that I hadn't returned. He was presumably on his way to me to get them back when he had a heart attack. He'd hit his head and someone called the ambulance. When I got the call, I had no idea who it was. I went to the hospital fearing it was someone I knew. They led me through the corridors and it was really sombre, like I was going to identify a relative. And then it was the body of this odd man I'd only met once. I had no idea what to tell them. I knew who it was, but I didn't really know him.'

Luke eyed her curiously for a moment. 'What were the photos of?'

'Me and my friends.'

'Why did he have them?'

'That's part of the long story. Maybe another day...?'

Luke's plate was more or less clean. He picked up Millie's and put it on top of his, then stacked the cutlery on top. The waitress was on her way to another table and said she'd grab them in a minute but Luke told her it wasn't a problem and carried them to the counter for her.

It might have been for show but Millie chose to believe he was one of those people who treated servers and retail workers like normal people, instead of servants.

'Do you want to hear something dumb?' Luke said as he slotted back into place.

'*How* dumb?'

'I read an article this morning for things to talk about on a first date. It was one of those lists, where it gives ten things you should ask.'

'My friend was trying to get me to go speed dating. She sent me something almost identical the other day. It was stuff like "What's your favourite colour?" – but even my eight-year-old has grown out of having a favourite colour.'

Luke nodded along. 'I think we might've seen the same piece. Favourite colour, movie, band, travel destination, all that.'

'Was the final one biggest fear?' Millie asked.

'Yeah. I thought, "Who talks about that on a date?" – but then you brought up having an affair and your parents in the first minute, so...'

He laughed kindly and Millie found herself joining in. Despite everything, it had been liberating to get so much out of the way at the beginning. Whenever she met a new person, those things would linger and niggle as Millie wondered whether they knew who she was. Whether they cared. Whether they'd already judged her. Luke had accepted it with a shrug and they'd moved on. It was a glimpse of the sort of life Millie hadn't believed she could have again.

'My biggest fear is dying alone,' Luke said. 'May as well get it out of the way. Bit morbid but there you are.'

It *was* a bit morbid – but it fitted with the nature of their conversation. Perhaps getting everything out at the beginning was the way things were supposed to be?

'I think someone betrayed me,' Millie said. She whispered it, because putting it into words made it more real. 'You know about my affair with the MP. Everyone does. It's in the past and a mistake. But someone tipped off the paper, or told a photographer. They knew where we'd be – and I guess I've wondered ever since if it was someone *I* know who did it.'

Despite the things they'd spoken about, it was only now that they felt serious.

Luke must have sensed it as well. He checked over his shoulder, making sure nobody was close enough to overhear, and then he leaned in. His whisper matched hers.

'Why would it be someone you know, not someone *he* knew?'

'Because he had so much more to lose than me. He's still got an election to fight and some people don't like that sort of thing. His party could've demoted him. He's married, with kids – and his wife could've left him. It doesn't seem like he lost anything in the end but it could have all gone.'

'Perhaps he was careless with messages, something like that? Someone he knows found out? His wife?'

'Maybe.'

'Did you tell anyone...? It's not my business but—'

'No one specifically – but that's why I think about it sometimes. Maybe someone I know figured it out? Maybe it *was* someone on his side? It's hard when you don't know. I suppose I'm always careful about what I say and who I say it to.' A pause. 'Not so much today...'

That got a smile and then Luke scratched his head and leaned in a fraction further. 'I know someone,' he said. 'An old friend of my uncle's is a private investigator up in Manchester. He mainly does background checks on employees for these big FTSE companies but, other than that, he takes on cases that interest him. He might be able to get a name for you...?'

Millie stared for a moment, wondering if it was a serious offer, before realising he had no reason to invent such a tale.

'No,' she replied, before repeating herself quickly. It felt as if she was trying to convince herself more than him. She wanted the reassurance and yet, deep down, she wondered if she actually did. Knowing could be worse than *not* knowing. 'Thank you for the offer,' she added.

Luke had been drinking from a giant mug of tea. He downed the final dregs and then asked if she wanted a refill.

'I've got to get home,' she replied. 'It's the Bay Burning and I've got my son...'

It was true – although she didn't have to rush off immediately. It felt like their conversation had gone well enough and she figured there was more chance of messing things up if they continued talking.

'Let's go out one evening,' Luke said. 'Drinks, or something like that? Doesn't have to be this week. We can go slow...?'

'I don't drink,' Millie replied, delaying, not wanting to commit. That sort of thing hadn't gone well in the past.

'Do you eat? I mean, I just watched you, so...'

Millie wanted to say yes, she really did, except she couldn't quite let herself. There would be hope and anticipation if she did – and with that might come disappointment.

'I've got so much on these next couple of weeks, with Christmas and everything,' Millie said, even though it wasn't particularly true. She had surprisingly little on, in fact. 'Maybe in the new year?' she found herself adding. 'I don't want to promise but... this has been good. Weird but good. I don't want to lead you on.'

'You haven't and you're not. If nothing else, the food was fab and so was the conversation.'

Luke slipped from the booth and stood. He stretched high as Millie joined him at the side of the table.

'What do we do now?' he asked. 'Do we shake hands?'

She offered hers and he shook it. Then, just as he was about to step away, Millie moved into him and pressed herself momentarily against his breastbone. He clasped her gently, then a little harder, and then she stepped away.

'Was that OK?' Millie asked.

She felt the weight of others in the diner watching them now. It had been an odd moment in a place where very little happened that didn't involve eating.

'It was good for me,' Luke said. He took a pace towards the door. 'I'll see you soon, right?'

Millie smiled as an answer. It was the only one she could give.

They walked together to the exit and he held open the door for her. They went out into the freezing car park and she was already back in her vehicle when she gave a proper reply, talking to herself.

'See you soon.'

TWENTY-FOUR

Millie was sitting in her car, again waiting for the windows to demist. Luke had driven off in his van and she'd watched him go while fighting the urge to send him a message. When she'd been younger, she'd hated the silly games of pretending not to like someone. The whole *treat 'em mean* nonsense.

Now, she wanted to tell him she'd enjoyed the afternoon – but wasn't sure why she simply couldn't do it. Perhaps she'd wait an hour? Or two? Or see if he messaged her? He'd listened to all her nonsense, barely batted an eyelid, and then asked to see her again. That meant something, didn't it?

Millie picked up the newspaper she'd taken from Guy the day before. It was still on the passenger seat, still folded open at the page with the article about Kevin Ashworth's charity walk. She'd read every word three or four times and couldn't escape the feeling she was missing something. It was like trying to think of an elusive word that was so close, yet wouldn't come.

And then Millie saw it.

It wasn't the words that carried a clue, it was the picture.

Millie was out of the car park and halfway to Guy's house

before she'd even thought to check he was in. He usually was – but there was no guarantee he'd answer, even if she called.

There was nobody following her on the track up to his house this time around. Her car bumped and bobbled across the uneven ground until she stopped outside his gate. There was a light on inside and Millie hurried along the path, paper in her hand. Guy had given her a key but the door wasn't locked anyway.

Barry was in the hall, although he wasn't even pretending to be a guard dog. He'd been snoozing between two stacks of papers and barely raised his head as Millie entered the hall. He lapped her wrist as she said hello, and then rolled onto his back for her to rub his belly. Millie obliged – but only for a few seconds.

Guy was in his office, working at the desktop computer. He didn't seem surprised to see her but he did stop typing. The windows were misty with condensation and the room clammy.

Millie was so excited, she could barely get out the words as she put the paper on the desk at Guy's side.

'It's the map,' she said, pointing to the image next to the main photo.

Guy picked up the page and squinted down to it. 'What about it?' he asked.

'It shows the route they took for the charity walk. They start in Whitecliff and go up to the moors, really close to the farm where Ashworth grew up. Then they take the route across to Steeple's End. It's the long way around because you can't go all the way along the cliffs in a straight line.'

Guy eyed the map and then looked back to her blankly. All that was already known.

'Look at the main picture,' Millie added. 'It shows Ashworth *on the walk* standing in front of a lake. But then you look at the map, and there's no lake on the route. I checked Google Maps and there's no lake there either. It must be somewhere on the moors – but where?'

Guy looked to the paper one more time – and then spun on his chair to take in the giant map of the area that was pinned to the wall. They crossed to it together and he pressed a finger to the spot that showed more or less where the Ashworth family farm had once been. There was a large expanse of green all around but, between there and Steeple's End, there wasn't a single spot of blue.

'You said that nobody ever asked where the car ended up,' Millie added. 'Everyone talked about the boys but never the car. But if Ashworth knows the moors better than anyone – including whoever made these maps – maybe we just need to find that lake.'

TWENTY-FIVE

Millie and Guy were back at the farm again. She didn't have long because she had to pick up Eric – but there was time.

It was the grimmest day of a grim month. The clouds were low and they were both wrapped in the full winter garb of coats, gloves, hats and scarves. Barry was happy to be out, regardless of the weather. As soon as Guy waved him on, the dog bounded along the path. He waited at the side of the farmhouse and, as they passed without stopping, he charged ahead onto the moor itself.

The map from the paper was small, with the charity walking route marked as a dotted line stretching across the moors. The roads were labelled, which gave them some idea of where they were – but it was far from exact.

They walked anyway, heading towards the trees in the distance. On the other side of the trees, miles in the distance, was Steeple's End. It was the next village along the coast, though there was no direct road between the two places. Drivers had to head inland, hop onto the main road, and then drop back down.

The nearest direct route was across the moors.

It was hard for Millie and Guy to talk because the sideways wind and drizzle threw their words into the void. They walked together, heads down, following Barry further away from the farmhouse. Fifteen or twenty minutes had passed when Guy touched her arm and pulled Millie close. They huddled from the conditions, checking Millie's phone and the photo she'd taken of the map from the paper. Her phone's GPS told her they were roughly on track – although there was nothing else to indicate that. There was no track, no trail, nothing except brush, moss, rocks and tufty branches.

'I can't go too much longer,' Millie said. Shouted, really. 'I've got to pick up Eric.'

Millie had been doubting herself ever since she'd pointed out the map and the picture to Guy. It felt logical in her head. Less so now they were in the middle of the squall.

'Why don't you come?' she added. 'To the Bay Burning.'

A fizzing, biting blast whistled through them, sending shivers through Millie's body. Her teeth chattered and then, as quickly as the chill had arrived, the rest of the wind dipped. A temporary truce. They turned and continued walking together, almost shoulder to shoulder.

'I've not been in years,' Guy said.

'All the more reason to go. You can toss your worries and grievances into the fire.'

Guy chuckled a little. 'Twenty years ago and it would have needed a big bit of paper. After Carol passed, I tend not to worry so much.'

'Come anyway. I think Eric would like to see you.'

The ground was bobbly, with rocks and roots hidden underneath the brush. Millie kept catching her foot and stumbling. Somehow, Guy was managing to walk as if they were on a pavement.

'That sounds good.' A pause. 'What problems are you going to be writing down?'

'I've not thought that far ahead.'

Guy didn't reply at first. It was a lie and he probably knew it. If Millie was going to write anything down, it would be that she wanted custody of her son. That she was worried Alex and Rachel getting married meant she'd see even less of Eric.

'How much longer can you walk?' Guy asked.

Millie checked the clock on her phone. 'Maybe fifteen minutes.'

A few paces more and Millie tripped on another hidden root. She assumed Guy had spent so many years walking his dog on the moors and through the woods, that he was somehow immune to it all.

'Maybe we should've shown the article to the police?' she said. 'Told them we were wondering if there's an unmarked lake somewhere out here.'

'I don't think we're in their good books. Well, I don't think *I'm* in their good books. Besides, it's not necessarily anything. The last thing we want is to waste more of their time.'

'Do you think there could be a lake?'

Guy thought on it for a little longer than Millie wanted. She wondered if he was humouring her. If he'd simply not wanted to shoot down her idea so instantly.

'It's not as far-fetched as it might sound,' he said, carefully, waving a hand off towards the trees. 'I realise there are satellite photos but most of this is uncharted. There are no real hiking routes, no shoots or hunts, not much of anything. People do walk over the moors, or ride mountain bikes. There are always the odd reports of people on scrambler bikes, too. In the time I was on the paper, we had at least six calls from people convinced they'd seen a UFO somewhere out this way.'

'Aliens live out here, then?'

A laugh: 'Seemingly. I'll tell you about my night covering the crop circle craze one day. Either way, you might be surprised at how much of this area hasn't been mapped in any real sense. It's a wilderness in many ways.'

'It would still be quite hard to miss a lake...'

'True.'

Millie took out her phone and moved her trembling fingers around the screen until she'd loaded Maps. She switched to satellite mode and pinched her way into where they were. The images must have been stored towards the end of the summer as there was a vast expanse of light yellowy, brown. The land was a different colour to the greeny moss on which they were walking.

Millie swiped around and couldn't see anything like a lake. There were a few spots that looked boggy, as if there might have been some heavy rain at some point, but that was it. No lake.

The walk suddenly felt like even more of a waste of time. Until Guy had mentioned satellite images, it hadn't occurred to Millie that there was an easier way to check. The photo of Ashworth on the walk must have been taken somewhere else, maybe even a different walk.

Millie continued anyway, wondering why Guy hadn't suggested turning around. Wondering why she hadn't. It was after a minute or two that she remembered there was more than one photo on the newspaper page. As well as the one of Ashworth in front of a lake, there was another of the finishers in Steeple's End – and he was wearing the same shorts and vest in both pictures.

They had to have been taken on the same day.

The wind had picked up again and was bristling sideways across the moor. Millie and Guy had achieved nothing except a bit of exercise. Somehow, the trees in the distance seemed as far away as they had been when they set off.

Millie slowed and stopped as Guy did the same. She turned and half expected the farmhouse to still be behind them. It wasn't. That was in the distance as well. They'd walked for almost forty-five minutes and it didn't feel as if they'd got anywhere.

Barry was a few metres ahead, tail wagging slowly as he looked back towards Millie and Guy. She had the sense he'd have walked all night if they'd kept going.

'How far do you think we've gone?' Millie asked.

'A mile and a half? Perhaps a little more.'

It didn't sound, or feel, like much. The terrain had slowed them but neither of them were quick walkers.

'I have to head back,' Millie said. She made the mistake of looking to the dog, who was giving it the big eyes. 'Fine,' she added, almost immediately. 'Five more minutes.'

Guy snorted but they continued over the uneven ground, up towards some sort of ridge that was ringed by a series of spindly low bushes. Barry bounded on, perhaps aware they were on the brink of turning around.

Millie was beginning to feel the strain in her legs. When she wasn't talking about speed dating, Nicola had been trying to convince Millie to join the same gym as her. She said they could do classes together, claiming it would be 'fun', which left Millie wondering if there was more than one definition of that word. She didn't fancy the exercise, let alone in front of other people.

Five minutes passed but they weren't quite at the ridge, so Millie said nothing. They walked silently for another minute. Two. Barry was sitting in a gap between the scrawny, windswept bush. There was no sign of leaves, only twigs.

And then she saw it.

They were almost on top of it before it was in sight. Hidden behind the bushes, pooled in a natural groove, was a murky, browny stretch of water.

Guy was half a step behind Millie but she heard him let out a long, low whistle as he slotted in at her side.

'The photo was taken somewhere around here,' Millie said. She had looked at the article enough times to know.

They stood together, staring over the ridge at the water. It was a muddy, swirling brown; the colour of tea with a splash of milk. Millie took out her phone and checked Maps, pinching her way in to where there was the merest dot of black among the barren land.

'A winter lake,' Guy said.

'What's that?'

'I don't know if there's an official name – but there's one in the woods near my house. For about three to four months every winter, it's impassable. All the rain runs into the valley and creates a pool across the trail. It's thigh-high at its peak, but, by summer, it's gone. You'd never know it existed if you didn't live in the area.' He glanced towards the dog. 'I always have to tell Barry off for trying to drink from it.'

Guy pointed towards the slope that angled above them. The road was a good couple of miles from the top, meaning all the rain, snowmelt, silt and mud would run into the ditch in front of them.

Millie turned back the way they'd come and, though it was subtle, now she was looking for it, she could see a slope in that direction as well. They'd been walking slightly downhill ever since the farmhouse.

'There's no natural water source here,' Guy said.

Millie had been thinking the same. There was no river, no stream, no outlet that would lead to the ocean. Over the course of the winter, the dip would fill with muddy water and then, presumably, through the summer, it would evaporate.

'Do you think the police searched this far out?' Millie asked.

'I doubt it. They put all their resources into the farmhouse and the immediate area. Even if they did, we only noticed the water when we were almost in it.'

That was true enough. It was also the sort of nowhere spot that hikers and dog-walkers probably wouldn't get to. Even if they did, a murky pool of water that was only prominent for a few months, during the wettest, grimmest time of year, likely wouldn't make much of an impact.

'Do you think it ever empties?' Millie asked.

'I... don't know.'

It felt strange that Guy wouldn't know something. Millie was used to him having an idea about everything. Before anything else could happen, Guy's phone rang. It was the default tone, because of course it was. The bigger surprise was that they had reception in the middle of nowhere. Millie checked her own phone, where there was one wavering bar.

Guy fumbled and fiddled before pressing to answer. There were a few pardons and sorrys. A 'Can you repeat that?', a couple of 'OKs' and then a 'Thank you for letting me know.'

When he slipped the phone back into his pocket, Guy sighed and slumped. He called Barry's name and then thumbed back the way they'd come. The dog set off at a canter, leaving Millie and Guy behind.

When he spoke, his tone was sullen and sad. 'Nicholas died at the hospice this morning,' Guy said quietly.

TWENTY-SIX

Millie and Guy didn't talk much on the walk back to the cars. She couldn't quite get her head around the fact that the man for whom she'd bought cake the day before had died. They'd said he was sick, and he clearly was, but he'd actually *died*.

He was a couple of years older than her and he was... *gone*.

It was unfathomable.

She found her thoughts drifting to Kevin Ashworth in his prison cell. She wondered who told him that his son had died and how he'd taken it. How could it be true that someone who'd robbed parents of *their* children could care so much about his own? She didn't want to feel sorry for him but it was impossible not to. She'd sat across from him when he'd asked them to pass on his message. It hadn't once occurred to her that it wasn't genuine.

And then Millie was thinking of Eric again, wondering how she'd cope if he was terminally ill. She couldn't stop thinking about it. There were the times he said he had a headache, or he felt tired. Maybe it wasn't *just* a headache. Maybe it wasn't *only* tiredness. She should have pushed Alex to make sure he went to the GP and had things looked at.

They were back at the farmhouse before Millie knew it, then she was on the road to the school. Picking up Eric was rare, let alone twice in a week. She was haunted by thoughts of him being ill as she waited a little away from the gates.

Eric was happy to see her and eager to talk about Chloe and the things they'd done in class. Millie listened and tried to push away thoughts that there could be anything wrong with him.

At home they had a quick meal before heading out into town. There was a crowd of people around the 'Welcome to Whitecliff' sign. It had been commissioned a few years before, and contained a mural of the pier, the promenade and the ocean. People were posing for selfies and live streaming themselves as, paces away, Guy stood by himself. He was in the same coat, scarf and gloves as earlier in the day, and asked Eric how 'my little man' was doing. They weren't related and had only met a handful of times – but Eric took it in his stride and was soon chatting away about the science experiment they'd done at school. From what Millie could tell, it involved tipping coloured water into differently coloured water. With the enthusiasm Guy showed, it was as if Eric had invented teleportation.

The three of them started to amble up the hill towards the cliffs that overlooked Whitecliff. The ones that gave the town its name. A long row of cars were parked on both sides of the road and police had closed access at the bottom. Families and groups of teenagers were walking in the road, chatting over one another as their chilled breaths eked into the dark sky. There was a festival feel, as couples held hands, while children skipped, ran, and, in the case of some of the boys, tried to trip up one another. A few other youngsters were using sparklers to weave patterns in the night sky. Eric was eyeing them a little *too* closely.

A burger van was parked in the lay-by a third of the way up, sending meaty smoke across the road as a queue gathered. A little past that, an ice cream van had been dragged out of winter storage and was doing a roaring trade, despite the temperature.

Guy waved to the man in the van and somehow managed to wangle a free 99 for Eric, who watched in awe at the newly discovered power.

'I used to know his dad,' Guy shrugged, by way of explanation. 'I gave him a driving lesson back in the day.'

Eric gasped a 'wow!' as he started to eat his ice cream – but Millie had seen and heard it all before. She'd known people who made themselves the centre of everything – but Guy was the real-life version of that, despite craving none of it. When it came to Whitecliff, he somehow did seem to know everyone. Or, more to the point, everyone's dad.

They continued up the hill, the pace slowing as the steepness started to hit their legs. Millie was huffing more than usual, after the excesses on the moors earlier. Guy was asking Eric about school, while Millie enjoyed listening. Eric was saying that tomorrow was the final day before Christmas break and that they would be allowed to wear their own clothes. He said how he'd been at Chloe's house the previous weekend and that they'd played together on her Nintendo.

Millie tried not to think about Nicholas. She'd watched him eat cake the day before and now... he was gone. He'd died with no family around him, no friends. It felt *wrong*.

The crowd was thickening as they neared the top of the hill. Millie tucked in tighter, sandwiching Eric between her and Guy.

'Keep hold of him,' Guy said, meaning Eric. 'But if we lose each other, we can catch up tomorrow.'

As they crested the hill, the volume was turned up to eleven. Thousands of people were talking over one another as, somewhere towards the cliff face, thumping music burst into the night. It was harder to move in any specific direction but that didn't stop a kid from appearing in front of them and blocking the way. He couldn't have been much older than twelve or thirteen and he thrust a thick wedge of paper slips towards them.

'Pound a sheet?' he said. 'Buy five and I'll chuck in a pen.'

Millie laughed, partly because it was so funny to hear a young boy talking like a market trader; partly because she had never once remembered to bring her own paper and pen. The whole point of the Bay Burning was to write down worries and concerns and then watch them get set on fire.

She looked to Guy, who already had a hand in his pocket. The boy gleefully stuffed the five-pound note in his pocket and then counted out five squares of paper. He dug out a felt-tip from a back pocket and passed that across, before heading off to accost the next person.

'I bet that kid makes more money tonight than I do all month,' Millie said, not talking to anyone in particular.

Guy handed Eric a piece of paper and the pen and said he should write down anything that he wanted to forget.

'Does burning it *really* make it go away?' Eric asked.

'Sort of,' Guy replied. 'If you want it to.'

Millie could see her son thinking. His features scrunched into each other and then he cupped the paper in one hand and wrote something on it with the other. When he was done, he folded up his sheet and passed back the pen.

'Your turn,' Guy said, handing Millie some paper and the pen. The felt-tip was slightly scuffed and looked suspiciously as if it might have been nicked. Probably from a school.

She needed a few seconds to think, partly because the list of grievances she had was so long. There were a lot of things she wanted to go away, or to be resolved.

Millie felt Eric watching her. The idea was to keep everything a secret, else the power of the burning wouldn't work. Millie didn't believe that... and yet, if she was honest, a tiny part of her did.

Millie wrote carefully, in tidy capital letters. Perhaps, if the power of the burning had to choose between making things happen, neatness would win over someone's messy handwriting.

She folded her paper into quarters and then gave Guy back the pen. 'Your turn,' she said.

A shrug. 'When you're my age, you don't have too many regrets or grievances.'

'How old are you?' Eric asked.

Millie was about to tell him it was rude to ask – but Guy answered anyway.

'I turned seventy today.'

Eric thought for a second. Millie was half-listening and only realised what he'd said after her son asked.

'It's your birthday today?'

'Shortest day of the year. I almost forgot myself. It's just another day when you're this age.'

Eric couldn't believe it. 'Don't you want a cake? Presents? How can you... *forget?*'

That got a laugh. 'When you're seventy, you don't really need more new things.'

'I'll still want stuff when I'm seventy.'

'Will you now...'

Millie had been momentarily speechless. 'I can't believe you never said anything,' she said. 'We walked together for an hour earlier. More. I was at your cottage and you never said a word. And what about last year? I didn't know then either.'

'We'd only recently become reacquainted then. I think I only remembered the day after anyway.'

Eric still couldn't believe it: 'You forgot your own birthday?!'

'I spent three years thinking I was a year older than I actually was. It was only when I failed a security check at the bank that I realised I'd added it up wrong.'

Eric turned between Millie and Guy. His eyes were wide, mouth open. The concept of missing out on presents, cake and a party was as existential as the breadth and depth of the universe. His mind was truly blown.

Millie thought of Guy sitting alone in his cottage, the radiators chuntering away, rain lashing the single-pane windows. The shortest, darkest, day of the year was his birthday.

'I wish you'd said something,' she said.

Guy didn't reply. Instead, he turned and guided them towards a line that had formed a little in front. It was moving quickly and it was only a few minutes until the three of them got their opportunity to approach the marionette.

The wood and paper structure was almost like a giant tent. There was a huge dome, with a thin wooden basket underneath. A series of long, heavy-looking stilts were attached, though laid flat.

Eric went first, walking up to the basket and dropping in his paper. After him, Guy and Millie did the same.

It was only as they moved further away that Millie realised this year's structure was in the shape of a dragon, for some reason. The papier-mâché lining was painted an earthy green, with scales, pointed ears, and a large snout.

Whoever had spent their time building and painting it was about to see their work set on fire and then hurled into the ocean.

The three of them drifted away from the dragon and joined the large ring of people who were surrounding it. Eric was telling Guy the story of the saint who'd supposedly founded Whitecliff in the thirteenth century. He'd slain a dragon and thrust his sword into the ground to claim the land in the name of the king. Eric had been taught the story at school, although it wasn't clear if he thought it to be fact or fiction. Millie had been taught it at the same age and it seemed some things never went out of fashion. Guy oohed and aahed in all the right places, as if he'd never heard the story before.

Millie listened in a not listening kind of way. The white

noise of people talking over each other was somehow both deafening and quiet enough that she could focus in on Eric if she chose.

It was as she was relaxing into the pageantry that Millie realised she was being watched. Something on the back of her neck tingled and, when she glanced off to the side, she saw Sharon with her arm linked with a man's. As best Millie could tell, it wasn't the same bloke from Sharon's photos. Dane Whateverhisnamewas. The two of them were duck-pouting as Zoe's sister took a series of selfies on her phone. Sharon swiped at the screen, showing them off to her companion, before tapping something quickly onto the screen. After a few more seconds, she lowered the device and started chatting to the man.

She didn't look across once, leaving Millie to wonder whether the sensation she'd felt actually was from being watched. It didn't seem as if Sharon had noticed her.

Millie was holding Eric's hand, even though he was at the age where it wasn't his thing. If any of his friends had been in the immediate vicinity, he'd have never let her – but she could feel the tension in his fingers. It was a big crowd, much larger than anything he was used to. Millie squeezed his fingers and then realised that Guy had somehow been lost among the numbers. She tried to ask Eric if he'd seen where Guy had gone – except it was too loud for him to hear. Instead, she held him tighter and gently pulled her son away from the front of the circle, ducking and pushing her way through the mass until they were nearer the back. There wasn't much of a view. It was mainly the backs of men who were tall enough to see over the tops of everyone else, or shorter people on tiptoes.

There was a better view in the other direction. Millie let go of Eric's hand and told him to turn around. They looked down on the deathly black waves smashing into the cliffs below. Beyond that, the lights of the town bled into the dark, while the blinking rainbow colours of the pier stretched into the ocean.

The clouds had cleared from earlier, leaving a bright, white moon to oversee the lot.

'Wow...' Eric said – and Millie couldn't have put it better. It was easy to see Whitecliff as the same old shops in the same old places. The tight terraces a little outside the centre, and the sprawling mansions on the hills beyond. The woods and the moors; the blustering gales and the summers of tourists. But it was beautiful, too... and it was home.

Eric wanted to know where his house was, so they sat on the ground and Millie pointed out the web of roads on the far side of town. They couldn't *quite* make out where Alex and Rachel lived but they got close enough. Eric looked for his school and Chloe's house, the points of reference in his young life.

And for those perfect few moments, a couple of simple minutes, it was only them who existed.

When they got back up, a woman was standing a few paces away. She must have been watching for a while and offered a closed-lip gentle smile.

'You looked so peaceful,' she said, talking to Millie, before lowering herself a little. 'And you must be Eric.'

'This is Genevieve,' Millie told her son. 'We were friends when we were a bit older than you.'

Eric began stumbling over her name. 'Genevul—' until she said: 'Call me Jenny. Everyone else does.'

The two women weren't friends now, not really. They were perhaps a little past nodding to one another on the street, while not quite close enough to plan a regular lunch or coffee. The sort of friends who'd not see one another for a couple of years and then spend a half-hour catching up in the Morrisons car park.

'Have you heard about Will?' Genevieve asked.

The name felt like a blow. Will knew something about Millie that nobody else did – but Millie knew things about him too. They had an unspoken pact of mutually assured destruction. If he didn't bother her, then she wouldn't bother him.

'Nothing,' Millie replied.

'He's moved to Mumbai. Or is it Bombay nowadays? Or the other way around? Either way, he's in India. Some sort of communal living thing. I think it's probably more to do with communal shagging but—' She cut herself off and glanced down to Eric.

'She means he's moved there to make carpets,' Millie said, before catching Genevieve's eye and grinning it away.

Before either of them could say anything else, there was a huge cheer. They were at the back of the crowd and Millie feared they wouldn't see much – but then, to the sound of a louder cheer, the marionette was hoisted high above everyone's heads. The giant puppet wobbled precariously on its stilts as the people lifting it began their slow march through the parting crowd.

Millie felt her bag rumble and checked her phone to find a text from Luke, asking how the burning was going. She fired back a quick: 'Busy!' and then dropped it back into her bag.

Eric was laughing and oohing as a second marionette – this one in the guise of a saint with a sword – began battling the dragon. The two puppets jousted and jabbed at one another, high above the crowd, who were cheering in support. People continued to move as the large structures were manhandled closer to the cliff edge until, as they neared the point of no return, there was a huge whoosh. Flames danced through the paper dragon, ripping through the head and down towards the belly. The heat stung Millie's face but it was pleasant, too: a burst of warmth among the ferocity of the cold.

Moments after the fire started, the dragon lurched forward, closer to the edge. It seemed to hover in the air, suspended miraculously against the laws of nature.

And then, with a rush and the loudest cheer so far, it toppled over the cliff and out of sight.

The puppet saint danced in victory as Millie realised, maybe for the first time, that none of it made any sense. If there was fire involved, wouldn't that have come *from* the dragon? Then she realised she was trying to rationalise something involving a fictional creature.

'Did you see?!' Eric called to her. 'It was on fire! It went over the edge!'

'I saw,' Millie assured him – but it was rare she saw such glee in her son's face.

She turned to say something to Genevieve, except the other woman had disappeared somewhere into the crowd. There was no sign of Guy, either – but, as she searched for them, Eric was tugging on her sleeve. It felt like something he was too old to do. When she looked he was beckoning her to crouch. It was too loud to be heard over the cheers and the shouts.

Millie lowered herself and her son leaned in to talk into her ear. She felt the air brushing her skin, making her tingle – but there was more than one reason for that.

'I want to live with you,' he said. 'That's what I wrote down. I don't want to live with Alex and Rachel any more.'

Millie almost asked him to repeat it. They were the words she'd been waiting to hear, *desperate* to hear, ever since she'd split with Alex.

'Can I live with you now?' he added.

Millie turned her head and cupped her hands around his ear. 'Not right away,' she said. 'It's not up to me.'

When they looked at each other, there was a sense of hurt in his face. He didn't like being told 'no' at the best of times – but this was more than that.

Millie leant towards him again. 'I hope it can happen,' she said. 'I'll have to talk to your dad. After the wedding, in the new year. I'll do it then.'

Eric nodded slowly, accepting, if not understanding. She didn't know how to tell him that it wouldn't be that simple. Alex would fight, if only to spite her. Probably Rachel as well. But Eric was saying clearly what he wanted was a fresh start. Millie didn't tell him that she'd written the same thing on her piece of paper. She didn't want to jinx it.

The crowd was slowly starting to move back towards the hill. Eager parents would be going on about being glad it was all over for another year; kids would be thrilled about staying up late. There would be a big line at the various fast food drive-thrus and the local chippies would be doing a roaring trade. Away from the summer tourists, it was probably Whitecliff's busiest night of the year.

Millie took Eric's hand again, holding him back and allowing people to move ahead. It was then that she spotted Guy on the far side of the crowd, close to where the dragon had been tossed off the cliff. He was illuminated by the moon, standing close to a group of teenagers who were hurling rocks over the edge.

He wasn't alone.

Millie had almost forgotten about the man she'd seen on the wall outside Guy's cottage. So much had happened in the previous days that there hadn't been room for him in her head. Except he was back – and he was here.

The man was around Millie's age, wrapped up in a big coat. She couldn't hear what was being said but they were shouting at one another; jabbing fingers and shaking heads.

'I need a wee,' Eric said.

Millie glanced from the arguing men, to where Eric was a couple of paces away. She muttered an 'OK' and had to drag herself away from watching the argument.

'I think that's your bag,' Eric said, when Millie was back at his side.

She checked her phone, expecting a text – but there was a

notification to say she'd had a direct message on Instagram. She almost didn't bother to look. It was an account for her business and the only messages she got were from people asking things that were already on her website. She'd check later... except curiosity got the better of her.

The direct message was from the account that had posted the picture teases of Zoe. Millie pressed to see it – and something tingled on the back of her neck.

There, on her screen, was a photo of Millie and Eric, standing close to the cliff edge. Their faces glowed orange from the flames as they'd watched the marionette go over the edge moments before.

She turned in a circle, expecting someone to be watching but nobody was. Nobody was paying them any attention at all.

'I need a *weeeeeeee*,' Eric pleaded.

Millie dropped the phone back into her bag – but not before sending the briefest of replies.

Who is this?

TWENTY-SEVEN

DAY SIX

Nicola's excitement had evaporated as they pulled up to the gates at the front of Zoe's house.

'I don't know if I can go through with it,' Nicola said.

'Go through with what?'

'They said you shouldn't meet your heroes. What if she doesn't like me? What should I say to her?'

'Just be yourself. Act like you would with anyone.'

Millie reached for the buzzer but Nicola hissed an anxious: 'Don't'. Millie did it anyway, which left Nicola muttering what sounded like a prayer to herself.

By the time the gates were open and Millie had driven along the drive, Nicola was imploring her to turn around.

'What do you say to a famous person?' she asked. 'Shall I ask her if she likes tea?'

'Why would you ask her that?'

'Because I don't know what to say!'

As Millie parked, the main doors of the house opened and Zoe appeared on the front step. Nicola had gone full goldfish in the passenger seat, gawping with a bobbing mouth.

Millie was out of the car but had to lean back inside to mutter a 'come on', before Nicola would eventually emerge.

They were a few paces away when Zoe beamed a friendly: 'You must be Nicola.'

'I'm Millie,' Nicola said. 'No. This is Millie... Oh, you already know that. You're Zoe, right? Oh, I already know that. I'm Nicola.'

Zoe laughed as she waved them inside – although Nicola didn't get out of the hallway. She stared in awe at the pictures and the tour posters. When she spotted the BRIT Award, she clutched at her chest and, for a moment, Millie feared her friend might faint.

'Is that a...?'

'It's a BRIT Award,' Zoe said, though she didn't add that it was a replica.

'Can I...?'

'You can pick it up if you want. It's heavy.'

Nicola reached slowly for it and then looked to Zoe again, presumably expecting to be told it was all a big joke. When nothing more was said, she lifted it from the shelf and weighed it in front of her.

'Wow...'

Millie kept the laugh to herself. The look of wonder was greater than what Eric had shown the night before at the Bay Burning.

Nicola carefully returned the award to the shelf and then straightened it, before focusing on one of the larger photos that showed the entire band. She pointed towards a younger Zoe, who was wearing a micro green dress.

'I *loved* that outfit,' Zoe said. 'I always wanted to know where you got it. I looked everywhere I could think of.'

'It was made especially for me. All of our outfits that night were from the same designer.'

'Wow...'

Millie watched, amused at her friend and happy that Zoe was getting the attention she craved. She started talking Nicola through the wall of pictures, mentioning cities where the photos had been taken. It was a largely one-sided conversation with a lot of 'oooooh's from Nicola.

'Do you want to see my wardrobe?' Zoe asked after a while. 'I wasn't allowed to keep everything but I've got quite a lot.'

'...Of your stage outfits?'

'I've still got the green one you like.'

'Are you joking?'

Zoe laughed. 'We're about the same size. You can try it on if it fits...'

Nicola gasped and clasped her chest once more. She looked to Millie: 'Did you hear that? I can try on the dress.' She pointed to the photo: '*That* dress!'

Zoe pointed towards a door at the other end of the hall. 'It's in there. You can have a look around. I'll be in soon.'

Nicola didn't need telling twice. She set off along the hall, only stopping to giggle to herself and point at the various pictures on the wall.

'I told you she was a fan,' Millie said.

Zoe didn't catch the humour. 'I love my fans,' she said. 'It's what it's all about.'

Millie wondered if it was sarcasm, though it didn't sound like it.

'It used to be like that all the time,' Zoe added. 'We did the Royal Variety Performance one year and met the Queen. We had more people lining up to meet us. There were loads of fans at the stage door. We always tried to sign anything that people brought – or let them have photos. It took us an hour to get out that night.'

Nicola stopped and there was a sad-sounding sigh.

'It's going to get out, isn't it?'

It took Millie a moment to realise she meant the naked

photos. 'If you want a proper investigation, you need the police,' Millie replied.

'Then it'll *definitely* get out.'

'I don't know what to tell you. Have you had any messages from the Instagram account? Any demands?'

'Nothing. I tried messaging but there was no reply. We're the only two people who follow it. I was worried all those papers tagged would end up following – but they've not even replied.'

Millie didn't say what she'd been thinking: that Zoe wasn't famous enough any longer for a big publication to worry about stolen nudes. She wondered if Zoe knew that deep down.

'How was the burning?' Zoe asked, suddenly sounding more enthusiastic.

'My son enjoyed it.' A pause. 'I saw Sharon there with a guy.'

Millie expected a reaction but there wasn't much of one. She thought about mentioning the direct message but it didn't quite feel like the time.

'What about your boys?' Millie asked.

That got a grin: 'I'm seeing them tomorrow, after school.'

Millie almost asked the question, stopped herself, and then went for it anyway. 'What do they think of the giant photo in your room?'

A dark look passed Zoe's face, although it was gone almost as instantly as it had arrived. 'They know they're not allowed in my bedroom.'

'Do they normally care about rules?'

Zoe's jaw stiffened and then she shrugged. 'I used to do all sorts of shoots for the lads' mags before they all went away. All us girls did. Bikini shots, lingerie, all that. There's nothing they won't have already seen somewhere.' She waited, wondering if Millie would accept that, then added: 'It was Harvey who wanted that photo in the bedroom. He paid for it. I came home one time and it was already on the wall. He said it was an early Christmas present to ourselves. I suppose I went along with it. When he moved out, I should've taken it down... but I guess it's a bit late now.'

'Is Harvey still in Bali?'

A nod.

'Do you think he could've had something to do with it anyway? Got a mate to take it?'

Zoe shook her head. 'Why would he? He's got his own stuff going on.' She let out another little sigh. 'Not that I want him back. He made his choice. Just like Brad and Louis. They all made their choice.'

Millie didn't say anything, not about that anyway.

'Can I look around upstairs?' she asked.

Zoe said it was fine – and then Millie went to the stairs, while Zoe headed off to her wardrobe – which was presumably massive.

The ceilings were high and Millie's footsteps bounced around the walls as she headed up. She noticed more of the flaws second time around. There were bare patches in the wallpaper, more dents and gouges in the wooden banisters. The chandelier in the upstairs hall had a cable hanging loose and no bulbs in the holders. The house was clean but slowly falling apart.

Millie didn't go directly into Zoe's bedroom. The first door she opened clearly belonged to a boy. There were football posters on the wall and an Xbox hooked up to a huge TV. It had that boyish smell that was partly too much Lynx and partly unflushed toilet.

The next room was similar to the one before – except this boy had posters of women on his walls. It wasn't lost on Millie that, a few years before, Zoe would have been the subject of posters on a teenager's wall.

Millie moved on – and Zoe's room didn't look as if anyone

had been in it since Millie had last been there. There was the wild pink bomb site and the wall of terrifyingly creepy, staring dolls – all with the huge four-poster bed in the middle. The large blank space was still on the opposite wall, with the faded rectangular lines.

It all felt a bit... lonely. A big house with only one person living in it. Millie didn't know her well but she doubted Zoe had bought it to live in by herself. It felt like a house, not a home.

As for the outline on the wall... it was massive. Millie approached the wall and stretched her arms wide, trying to figure out how someone could have lifted it off. It surely would have needed more than one person to carry it down the stairs, unless...

And then she saw it on the wooden floor.

Millie would have never noticed if she wasn't looking. Close to the bed, etched into the hardwood, was a gentle scuff. It was almost the same colour as the wood itself – but a little lighter. The colour of sand.

Millie knelt and ran a finger along it. Ahead of her, the bedclothes were touching the ground. An enormous bedspread on a massive bed, which was only a foot or so above the floor.

Millie lifted the bedspread, which was on top of at least three layers of sheets. She flipped everything up onto the bed and then shone the flashlight from her phone underneath.

And there, sitting neatly in the dark, obscured by the bed itself, was an enormous picture frame.

TWENTY-EIGHT

Millie almost had to crawl under the bed to get a hand around the frame. Her shoulders ached as she dragged it across the floor and partially into the open.

The frame was empty.

It wasn't a surprise. Whoever had hauled it off the wall had removed the picture, presumably rolled it up, and then slid the frame out of sight. It was an easier alternative than getting the whole thing down the stairs. Millie was silently impressed. Why would anyone bother looking under their own bed?

Millie headed downstairs and along to the door into which Nicola had disappeared. Music was playing from inside and it took Millie a moment to realise it was one of Girlstar's songs. She'd not heard the tune in years but it was one of the ones that had been impossible to avoid. It had been on in supermarkets and shops; used for adverts and in TV shows. Millie knew the words, even though she'd never gone out of her way to listen to it.

She pushed open the door and headed into what looked like a TK Maxx at the end of a busy Saturday. There were so many rails of clothes that it had created a series of aisles running the length of the room. Everything seemed to have been sorted by colour and Millie was dazzled by the rainbow. At the furthest end, shelves had been built into the wall and there had to be at least a hundred pairs of shoes and boots tucked into the space.

Nicola was half-naked, balancing on one foot as she squeezed herself into a short silver dress, as Zoe wrenched the two halves together at the back.

'Breathe in,' Zoe said.

'I am.'

'From your diaphragm.'

Nicola gasped as she tried to inhale deeper and, as she did, Zoe quickly pulled up the zipper.

'You're in.'

Nicola let out a loud gasp, though the dress held strong. When she spotted Millie, Nicola let out an excited squeal and then added: 'She wore this at the MTV Awards!'

Nicola was bare-footed, though a pair of matching silver boots was at her side. She tried to sit on the nearby chair but the dress was too tight, so she ended up squatting as if she needed the toilet. Zoe caught Millie's eye and smiled, before she crouched to help Nicola squish the boots onto her feet. When she was all set, Nicola attempted to spin but couldn't quite manage it. She ended up waddling off to the mirror to look at herself.

'I was thinking of selling some of this stuff,' Zoe said.

'No way...' Nicola replied.

'It just sits in here. I don't know why I kept so much. I've only worn most of it once and can't fit into much.'

Nicola smoothed down the front of the dress. It was silky soft, with a series of glimmering sequins sewn around the seams. 'How much do you want for it?'

Zoe shrugged. 'That's the thing. I have no idea how much anything is worth. Then, where do you sell it? eBay? Buyers would know my address, wouldn't they? I don't really know what I'm doing.'

It hadn't answered the question but, as Nicola half turned to look at her bum in the mirror, Zoe continued: 'You can have it. I'm never going to wear it again.'

Nicola started to say 'Are you sure?' before cutting herself off, not wanting to risk Zoe changing her mind. 'Thank you so much,' she said instead. 'I'll look after it, I promise.'

Millie didn't want to burst her friend's bubble – but she couldn't think of a time when Nicola would ever wear the dress. It was too short and too shiny to realistically wear outside, let alone in the pubs of Whitecliff. Still, even if she wore it around her own living room, what did it matter? It would make her happy.

'You're so kind,' Nicola continued. 'You were always my favourite.'

Zoe did the thing where she touched her palm to her chest. 'It's my pleasure,' she replied.

The song that had been playing had switched to another from Girlstar. Millie vaguely recognised it, though it hadn't been as popular as the one before. It felt like they were probably listening to the band's greatest hits.

'Can you help me out of it?' Nicola asked. 'I need a wee and don't think I can sit in this.'

Zoe unzipped it for her and Nicola gasped with relief as she could finally breathe again. She slipped off the boots and gathered up her actual clothes, before Zoe told her where the downstairs bathroom was. Nicola said she'd be right back and then disappeared out the room.

'That was kind of you,' Millie said.

Zoe tilted her head a fraction, acknowledging the point. 'She'll make better use of it than me.'

Millie laughed, because it was true – and because she could

easily picture her friend squeezing herself into the dress, solely to wear around her house.

'I've got something to show you,' Millie said.

She nodded upstairs and then led Zoe up to the bedroom. Millie entered first, Zoe a pace behind. As soon as Zoe saw what was half poking out from underneath the bed, she stopped and stared.

'Where did you find that?' she asked. Millie didn't need to answer, as it was evident.

Zoe crossed the room and crouched, then touched the frame as if to make sure it was real.

'I... don't understand,' she said.

'It's very heavy. I figured it would've needed a couple of people to get it down the stairs and out the house. Then I wondered whether someone took only the picture. If they did that, they'd have left the frame – and your bed is massive. I looked under and there it was.'

'I can't... It's just... I've been sleeping in here the whole time. I've been on top of it and didn't realise. Who looks under their bed?'

Zoe got onto her knees and peeped fully under the bed. She tried hauling out the frame but could barely get it to move until Millie helped.

'Has the cleaner been in here?' Millie asked.

'I always make my own bed,' Zoe replied. 'It was the same on tour. I didn't like the maids doing it in the hotels. When the band started touring, Dad told me doing something simple like making my bed would help remind me where I came from. He used to say that you have to remember your roots. I think that's why I moved back here in the end.' She stopped and then added: 'I feel so stupid. Why didn't I look?'

'I couldn't see the print anywhere,' Millie said. 'Not that I was expecting to. I wondered if maybe it hadn't been stolen at all? Perhaps someone took those photos and they're posting them on that Instagram account to make you think they stole it...?'

Zoe stared at Millie for a second, then the frame, then the empty wall. 'I never thought of that...'

'It's a big house.'

'But why would someone want me to think they'd taken it?'

Millie couldn't answer that, although she had some suspicions. 'It wasn't taken – or hidden – on a whim,' she said. 'Whoever did this knows your house.'

Saying that made Millie think of Luke and how she should have sent him a better reply the night before.

Zoe didn't reply because Nicola's voice was echoing up from the floor below. 'Zoe...? Mill...?'

Zoe stepped towards the door but Millie stopped her. 'Don't tell anyone we found the frame,' Millie said.

'Why?'

'Because it's something we know that whoever moved it doesn't.'

Millie nudged the frame with her foot and then Zoe joined her to shove it back under the bed. From below, Nicola was still calling. They left the bedroom together and headed along the hall towards the stairs.

They were halfway down when Millie next spoke. 'If I don't see you before, then enjoy Christmas with your boys.'

Zoe paused on the stairs and Millie only realised when she was two steps ahead. 'Thank you for remembering.'

They continued to the bottom, where Nicola was waiting, back in her own clothes and shoes. 'We're not going already, are we?' Nicola asked. She sounded like Eric when Millie told him it was time to go home.

'If it's OK with Zoe, we don't have to leave right away,' Millie replied, which got a little squeal. It really was like babysitting, not that Millie minded too much.

They all returned to the room that had been converted into

a wardrobe as Nicola asked what the other bandmates were like. Millie wasn't listening to much. She checked the Instagram account again, where the two photos were still up. She hadn't told Zoe about the photo she'd been sent from the Bay Burning. She'd seen Sharon there, but that didn't necessarily mean Zoe's sister was the one who sent it. There had been no follow-up message, no words at all. Millie wasn't sure what to make of it. Was it a threat? It felt like it might be, especially as Eric was in the photo alongside Millie.

Zoe was busy telling Nicola a story about being backstage at a gig, where one of the band members had lost her boots. It was long and rambling, but Nicola was enjoying listening to it almost as much as Zoe was revelling in the telling. They were a good fit for the moment. The celebrity who feared she was past it, with a fan who'd recently divorced her husband, desperate for an escape.

Millie knew she wouldn't tell Zoe about the message. Not today, in any case. For now, she would let the women have their moment.

TWENTY-NINE

Guy's front door was locked for once, which left Millie digging around in her bag, trying to find the key he'd given her. She checked over her shoulder, looking back towards the track, half expecting someone to be watching. It was hard not to feel vulnerable after the direct message from the night before – let alone the reappearance of the mystery man, with whom Guy had been arguing at the Bay Burning.

Millie found Guy in his office. He was sitting on a chair in the window, knees crossed, Barry at his feet, as he scanned the pages of a hardback notebook. He didn't appear remotely surprised to see someone appear in his house, instead calmly closing the book.

'I wasn't sure I'd see you today,' he said.

'I brought you a present.'

'Really?'

Millie removed the gift from her bag and passed it across. She knelt to ruffle Barry's ears and he rolled onto his side so she could give his belly a rub. Millie obliged as Guy weighed the present.

'You didn't have to,' he said. 'I'm not really a birthday kind of person.'

That didn't stop him digging his thumbs into the gaps of the paper and pulling. Inside was a framed image of Guy and Barry.

'Someone I used to go to school with runs the art studio in town,' Millie said. 'I commissioned him to draw you both and was going to give it to you for Christmas. You can have it for your birthday instead – and I'll get you something else for Christmas.'

'You didn't—'

'Yeah, yeah. I know I didn't have to but I did.'

Guy held up the picture into the light and looked at it properly. Millie's friend was an expert with pencils and had drawn it from a photo Millie had on her phone. Guy placed it on the windowsill and said he'd find a place for it. Millie knew it would remain in the window but didn't mind. Guy urged Barry to look at the illustrated version of himself but the dog was having none of it.

'He's still tired from the walk on the moors,' Guy said. He was smiling, clutching his notebook.

'I saw you arguing last night,' Millie said.

Guy flinched momentarily but then reopened the book as if it hadn't happened. 'Really?'

'With the man we both saw hanging around outside here last week...?'

Guy nodded along, not contradicting but not answering either.

'Who was it?' Millie asked.

'No one, really. A misunderstanding. I thought I saw him pickpocketing.'

It was such an obvious lie that Millie didn't quite know how to address it. To a certain degree, she expected that sort of thing from an eight-year-old. Not from a seventy-year-old man.

'Did Eric enjoy the Burning?' Guy asked, obviously changing the subject. He was avoiding Millie's gaze, too.

Millie paused a second, the momentary silence letting him know that *she* knew he hadn't properly answered.

'He seemed to,' she replied. 'It's his last day at school before Christmas today. He... told me he wants to live with me.'

Guy looked at her properly. 'That's wonderful.'

Millie realised she was smiling, despite everything. It was hard not to.

'And how's Zoe?' he added. He was moving the conversation on quickly, avoiding what Millie really wanted to know.

'I found the frame,' Millie replied.

'Really? Well done.'

'There was no print inside but it was under the bed.'

Guy was nodding along. 'Of course. There was no reason to take the heavy frame when the image could be removed so easily. I hadn't thought of that.'

'Someone's putting up teases on Instagram.' Millie swiped through her phone and held it up for Guy to see. It was the first post, that showed a snippet of Zoe's thigh. 'They tagged in the *Sun* and the *Mail*. A bunch of other papers and magazines. I think they're trying to get attention – but nobody's bitten yet.' A pause. 'Except me.'

'Things have been a lot tighter on privacy since phone hacking, and Meghan suing, and a few other things.'

'It feels like a cry for attention,' Millie said, 'but I can't figure out who wants that attention. Zoe's sister says Zoe still wants the fame. Zoe says she doesn't. Zoe's sister *definitely* wants to be famous. I don't know what I'm missing.'

'I figured wanting a way back to fame might be why she wanted us involved...'

Millie thought on that for a second. Guy had never specifically said why he hadn't wanted to be involved, though she suspected this was the reason. 'She told us not to write anything. She didn't call the police in case something was leaked.'

'What else was she going to say? If she'd asked us to write something, it's easy to say no. If she says she *doesn't* want us to write anything, it sews intrigue.'

Millie didn't know what to say. There was truth in that... but she also believed Zoe.

Millie swiped around her phone again, loading the DM from the night before. It was still only the photo of her and Eric. No words, no demands.

'I was sent this from the account,' Millie said. 'Zoe and me are the only followers.'

Guy examined the picture and frowned. 'Was there anything else?'

'No.'

'That *is* curious.' Guy stood and crossed to his desk. He started opening drawers, taking things out, then putting them back in again. Guy hunting for something happened regularly – and it was rare he found what he was after.

Defeated, he perched on the edge of the desk and turned back to where Millie was still stroking an appreciative Barry.

'I once got Polaroids in the mail,' Guy said. '*Years* ago. I was doing a story about travellers moving onto a piece of land on the edge of town. I spoke to them and they didn't really want to talk but it ended up OK. One of them recognised me because I'd written a letter on their behalf to the council a few years before. I can't remember quite why – something to do with trying to get them access to running water.'

'Why am I not surprised?'

Guy didn't break his thought process: 'I interviewed them on one day and then, the next, an envelope arrived at the office. There was no note, just Polaroids of me on the traveller site. I didn't know who'd sent them, or why. I hadn't finished writing the piece, let alone had it published. I had no idea if they were meant to intimidate me...'

'Did you find out who sent them?'

A nod. 'The son of the man who owned the field and farm next to the travellers' site. He didn't like that I was talking to the people he considered the enemy. He wanted them evicted and thought I was holding that up, even though he didn't know why I was there. His dad didn't know anything about it. He told me later that his lad wanted me to think it was someone from the travellers' site who'd taken the photos.'

'Why would they have done it?'

'To scare me off – although I never quite understood the reasoning.' He nodded towards the phone that Millie had put at her side. 'I'm not saying it's relevant, just that people act strangely when they want you to do something but don't feel they can ask directly.' He stopped for a moment, then added: 'Or when they want you to *stop* doing something.'

Millie had been thinking along similar lines, except she had no idea who was trying to either get her to do something, or stop her from doing it.

Guy opened one of the drawers again, pushed something deeper inside, then closed it again. As soon as he'd done that, his landline started to ring. There were multiple handsets through the cottage and they all chimed a cacophony as one.

Millie had an idea of who'd be calling and why. It almost felt inevitable after what had happened to Nicholas the day before.

Guy answered the handset near his desk and there were a lot of 'yes' responses and 'I see'. He nodded gently to Millie, confirming what she'd guessed, even though neither of them had spoken of it.

When he hung up, Millie was already on her feet as Barry looked up to her, wondering why she'd stopped rubbing his belly.

'Kevin?' Millie asked.

'He wants to talk to us again – and our old friend, Chief Superintendent Baker, has apparently given his blessing... with one condition.'

THIRTY

As far as conditions went, things could have been worse. Chief Superintendent Baker had agreed for Ashworth to talk to Guy and Millie *if* he got to brief them first and in full. There were ground rules to be set, apparently, which left Millie biting her tongue as she knew Guy wasn't the type who simply agreed to that sort of thing.

As it was, they were sitting in the café across the road from the prison. Baker was nursing some sort of macchiato, syrupy, foamy thing – which was the last drink Millie would have predicted for him. She'd have guessed flat white, or straight black, no mucking about. 'Normal tea' was Guy's order, because of course it was. Millie was nursing a flat white, wondering how long it would be before she needed to act as peacemaker for the two grown men.

A vein had appeared on Baker's neck that was throbbing as if there was something trying to escape.

'I tried to interview Kevin Ashworth last night,' he said.

'After telling him his son had died?' Guy replied.

'Not *directly* after.'

'It was still the day his son died.'

'Regardless, I asked if there was anything he wanted to say about what we found on the moors, or if he had anything to add about the location of those boys.'

'What did he say?'

'He said your name forty-one times.'

Guy picked up his tea and sipped. 'Perfect,' he said, presumably talking to himself about the quality of the tea.

'What do you have to say about that?' Baker demanded.

'What do you want me to say?'

'I want to know the same thing I've wanted for the last week and a half. What is the relationship between you and Kevin Ashworth?'

Guy took his time, first blowing on his tea, and then having another sip. He placed the mug back on the table, then picked it up again. Millie wasn't sure she liked this side of him. She could more or less understand his attitude to authority in general – but deliberately winding up Baker felt a little... *childish*.

'I don't know what to tell you,' Guy replied. 'I've already said that we don't have any specific type of relationship. I interviewed him a few times twenty-odd years ago. I covered the case when the boys went missing – and I was there for every day of his trial. Until last week, I'd not seen Kevin Ashworth since the day he was taken down from the dock.'

Guy sipped his tea again as Baker picked up his drink and did the same. It really was hard to take a man seriously when there was milk foam on his top lip. Even harder when it was combined with a bulging neck vein and a quivering eyebrow. It was clear enough that Baker didn't believe Guy and, if Millie was honest, she wasn't sure she did either.

'Kevin doesn't have anyone,' Millie said. 'Nicholas was his final link to the world. You don't expect to outlive everyone around you. He was attacked in prison, so probably doesn't trust anyone in there. He obviously doesn't trust the police, no offence. Perhaps Guy was kind to him one time years ago? You'd remember that sort of thing...'

Baker reluctantly dragged his gaze across to her, as if only then remembering she was there.

'The pair of you are on very thin ice,' he said.

'Or what?' Guy replied.

The two men glared at one another and Millie felt embarrassed to be sitting in the middle of it. For what was probably the first time, she saw a hint of her father in Guy – and she didn't like it.

'Is this really necessary?' Millie said. Neither of the men looked to her. She pointed to Baker. 'We all know you need us, because this is never getting solved if he won't talk.' She switched her attention to Guy: 'And we all know you're going to get to break a story that's been building for all these years. So can we just get on with it?'

Guy was cradling his mug between his fingers but he put it down and started to nod. 'You're right... and I apologise.'

The vein was still bulging in Baker's neck, his eyebrow still twitching, the foam on his top lip. 'I don't have time for this,' he said. 'That man's been stringing us along for days. If this is some sort of scam to get out, you might as well tell him it's not happening.' He stood so abruptly that his chair scraped on the floor and fell backwards. 'I'll see you over there,' he added, not bothering to right the chair before storming out.

Guy got up and picked up the chair himself, before returning to carefully sip his tea. 'You're right,' he said again. 'It's not about me.'

Millie didn't have anything to say. The very fact he'd acknowledged it wasn't about him was something that differentiated Guy from her father. Perhaps they shared a few tendencies – but not the worst ones.

. . .

Millie was becoming used to the process of getting into prison. There were metal security gates, like the ones at airports; plus hand scanners and actual pat-downs. There was a locker in which to leave her things, one final check, and then corridor after corridor until she and Guy ended up back in the room with the sofas from what felt like weeks before.

Plastic cups of water were on the low table, although it was unclear if they'd been left specifically for them, or if they'd been there a while. There was no clock on the wall and Millie didn't have her phone. It might have been five minutes that passed but it could have been longer. She didn't know what to talk to Guy about – and she knew that whatever they said would likely be heard by whoever was watching live footage from the camera.

Time passed and then there was the distant clink of doors, then footsteps, then more rattling. The door opened and a prison guard ushered Kevin Ashworth into the room. Millie couldn't stop staring at him. His skin was pale, except for the dark bags under his eyes and the pinky-purple bumps of his scar. It didn't look as if he'd slept and his eyelids hung heavy as he was released from his cuffs.

The second sofa almost swallowed him as the guard told him to sit. He yawned, tried to cover it, and then yawned again. In the days since they'd last seen him, he'd lost so much weight that his cheekbones looked as if they were trying to burst through his skin.

The guard asked Guy if everything was all right and, when told it was, he left the room.

Ashworth yawned again but didn't bother to cover his mouth second time around.

'I'm sorry to hear about Nicholas,' Guy said.

'Did you talk to him?'

'We did. We passed on your message. Millie bought him a cake.'

Something that wasn't quite a smile crept onto Ashworth's face. 'You bought him cake?'

'That's what he wanted,' Millie replied.

'Chocolate, I'll bet. He always had a sweet tooth.'

'Chocolate. We gave him a spoon and he managed about a quarter of it. Didn't bother to cut it up.'

Ashworth squeezed the bridge of his nose. When he next spoke, it sounded almost choked. 'Thank you. You didn't need to do that.' He took a breath and then added: 'Thank you. Really.'

Nobody spoke for a minute or so. There was a lot going on but none of it was said out loud.

Ashworth rubbed his eyes and took a series of deep breaths. He scratched his temple, pressed thumbs into his cheeks, leaned forward, angled back, rocked, mumbled something to himself – and then, finally, looked to Millie. When it came, he was speaking to her.

'The year before Nicholas was born, my wife, Tina, was pregnant. We'd been trying since we got married but it hadn't worked. We went to the doctor and there were appointments with specialists. They took samples and ran tests... and it was all inconclusive. There was no reason why Tina couldn't get pregnant – except it wasn't happening. And then it did. She felt sick one morning and went to the doctor – and she was pregnant.'

Ashworth reached for one of the plastic cups. His hand was trembling and water sloshed over the side as he lifted it to his mouth. He drank, though it seemed as if more of the water ended up on his hand and leg than it did in his mouth.

'This was before mobile phones,' Ashworth added. 'I've never owned one – but you probably know that. It was the year of the storm.' He looked to Guy. 'Do you remember? It washed away part of the pier. There were trees down, the power was out.' A nod to Millie. 'It was probably before your time.

'I remember,' she said – and she did. It was one of her

earliest memories, when there were tiles coming off the roof of their house. She'd heard them shattering on the ground as she hid under her bedclothes, wondering if the roof itself would blow off.

'I couldn't get the car to start,' Ashworth said. 'You expect labour to last a little while – but Tina started to get contractions one minute and then the next...'

Ashworth finished the water and then crumpled the cup.

'She gave birth on the stairs,' he said. 'Except there was no crying. No anything. He was just... still.'

Ashworth opened his palm, balancing the cup before letting it fall.

'She went more or less the full term. There was no sign anything was wrong. She had the scans and the tests. It's just he wasn't... alive.' He bit his lip, then added: 'That's who was on the moors. We called him Bryan, with a "y". "Our Bryan". We sat there all night in the house, just him and us. The wind was rattling the windows and the rain hammering the roof. We just sat, listening to it all. The three of us.'

There was a lump in Millie's throat. She tried to swallow but it was stuck and, for a moment, it didn't feel as if it would ever shift. It was impossible not to think of her own labour, her own son. Alex's parents had insisted on paying for a private hospital, where she had a separate room. It wasn't particularly her choice but she wasn't going to argue. She and Alex had chosen a soundtrack and they had designated nurses

It was such a long way from what Ashworth was describing. From what *Kevin* was describing.

'Someone must've noticed...?' Millie managed.

A nod. 'We didn't have a massive circle of friends and family. We told the people around us it was a stillbirth – but not how it happened. It's not the sort of thing people want to ask. You say "stillbirth" and all anyone says is sorry. They don't want details.'

That was true enough. When Millie was in her twenties, one of her friends had miscarried – and the idea of asking for specifics would have felt obscene.

'There must've been a social worker?' Millie said. 'Someone like that?'

'We didn't try to hide anything, necessarily. We told her he'd been stillborn and that we'd been to the hospital. Nobody ever asked what happened to him. I think everyone assumed it had been dealt with by someone else. Meanwhile, we wanted our own spot to remember him.'

Ashworth reached for a second cup of water and drank.

'*I* wanted a spot to remember him. Tina never visited. Not once. She wasn't even there when I buried Bryan. She tried to pretend it never happened. I don't think she ever said Bryan's name after that night but I'd go up to the moors by myself. I'd walk a lot and sometimes just sit on the rock at that spot where I took you. I never told anyone where he was until the other day. Not even Nicholas.'

The mention of his other son's name brought a cloud to Ashworth's face.

'Tina was pregnant again not long after – and everything was fine second time around. We worried, of course, but Nicholas was perfect.'

There was a moment of silence. Those few seconds of recognition.

'Why did you show us Bryan's resting place?' Guy asked.

Ashworth didn't answer at first and, for a while, Millie wondered if he'd say anything at all.

'It was important you knew,' he said eventually. 'Sometimes you need to see something...'

Ashworth scratched his scar and then seemed to catch himself doing it.

'Do you believe in karma?' he asked. It wasn't clear to whom he was speaking but, when he glanced up, it was Millie's eye he caught. 'Or payback? Whatever you want to call it. That, if you do bad things, they catch up to you in the end.'

Millie hadn't expected to be asked any question, let alone something so existential.

'I've seen good things happen to bad people,' she said. 'And awful things happening to some of the best people I know. I think people only talk about karma when they're trying to convince themselves there's some sort of order, or fairness, to the world.'

She wasn't quite sure from where that had all come, though it felt like the truth. Her truth, at least.

Ashworth looked back to the ground and continued cradling his cup of water.

'Do you think Nicholas getting leukaemia is payback?'

His voice was almost a whisper. It didn't seem as if he wanted an answer, not from them. It felt like something he'd been asking himself for a long time. If the sins of the father truly had been passed onto the son.

Nobody spoke for a minute or so. Millie glanced up to the camera in the top corner of the room, wondering what Baker was making of it all. They now knew what they had discovered on the moors, though there were still no answers for Victoria about what happened to Wesley.

Guy must have been thinking something similar. 'This might be the last time they let us speak,' he said. 'It sounded originally as if you wanted to tell us about Wesley and Shaun...'

Ashworth had been lost since he'd last spoken. He'd sunken deeper into the sofa and was battling with a yawn.

'I need to show you something,' he said.

'They're not going to let you leave again,' Guy replied.

'I'll show you where the boys are.'

The air had left the room. As far as Millie knew, it was the first time Ashworth had specifically promised such a thing. It was definitive.

Millie had no idea what to say and, seemingly, Guy didn't either.

It wasn't a surprise that, seconds later, there was a knock on the door.

Ashworth didn't move and neither did Guy. It was Millie who stood and crossed to the exit. Baker was there, a couple of paces from the door, apparently unwilling to enter. Probably wary of spoiling whatever was happening. Millie closed the door behind her and followed Baker to the other end of the hall.

'There is *zero* chance of him leading us anywhere a second time,' Baker hissed. 'I'd tell him myself if I thought for one second it would do any good. He had his chance and he blew it.'

'He did tell us about Bryan...'

'We already knew it was a male relative of his! Who's to say that stillbirth stuff wasn't a load of nonsense and he killed his own son?'

'If that was true, why would he lead us to it?'

'Who knows what goes on in that mind of his? He's been stringing us along for over a week now.' Baker stopped and jabbed a finger towards the room at the end. 'Actually, he's been stringing us along for more than twenty years. Getting on for thirty. If he has anything to say, tell him *this* is the time. There'll be no more cosy chats on the sofa after this. If it was up to me, he wouldn't be out of the cuffs.'

Millie considered what to say for a moment – and then it came to her. 'I saw a map of Whitecliff on the wall in reception,' Millie said calmly. 'Do you reckon somebody might be able to get it for me? And a pen?'

His eyes narrowed and, if she'd been at the right angle, Millie felt sure she'd be able to see Baker's neck vein convulsing again. He had that *one-bad-day-away-from-a-heart-attack*-vibe about him.

'Wait there.'

Millie did as she was told.

Obviously it wasn't Baker who went on the fetch and carry mission himself. He ducked into the room at the end and then, a few seconds later, a prison guard slipped out. He smiled gently at Millie and then hurried into the maze of corridors and out of sight. It was a few minutes until he was back but he didn't have the map she had seen on the wall. Instead, he was clutching a road atlas, the type which used to live in the pocket on the back of every driver's seat. Millie couldn't remember seeing one in at least ten years.

'Best I could do,' he said, as he dug into an inner pocket. He passed across a red crayon. 'He's not allowed pens.'

Millie took both, thanked him, and then headed back to the room with the sofas. It didn't look as if either Guy or Ashworth had moved since she'd left. Millie flipped through the atlas pages and opened it at the one showing Whitecliff. There was an expanse of blue, then the webbed roads of the town, surrounded by a huge splodge of green.

Millie handed Ashworth the map and the crayon. 'They're not going to let you out again,' she said.

He clutched the crayon and, for a mad moment, Millie thought he was going to put it in his mouth. Instead, he put down the map on the sofa and used a finger to trace the A-road that wound across the moor. He marked a cross somewhere along the road.

'That's Dad's farm,' he said.

Millie didn't say that she already knew.

Ashworth leaned in closer to the page and said something about needing glasses. He squinted and poked the paper, then marked a second cross.

'That's where I took you,' he said.

Considering how long they'd walked in the dreary conditions, the crosses were ridiculously close together.

Millie knew what was coming before it did. Ashworth flipped the page to the one that showed Steeple's End, then turned back to the first. He marked a cross on the Whitecliff page – and then handed everything back to Millie.

'I always assumed someone would find it,' he said. 'There's a patch of water that's not on any maps I've ever seen. It's not a lake, not quite. It gets low in the summer and fills through the winter. Dad used to take me there as a kid. We'd float on rubber rings and have the whole place to ourselves.' He pointed towards the atlas in Millie's hand. 'It's somewhere close to that cross but maybe not exactly there. Start at the farm and walk east south-east. It's more or less all downhill and you'll find the water eventually. It will be deep and dangerous at this time of year.'

Ashworth looked across to Guy.

'Tell them to look in the water,' he said. 'Make sure the car's still there and then, if you take me to Dad's farm one final time, I'll tell you everything.' He glanced up to the camera. 'Promise.'

THIRTY-ONE

DAY SEVEN

Millie and Jack were in the smoking area at the back of the nursing home. Jack was busy with his Rubik's Cube again, anything that stopped him having to light up. It was two days until Christmas and he was wearing a Santa hat, with a green and white jumper.

'It feels like the last day of term,' Millie said.

'It's my last day at work. You?'

'I'm doing the morning here but I've got no dogs booked in before Christmas. I'm essentially already off.'

Jack wasn't looking at the cube as he spun the sides. 'Remember when you were a kid and you looked forward to Christmas all year? You'd go through the Argos catalogue and put a circle around everything you wanted – which was all of it. You'd get the *Radio Times* and mark all the things you wanted to watch. Then the day would come and you'd eat cake and Quality Street for breakfast. There'd be a massive dinner, then Christmas pudding and cream. Then you'd have seconds of turkey and be so full you could barely move. And, now, it's just... a pain in the arse.'

Millie laughed. 'Surely Isaac's looking forward to it?'

'Yeah...' He didn't sound so sure.

'Are you still coming round tomorrow?' Millie asked.

'That's the bit I'm looking forward to. We're coming to yours and then driving up to spend Christmas with Rish's parents. They don't celebrate the day itself but his mum cooks a load of Indian food for anyone on the street who wants it.' The clicking of the Rubik's Cube stopped momentarily until he added: 'Actually, I'm looking forward to that as well.'

'Do they know about...?'

'No peanuts,' Jack said. 'No cashews or nuts of any kind. Rish says his mum keeps calling him to ask if there's some other sort of nut she can use. He keeps telling her no.' Jack checked over his shoulder, which set the bell on the end of his hat jangling. There was nobody there. 'I heard there are a bunch of police vehicles up on the moor. I've not told anyone what you said but I wondered...'

There wasn't quite a question there.

'It's all over Facebook,' he added.

'What are people saying it is?' Millie asked. She avoided Facebook where and when she could.

'Someone reckons they've found an unexploded bomb.' He checked over his shoulder again and then leaned in to whisper. 'I wondered if it's... y'know, Ashworth...'

He hissed the name, like a fundamentalist preacher mentioning the devil.

'I don't know what's happening,' Millie replied. She didn't like lying but also didn't want to talk about what she knew. She assumed that, after she'd handed the atlas to Baker at the prison, some sort of search team would be dispatched to the spot Ashworth had marked. Millie and Guy had been able to find the pool of water, so there shouldn't be any issue with them stumbling across it.

As for dragging Ashworth's car from the water, that might be harder, especially considering the vehicle would've been submerged either wholly, or partially, for more than two decades. Millie had no idea what they'd find but she doubted it would be pleasant.

She had no idea whether Ashworth would be allowed to return to his father's farm to explain why he'd done whatever he'd done.

At the bottom of the valley, the Christmas lights were again blinking in the house. Millie found herself staring out to the roof where one of the nursing home's residents, Ingrid, said she'd seen a girl pushed. It had been a little over a year ago.

'I heard the house was sold,' Jack said, following her gaze.

Millie had heard the same. She'd never be able to look without remembering how it had changed her life.

Neither of them spoke for a while. Jack wasn't one of those people who needed to fill every pause with words and neither was Millie.

'Can I ask you something?' Jack asked. He'd put down the Rubik's Cube, which made it seem serious.

'Of course.'

'When you had Eric, did you...? Was it immediate...?'

'Was *what* immediate?'

Jack gasped a long plume of air. 'You know when you first start seeing someone. You don't instantly fall for them, do you? Love at first sight is this dumb movie thing. You get to know them and it grows. But when you had Eric, was it... immediate...?'

Millie didn't like where the conversation was going. She continued watching the house at the bottom of the valley because she didn't want to risk looking at Jack. She hoped he wasn't asking what it sounded like he was.

'Are you asking if I loved him right away?'

'Yes.'

'The first time I held him, I knew everything was different. I thought I was in love with Alex, and I probably was, but it wasn't the same sort of love. I'd have never jumped in front of a bus to save my husband – but I wouldn't have thought twice about doing it for my son. It's like I had two lives. There was before Eric and after. Nothing's ever been the same since.'

Jack was quiet and yet he wasn't. He fidgeted, he scratched his ear then his bum. He didn't breathe for a while and then let out a long, low huff.

'What do you want to say?' Millie asked.

She almost didn't want to know – but this was what friends were for. Or what they were supposed to be for.

'When Isaac collapsed and he couldn't breathe, I was terrified. Really scared. I've never been like that before but...' He let the sentence hang for a while, then added: 'I thought about it later and I think I was scared for me. I was worried what would happen *to me* if he choked in my care. I don't know how to explain it. It's not like I wanted him to... *you know*... it's just...'

Jack picked up the Rubik's Cube, turned a couple of edges and then put it down again.

'I don't know how to put it without it sounding bad.'

'Just say it.'

He did: 'I miss my life before. I miss sleeping, without Isaac's night terrors. I want to watch what *we* want on TV and not have to worry about swearing or shagging. I miss going out without having to plan everything. I miss having a lie-in on the weekend. I miss just doing nothing...' He paused for breath, and then: 'I'm awful, aren't I?'

Millie rested her head on his shoulder. 'Everyone feels like that,' she said. 'After Eric, I missed lie-ins. I didn't like having to plan everything. That doesn't mean I didn't love him. When you adopted Isaac, your life changed in a day. Nobody's going to suddenly be used to that. It takes time.'

Jack rested his head on hers. She could feel him breathing. It was impossible to forget that she was the person who'd vouched for them as a couple, despite knowing Rishi wanted the child more than Jack.

'It's just, Isaac feels like someone who's living in our flat,' Jack said. 'A lodger, or a housemate. When you said you had Eric and knew everything was different. That you had two lives, the before and after, I don't feel that. I just... want my old life back.'

He lifted his head and picked up the Rubik's Cube, then sat on the bench. Millie lowered herself so she was at his side.

'What do I do?' he asked.

Millie touched him on the knee and then put an arm around his waist. She said nothing, because the alternative was telling him that she had no idea.

THIRTY-TWO

A tinsel bomb had gone off in the rec room of the nursing home. It was across the ceiling, around the doors and window frames, covering the entirety of the tree in the corner, and even around the wheels of Mick's wheelchair. Millie suspected that, if she stayed still for too long, someone would hang tinsel around her neck.

Millie spent a few hours a week at the home, talking to the residents or playing board games with them. Sometimes, she managed a bit of low-level tech support with various phones or iPads. Most of the time, she simply hung around. There was always something to do, or someone who wanted company. Ingrid was the resident to whom Millie spoke the most.

Ingrid nodded across to the television. There was a semi-circle of chairs around it, though nobody was really watching. Everyone in the corner was either on a tablet or phone. 'Everyone's already complaining that Christmas TV isn't as good as it used to be,' Ingrid said.

'What do you think?' Millie asked.

'Everyone gets to about thirty and thinks whatever's new is rubbish. The best music is what you liked when you were eighteen. The best TV is what you grew up with. If I have to listen to one more person tell me how great Morecambe and Wise were...'

'Dad always used to go on about that.'

'Here's the thing about Morecambe and Wise, *Monty Python*, and everything from then... most of it was *rubbish*. People remember the odd sketch but it was all hit and miss. For every one good thing they did, there were five that were nonsense.'

Millie let Ingrid rant. She knew that feeling herself.

A wicked grin spread onto Ingrid's face.

'What are you doing for Christmas?' she asked.

'It's my ex-husband's wedding tomorrow.'

'They're getting married on *Christmas Eve?*'

'I'm going to the reception. They asked if I'd go to look after Eric.'

Ingrid picked up the deck of Uno cards from the table and shuffled them like a veteran casino dealer. There was a blur of fingers and cards, then she flicked a card to Millie and one to herself.

'And you said yes...?'

'For Eric. There aren't going to be many kids there and he'd have had a miserable time. I still don't know if it's the right thing to go.'

Ingrid continued dealing until they each had seven cards. She put the leftovers into a pile between them and picked up the ones on her side.

'I've done a lot of things in my life,' she said, 'but I've never gone to the wedding of an ex-husband.'

That didn't make Millie feel any better – and neither did the hand she'd been dealt. There were no special cards and no matching numbers. She rearranged them in an attempt to make it look as if she had more interesting cards than she did.

'Eric told me he wants to live with me,' Millie added. 'His

dad doesn't know yet. I suppose I'm hoping that, if I go along with everything, things can't be held against me if it goes back to court.'

Ingrid lowered her cards and peeped over the top. 'Something that *looks* good isn't always *actually* good.'

'No...' Millie put down a red three. 'But I'm also worried about him being on his own at the wedding. Last summer, on his birthday, he got a dress from his friend. I think he was just curious about how it would fit, or look. Something like that. Loads of people were there. I figured it was one of those things. If he wants to wear a dress, what does it matter? Alex's wife-to-be didn't see it like that. She made a big scene and tried to get him to take it off. Then, later, after everyone had gone, she put it in the bin when she thought he wasn't looking.'

Ingrid played a blue three on top of the red, so Millie put down a blue four. Ingrid re-sorted her cards.

'I can see why you might be worried about others judging him at such a formal event,' she said.

'I suppose I'm worried why they asked. If they weren't planning on involving Eric, then why even have him there?'

Ingrid put a second blue four on top of Millie's – and, because Millie had no other blues, or fours, she picked up a card.

'I'll never understand the brides who think the wedding is about them,' Ingrid said. 'If you make it about your guests, and they have a good time, then you'll have a great time by default. You can't expect to enjoy yourself if you've made everyone around you miserable.' She shrugged, as if this was the most obvious thing, then added a blue five to the pile.

'Sorry to keep dumping stuff on you,' Millie said. 'That's not why I come here.'

'Oh, don't you worry about that. I'll happy live vicariously through others. I just wish you had a few stories of brawny men sweeping you off your feet. I'd listen to that all day long.' A pause. 'Or brawny women, if that's your thing. I'd happily listen to either.'

Millie grinned. 'Now that you say that...'

Ingrid squealed like someone sixty years younger. 'Ooooh... tell me all about it. Do not miss a single detail.'

Millie put down a red five, leaving her five cards. Ingrid added a red two, which left her three. The game became a temporary afterthought as Millie said that she'd gone on a lunch date with a man who worked as a kitchen fitter. Ingrid was disappointed Millie had no photos but speculated that someone who fitted kitchens was probably good with their hands. 'Strong, too,' she added.

Millie added a draw two card to the pile. Ingrid pulled a face and picked up a pair of cards, then Millie picked up one herself.

One of the reasons she enjoyed talking to Ingrid was that everything was said in isolation. There was no risk that anything would end up on Facebook, or that Ingrid would tell anyone else. They could each talk about anything, everything, or nothing – and it would never leave their table.

'I've only been in one proper relationship,' Millie said. 'I didn't think it would end but it wasn't right for a long while and then it was over. So what do you do then?'

Ingrid snorted with some degree of amusement, then she put down a yellow draw two, paused, and then a second version of the same card. Millie mumbled 'cheat' under her breath, making sure Ingrid heard, and then picked up her four cards. She was up to nine as Ingrid put down a yellow nine, to leave her with two.

'Do whatever you think is going to be fun,' Ingrid said. 'I've never regretted the things I *did* do – but I certainly regret missing out on some of the things I chose not to.'

Millie put down a yellow eight and then Ingrid added a yellow six.

'Uno,' Ingrid said.

Millie eyed the back of the single card in the other woman's hand, trying to second-guess what it might be.

'I'm holding a yellow,' Ingrid said.

Millie placed a yellow two on the pile. 'I don't believe you,' she said.

Ingrid feigned to put down her final card but then laughed to herself and picked up a card instead. 'I was never much good at bluffing,' she said, as she pressed back into her chair. 'Here's the other thing – and I know how hard it's been for you – but, when you're a child, the most important thing in your day might well be the painting of a rainbow you do. Or maybe it's playing with your favourite toy. And then, a year later, that one thing that was the most important thing in your life... is something you don't even remember. When I got divorced, times were a bit different than now. There was more of a stigma. You used to get stared at and there was this great sense of shame. I didn't think I'd ever get over it – and now... I couldn't care less.'

Millie put down a yellow one and Ingrid immediately added a yellow nine. 'Uno,' she said, before adding: 'I suppose what I'm saying is that, if there's some brawny kitchen fitter you want to snog, then go for it. What's the worst that can happen? Give him a snog for me while you're at it.'

'I don't think I'd be able to explain why I was snogging him on behalf of an old woman...' Millie placed a green nine on the pile. 'No offence.'

Ingrid laughed at that. 'If being called "old" is the worst thing someone says to me, then I'm doing all right.'

She delicately placed a four-colour wildcard on the pile, meaning she'd have won regardless of what colour Millie played. Millie turned over her remaining cards, for the values to be counted. Her complete defeat and surrender wouldn't be far off.

There was a murmur of noise from across the room and

Millie looked up to see that the television was now showing the local news. There was no sound, as ever, but the image on the screen was unmistakeable.

'I'll be back,' she said, though she was already on her feet, drawn inexorably to the corner.

There was a man standing in front of the dilapidated farm on the moors outside Whitecliff. He was talking into a microphone but Millie was watching the large trailer being driven past the no trespassing sign, through the farm gate behind. Her phone was in her hand and it felt inevitable that it started to buzz. It was a call, not a text, which meant it had to be Guy.

And that could only mean one thing.

THIRTY-THREE

Huge white screens had been put up across the farm gates, blocking anyone on the road being able to see what was happening on the other side. When Millie had arrived, she'd had to park a few hundred metres along the road, behind the series of satellite trucks. There were people with cameras and boom mics, plus presenters straightening their suits, before getting ready to do their pieces.

Millie told the uniformed officer at the farm gate who she was – and then he sent a colleague off behind the screen to find out if she was allowed in. One of the news presenters was eyeing her curiously, wondering who she was, or, perhaps – worse than that – he *knew* who she was. Millie didn't get recognised as much as she had a year ago, or a year before that, but she still knew those sideways stares.

A minute or so passed and the officer returned. He beckoned Millie around the gate and then made a point of getting her to spell out her name to go on a list he was holding. After that, he escorted her along the path, to the side of the farmhouse – where Chief Superintendent Baker was standing next to the rusting tractor frame.

He'd been staring off into the distance but turned to take her in. His nose wrinkled and then he went back to looking towards the expanse of the moors. It was somehow colder than it had been any of the previous times Millie had been at the farm. Colder than Whitecliff itself, colder than her house. Like some sort of micro-climate. There was a hint of snow in the air and it wasn't going to be long until it was dark.

Millie hadn't seen Guy's car and assumed he was on his way. Instead, he ambled across from the other side of the house. He was unescorted and apparently had free rein.

'You're here,' Guy said, talking to Millie.

Baker glanced to the pair of them and then away again.

'Divers went down this morning,' Baker said. It wasn't clear he was talking to them – except nobody else was there. 'They found a rusted car at the bottom.'

Millie pictured the murky pool she and Guy had found.

'We've got to be careful removing it, so it's not happening today. It's Christmas Eve tomorrow, so I doubt it'll be then either. We're not quite sure how we're getting the equipment across the moor yet. They might need a helicopter. We might even be looking at New Year.'

'Is there a specific reason you have to be careful removing it?' Guy asked.

It was an odd question, Millie thought, and then she realised what Guy was *actually* asking. This time, it wasn't about the car.

Baker didn't respond, so Guy said it instead.

'Bones...'

Millie shivered – and only partly because of the cold.

Baker didn't acknowledge them with words but Millie was certain she saw the merest of nods. Of course that's why they were being careful with the car. It wasn't the only thing they'd found. That's why they were at the farmhouse and why Baker's promise about Ashworth never again leaving prison had been broken. Ashworth had known they'd need him one last time – and here they were.

Baker made a point of rolling up his sleeve to check his watch: 'They're late,' he said.

Nobody spoke for a while. Various uniformed officers were coming and going around the property, although it wasn't clear what any of them were doing. Millie knew that sort of *look busy* energy from her years of working in an office.

She fiddled with her phone for a while, trying to keep her fingers warm. There was a text from Luke, asking what she was up to. Millie laughed silently to herself as she wondered how to reply. 'I'm on the moors, awaiting the arrival of a convicted murderer' wasn't going to cut it.

All of a sudden, the officers moved as one towards the white screen. Millie and Guy turned to watch, Baker at their side.

'There is a condition,' Baker said, the first time he'd properly acknowledged them.

'What?' Guy asked.

'Ashworth said he'd tell you everything if we brought him back here. We agreed, reluctantly, but it's only valid if he'll talk while I'm present. We're not going to accept you relaying things back to us. It's going to be recorded, too.'

He started fiddling with a series of cables that appeared to be wrapped around his body and attached to a radio mic that was clipped to his jacket pocket.

'There's not a lot I can say to that,' Guy replied. 'I'm in the middle here. I always have been.'

Activity was continuing around the gate. The large screen was still up but there was a grumble of an engine from the other side.

'Why you?' Baker asked.

'I told you,' Guy replied. 'I don't know – but I have a condition of my own.'

Baker's mouth dropped as he turned to look at Guy. 'Are

you joking? You know this has been arranged with the Home
Office and Ministry of Justice? It was signed off by the Justice
Minister this morning.'

Guy didn't react to any of that. Millie wondered if he
already knew because she certainly didn't. 'Kevin asked for *us*
to be here – but you, the prison service, the Home Office and
the Ministry of Justice all decided to make an arrangement
without talking to either Millie or myself…? You assumed we'd
do whatever you wanted.'

Baker's vein was pulsing again. 'You're here, aren't you?'

'And I have a condition.'

The screen was folded to the side as an officer opened the
gate. A set of headlights flared from the other side, swinging
around towards the farmhouse.

'What is it?' Baker hissed.

'If Kevin tells us what we think he might, I want to be the
one to tell Wesley's mother, Victoria.' Guy waited as an
unmarked white van started to edge through the gate towards
them. 'It's not ego. She's been unhappy with the police for years
because she says nobody tells her anything. I think it'll be a bit
rich if the first thing she hears in years is this.'

Baker was chewing, even though Millie didn't think there
was anything in his mouth. It was a bit late for negotiation
considering the van was past the gates and the screen was being
put back up again.

'Fine,' he said, not that he had much choice. Guy didn't
react.

The van slotted in behind the farmhouse. There were no
markings and it wasn't the same as the one that had brought
Ashworth to the moors a week before. It was a grubby grey, with
mud around the wheels and the rims. It could easily have
passed for some tradesman's on his way to a job. As it was
edging into place, the front wheel dipped into a grimy pothole
and span with an aching, grinding sound. Mud splattered the

crumbling wall until the engine stopped. Moments later, Ashworth was guided from the back of the van. His hands were cuffed but his head was up, blinking at the surroundings. They'd set off from this spot a week before, on the first morbid treasure hunt – and here they were again. Ashworth had grown up on this spot and he'd know this was the last time he'd ever see it.

A pair of prison guards guided Ashworth across to the trio of Baker, Guy and Millie. The six of them stood across from each other for a moment, nobody entirely sure what should happen next.

'Shall we uncuff him?' one of the guards asked.

Baker let the question hang but it was a ludicrous one. Where was Ashworth going to go? There were journalists on the road and a dozen officers milling around the farm. In the deepest distance, out towards the trees and the hidden pool, there were lights.

'Do it,' Baker said.

After being released, Ashworth moved slowly, achingly, across the crunchy gravel. It was only three or four steps but Millie could feel the pain in his joints as he tried to straighten himself.

Baker pushed himself up onto the balls of his feet, even though he was already the tallest of the four. He was at his pompous best as he pointed out the microphone.

Ashworth didn't appear to pay much attention to any of it. He was looking around the farm, taking in the rusty tractor and the shattered barns. His stare was distant and haunted.

When Baker had finished, he looked to Ashworth, expecting some sort of confirmation. Ashworth himself clearly hadn't been listening. He pointed in the vague direction of town, his hand shivering. He was the only one not wearing gloves.

'When I left the football club with the boys, I was supposed to be driving to the game. We were away and it should have taken about an hour to get there. Everyone hated playing us because Whitecliff is so far out of the way. There were some clubs in our league who were ten minutes apart – but we were always the outlier. Every other week, we'd have to trek along the coast, or across the county.' He looked to Guy and smiled sadly. 'Did you ever come with us?'

'No. I did a few adult games. I think they got to the first round of the FA Cup once but that was at home.'

A nod. 'Nicholas was home alone. He was sixteen or seventeen but had a habit of not eating when he was by himself. I told Tina I'd make sure he had something but I wasn't going to be at the house. There was always a burger van down the road from the ground, so I figured I'd take him with us. He wasn't into football and probably wouldn't have gone – but there was a scrap yard at the back of the pitches. He'd built this off-road, ATV cart thing himself. He couldn't ride it around town because it was unlicensed – and so was he.' Ashworth pointed across to the remains of the barn. 'We hid it out here. Nobody ever came this way, so it was safe from thieves. I'd bring him out once or twice a week and he'd fix bits and pieces and then ride around the moors.'

He stared longingly towards the place where he said the kart used to be stored. In the gloom and the gently falling snow, Millie could easily picture a teenager tearing around in the middle of nowhere. Guy had mentioned reports of scrambler bikes the last time they'd been on the moors – and where else would be better?

'We had to drive past here on the way to the game,' Guy said. 'Because Nicholas was going to the scrap yard, he asked if I could stop so he could check something. I assumed he was after a replacement part, that sort of thing. We were on our way out of town and I suppose he couldn't resist: he ended up telling the other two boys about his hidden kart. They were eight or nine and he was twice their age, so they were in awe. Like little brothers looking up to a bigger one.'

Millie thought of Eric, who was the same age as Wesley and Shaun had been. On the evening they'd walked up to the Bay Burning, Guy had acted as that sort of figure to her son. He'd listened and talked to him as an equal. She knew the type of relationship Ashworth was talking about. Young boys could easily end up in awe.

'I should have stopped it,' Ashworth said. 'But we were early and Nicholas had got the pair of them wound up. I think they were more excited hearing about his kart than they were about the football. So I stopped there.' Ashworth pointed across to the large white sheet at the front of the farm. 'Nicholas had this enthusiasm about him when it came to engines. It was infectious. He asked me if the boys could have a go. He knew what he was doing. He'd spent fifteen minutes telling them all about it, so I couldn't say no. He wanted to show off and didn't have lots of friends, so I figured there couldn't be much harm.'

'My son went karting a couple of months back,' Millie said. She hadn't planned to speak but it felt right. Ashworth paused to look at her and nodded. 'It was a birthday party for one of the boys in his class. They're only eight but the centre have these mini karts and they all got to race and go on the podium. Eric wasn't very good but he had fun.'

Ashworth bit his lip. 'Nicholas would've loved that growing up,' he said. 'There was nothing like that back then. He couldn't wait to turn seventeen and start taking driving lessons.'

He twisted back towards the barn and then pointed to a spot on the moors a little past it.

'The boys took it in turns to have a bit of a ride around on Nicholas's kart. Nothing complex, just going in circles. It would have been the first time any of them had a chance to drive anything – but we had to get going to the game. I told Nicholas to hide it away but, as he was doing that, I saw a dog, or... *some-*

thing over there.' He pointed across to the far side of the farmhouse. 'There were always stories of big cats prowling the moors. Dad always said he'd seen a panther and Mum used to tease him about it. There was this flash of black so I went over to see what it was.'

Guy barely moved but Millie felt his gaze shift momentarily across her. It was a year ago that they'd been on their own search for a big cat. It felt otherworldly now.

'I was probably away for a minute or two, not long,' Ashworth said, pointing towards the front of the farmhouse. 'I was on the other side and there was this squeal and a bang and...' He motioned towards the spot on which they were standing, a short distance from the house.

'What are you saying?' Millie asked. It felt as if the other two men had lost their voices.

'There was blood. Just so much blood.'

He was looking to Millie now, blinking and dazed.

'Both boys were under my car. I remember a pair of legs sticking out of one side. They used to wear their kits to the games and I could see the long socks. It started raining almost immediately, as if... I don't know. Divine intervention.'

There was a few seconds of silence and Millie presumed the men were as lost as she was.

'I don't understand,' she said and it felt as if she was speaking for all of them.

There was a long, solemn sigh. 'Nicholas was showing off. He'd hidden his kart but he wanted to show them he could drive a proper car too. When I'd gone over to look for the dog, he'd got into the driver's seat of my car. I think... I mean I didn't see it but... He couldn't really talk afterwards...'

Ashworth scratched at his scars. He was pointing around them; to the gate, the barn, the ground, the farmhouse itself. He mumbled something to himself, coughed and then grabbed Millie's hand.

'You have a son, so you understand. I know you do. Nicholas said he was trying to reverse but he put it in the wrong gear. He went forward instead of back, then he tried to go back but they were already underneath.'

Ashworth squeezed her fingers, imploring her to understand. And, in that moment, Millie did. It was as she'd told Jack hours before. Her life had changed the day she'd given birth. There was a before and an after – and the difference between the two was that she went from being her own number one, to being her own number two.

He let her go but it felt as if it was only them. Guy and Baker were watching but they might as well have not been there.

'Nicholas was panicking,' Ashworth told her. 'He was saying he was sorry but it was too late. I didn't know what to do. I'd lost one son. I couldn't lose another. It's why I needed you to see for yourselves what was up by the rock. You needed to understand why I did it.'

Millie hadn't known what to think of what they'd found the week before. The self-made coffin and what was inside. Now she knew. Bryan.

'What did you do?' Millie asked.

'I told Nicholas to go home. It was a long walk but he'd done it before when he'd been up here working on his kart. I told him to not tell anyone what happened, not even his mum. Nobody knew he had left the house. As far as anyone else knew, it was only me and the boys. Me and... Wesley. And Shaun.'

It was the first time he'd said their names and there was a crack in his voice.

'I told him to never, *ever*, tell anyone what happened. He asked what I was going to do and I shouted at him. Told him to run. That was the last thing I said to him for maybe ten years.'

Ashworth was breathless. He kept scratching his arms and his scars. It almost felt as if the story was bleeding from him.

'I got the boys into the back of the car,' he continued. 'I knew about the pool on the moors and how deep it got. I just drove. The car bumped up and down and the wheels spun a few times. I wasn't sure I'd get there and I had no idea it would stay hidden this long.' He pointed towards the lights in the distance, in the direction of the trees. 'The kart's in there too. Every year I was inside, I thought someone would come and say the water had dried up and that the car had been found, that the boys had been found, and every year it didn't happen. I spent all this time trying to think of what I'd say to make sure Nicholas was kept out of it – and now... it doesn't matter. There's nobody left to protect.'

Millie couldn't speak. She'd spent the past week confused that nothing made sense – but now it did. She had been trying to separate Eric from everything in her mind and yet the parent–child relationship was key to it all.

'I didn't mean to hurt the other parents,' Ashworth said quietly. 'But if I had to choose between my son and theirs...'

It was snowing properly, airy puffs of white drifting on the air. Ashworth pushed his hands into the waistband of his pants in an attempt to keep them warm. Millie tugged off her gloves and handed them to him, before cramming her hands into her jacket pockets. At first, it was as if Ashworth had forgotten what to do with the gloves. He held them and stared, before squeezing his fingers inside. They were probably too small but he made it work.

'Will you tell them?' he said, talking to Millie. 'The other parents. Tell them I'm sorry but I had to protect my son. I'm not expecting forgiveness...'

Millie didn't reply, mainly because her throat had narrowed to the point where she couldn't get out any words.

It was Baker, predictably, who brought them back to reality.

'Is there any proof this happened?' he asked.

'What proof could there be?'

Baker mumbled something that Millie didn't catch but would probably be picked up on his microphone.

Around them, the snow was melting as soon as it touched the ground. The officers who'd been shuffling around, trying to look busy, had started to bunch together, wondering what was next.

'Why me?' Guy said. 'I know it isn't about me but it's been hard not to wonder...'

Ashworth smiled kindly towards him. 'Because there was a time when someone was trying to make a documentary about all this. They wanted to talk to Nicholas and you kept them away.'

Guy's brow creased curiously. 'How do you know that?'

'Someone told Nicholas and Nicholas told me. He started visiting me in prison when he moved back. My dad always used to say that the kindest acts are the ones you're not supposed to know about. And you never boasted, you never even told Nicholas you did it. But you went out of your way to protect him, for no reward and no acknowledgement. I needed to tell this to someone like that. I don't *know* anyone I can trust – but I knew I could trust you.' He turned to Millie. 'And you.'

He stretched out a hand and, when Guy took it, they shook.

'Thank you for protecting my son,' Ashworth said.

The way Nicholas looked to Guy in the hospice now made sense. He told Guy he knew who he was, even though they'd never met.

Guy didn't reply. He'd never been much for praise. He withdrew his hand and nodded a little.

Baker didn't seem convinced. 'Are we done?' he asked, as he held up a hand to the sky. 'I don't know why we couldn't have done this last week. Or indoors.'

Millie knew why.

'One last thing,' Ashworth said. He took a step away and turned slowly, taking in the moors, the snow, and the gloom. He breathed in the cold and closed his eyes.

'What?' Baker snapped.

There was no reply, because this was it. Ashworth was never getting out of prison and he knew it. When he found out his son was close to dying, he'd set these events in motion because it was his final chance to tell the truth, to give Wesley's mother an answer – and, selfishly, the last time he'd stand on this spot.

As the guards descended, ready to pack him pack into the van, Ashworth's eyes were still closed and the snow still falling.

'I'm sorry,' he whispered.

THIRTY-FOUR

A red felt stocking had been pinned to the wall next to Victoria's Christmas tree. A white letter 'W' was stitched to the front and there was something lumpy in the bottom.

'I only ever put the tree up a few days before Christmas,' Victoria said as she ushered Millie and Guy into her living room. 'Every year I tell myself I'm not going to bother but then I see the lights in people's windows, and their trees, and I end up giving in. Then it gets to Boxing Day and I'm dragging it into the back alley so the council can get rid of it. Waste of time, really.'

She wiped her hands on her front but there was already the hint of wetness in the corners of her eyes. She knew.

'I'm sorry,' Guy said.

Victoria nodded acceptingly as she bit her bottom lip. 'Do you want tea, or—'

Guy pulled Victoria towards him and wrapped an arm around her. She pressed herself into him and allowed him to hold her for a few seconds before pulling away.

'I'm all right,' she said. 'I can boil the kettle if you want. Won't take long.'

'Perhaps we should just sit here...?'

Victoria seemed glad that someone was telling her what to do. She sat in the armchair, her back straight as if she ready to spring up at any time. Guy and Millie slotted onto the sofa next to each other.

'Did he tell you?' Victoria asked.

'Yes,' Guy replied.

Two decades in the making, and the question came in one word: 'Where?'

'There's a body of water on the moors, a couple of miles or so from the farm. It's not a lake, as such – and it's not marked on maps. It shrinks in the summer and fills during the winter. It's not easy to reach at this time of year but the police are up there now. It might not be today or tomorrow, then there's Christmas, but he's there.'

Victoria was nodding quickly as she drummed her fingers on her leg. 'Right, yeah, of course. Yeah. On the moors. Right.'

Guy told her everything Ashworth had said to them at the farmhouse. About the kart and the car, about Nicholas and the accident. How Kevin took the blame to protect his teenage son. Victoria didn't say a word as she continued to nod and drum her fingers. There was a sense that she was being told something she already knew, even though that wasn't possible. Millie thought she must have been preparing for something like this for so long that it almost didn't entirely matter what had happened and how.

When Guy was finished, there were a few moments of quiet. Victoria glanced across to the stocking on the wall and Millie could tell she was going to take it down the moment they left.

'Are you sure you don't want a cup of tea?' she asked.

'How about I make you one?' Guy replied.

'All right...'

Guy stood and hovered in the space between the sofa and

the chair. With his back to Victoria, he mouthed 'OK?' to Millie and she nodded. That done, he headed into the hall and out of sight.

Millie didn't know what to say, or whether Victoria wanted to hear anything. She tried not to look at Wesley's mini-shrine in the corner as she wondered if that, too, would soon be gone.

'Were you there?' Victoria croaked. 'On the moors, I mean. When he told you...?'

'Yes.'

'Do you believe him?'

Millie nodded another yes as she remembered Nicholas in the hospice, saying that he never quite loved driving the way he once did. Something about it had stuck with her, though she'd not been sure what. She'd almost asked what he meant but he'd been talking about things not being the same after he'd run over the two boys.

How could it ever have been the same?

His dad had spent getting on for thirty years in prison to protect him – but, in doing so, had tormented Victoria the same length of time.

'There's no proof,' Millie added. 'The police will probably tell you what they've found at some point but they'll never be able to verify Kevin's story. As far as everyone knows, he was still the only person responsible...'

Victoria was nodding again, although Millie wasn't sure she'd taken it in.

'Do you have children?' she asked. 'I can't remember if you told me last time.'

'I have a boy,' Millie replied. 'He's eight.'

A nod. 'They're lovely at that age. Wesley was so inquisitive. They're old enough to understand most things while, at the same time, there's still so much to learn. The perfect age because they've not quite learned how to back-chat.'

'Mine must have learned that early.'

Victoria laughed. 'You have to cherish these days,' she said. 'They go so fast. Then they're off with their friends and you never see them. Or they're at home – but they're locked in their rooms and they don't want you anywhere near them.'

'I think I've got that to come...'

Millie wished she hadn't said it as Victoria gulped and spent another few seconds looking towards the stocking on the wall. Millie wondered if she'd been putting something out for her absent son every year since he disappeared. Victoria had said she knew Wesley was gone at the time – and yet it was easy to put into words, not so easy to push away that little voice saying there was a chance.

In the other room, the kettle had started to boil.

'I think I'd have done it, too,' Victoria said. 'If it was Wesley who needed protecting. You do, don't you? When it's your kids. You know how it feels...'

Millie didn't know how to reply. It was hard to imagine doing something like Kevin Ashworth had done – and then staying quiet for so long. But then it was hard to imagine watching on if Eric was ever in a similar situation to Nicholas. It was a terrible accident and yet there was definitely recklessness that led to it.

Guy bundled back into the room, carrying a tray of mugs, a small bottle of milk, and a bag of sugar. 'I didn't know what everyone wanted,' he said. He placed the tray on the table, then went around the room, playing the host, even though it wasn't his house.

They all sat and sipped their tea, as the lights on the tree winked in the corner.

There wasn't much left to say. For a conversation that had been more than two decades in the making, it was almost anti-climactic.

'Will you ever see him again?' Victoria asked, talking to Guy.

'Kevin? I very much doubt it.'

A nod. 'It's just... if you ever do, you can tell him I understand.' She waited a moment, lips pressed on the rim of her mug as she thought. 'It's not forgiving, it's understanding. I'd need him to know that. They're different things, aren't they?'

Guy considered what she'd said and then replied carefully. 'You're right,' he said. 'But it doesn't make it any easier.'

THIRTY-FIVE

CHRISTMAS EVE

There was a dusting of Christmas Eve snow across the Big Tesco car park. Millie was in the passenger seat of Guy's car, staring across the frosty tarmac towards the store, where a line was beginning to form near the locked front doors. There was no twenty-four-seven malarkey in Whitecliff, not even on Christmas Eve. Stores opened, and then they closed. It's how it was and how it would always be.

Barry poked his snout through the gap between the seats. He didn't like being cooped up in the car and was desperate to get out and chase snowballs. Millie rubbed his nose and he nuzzled his head on her shoulder, trying to tell her to get on with whatever it was they were up to.

'I've been wondering if I should say something to you,' Guy said quietly, from the driver's seat.

He sounded hesitant, which was enough to send a gentle prickle of worry through Millie. 'Say what?'

'It's just... yesterday, when Kevin said the kindest acts are the ones you're not supposed to know about, I thought it was true of you as well. But the *cleverest* acts. *You* spotted the discrepancy with the map. *You* found the place that everyone's been searching for all these years. You solved something nobody else had... and then, when Kevin told us anyway, you didn't flinch. Didn't try to take credit. Didn't try to let everyone know how smart you are.'

He paused.

'I thought it was incredibly humble of you. Genuinely one of the most impressive acts I can remember.'

Millie had been so ready for something negative that her mouth was hanging open. It was one of the kindest things anyone had ever said to her – and she had no idea how to respond.

'That doesn't mean I like this,' Guy added. 'It's not the sort of thing I do.'

'I couldn't think of another way,' Millie replied, suddenly finding her voice. She waited a second, unsure if she should say it, before going for it anyway. 'There have been a lot of things I don't really do. Tell a woman what happened with her missing son. Trek across the moors with a convicted killer. Visit prison...'

Millie's relationship with Guy had been one in which she'd been slightly in awe of him. They were a partnership, except there was no question he was senior. She'd accepted that, partly because life had become exciting when they worked together. He'd told her that the town harboured secrets and he'd been right. The other part was because the contacts, archives, and notes were his. With the things that they had seen and done in the past year, she couldn't have done it alone.

Except, now, with Zoe... she *had* done things by herself. Right up until this moment.

Guy thought for a moment. 'You're right,' he said – and that was that. No need for a long, in-depth chat about power dynamics, because he'd said it in two words.

'It happened quickly last night,' Millie told him, as she nodded across towards the supermarket. 'I had the idea and... hopefully it's worked...'

She suddenly felt vulnerable. The thing about trusting Guy's judgement on things was that, if they went wrong, Millie didn't' have to bear responsibility. Now, this was all her. What if things *did* go wrong? What if they *were* dangerous?

There were at least ten people in the queue, waiting for the supermarket to open. Coats were snuggled tight, hats pulled low, scarves wrapped. There was no particular reason to wait away from a car, except that nobody wanted to miss out on their last-minute Christmas buy.

'Have you heard anything else from the moors?' Millie asked, wanting to change the subject.

'I know there was more heavy equipment up there late last night. People were talking about big spotlights being visible from town. The cameras are still up there but the police aren't saying anything more than there being a major development in the Kevin Ashworth case.'

'Do you think you'll try to pass on Victoria's message to him?'

Guy pursed his lips 'She didn't ask either of us specifically to do it. Just if we ever saw him again – which seems highly doubtful.'

'When will you write everything up?'

'I've already written most of it. Solving a case this old, finding those boys' remains, is going to be a big win for the police. They won't announce anything until they're certain, so I'll publish then. Unless you have alternate thoughts...?'

Millie needed a moment to register that he'd asked. When it came to his news site, she'd written things but he'd never specifically asked her opinion on his work. She'd never wanted to offer it.

'I think you're right but are you going to write up what Ashworth told us about Nicholas? I don't think the police will announce that.'

Guy was quiet at that. Across the car park, a child climbed

out of a car and ran to save a spot in the line. Whoever had driven remained in the vehicle.

'I haven't decided,' Guy said. 'I don't like reporting something that can't be sourced – and Kevin's version of events can't be proven. I think I might wait and see what the police release – and then ask Victoria what she thinks. Whatever comes out in the next week or so will be the official account, regardless of whether it's true.'

Millie considered that for a while. There was always that saying about history being written by the winners. Conquering armies would see themselves as sophisticated liberators and that would somehow become fact. Everything Kevin Ashworth had told them at the side of the farmhouse could, and maybe *would*, be lost. She finally realised why he'd been so keen for Guy to witness everything.

Guy plucked the envelope from the footwell behind Millie's seat. Barry snuffled around his arm, trying to figure out if there was a treat involved. When he realised there wasn't, he lay on the back seat, ears high, waiting for movement.

He had already checked it once but Guy lifted the flap of the envelope and flitted through the packed, padded scraps of newspaper. For someone who was usually calm, he was fidgety and unsure. He folded the flap of the envelope back down and hooked the clasp, sealing it closed. It was around the size and shape of a hardback book.

Across the way, the double doors of the supermarket opened and people started to head inside. A woman jumped out of the car next to the trolley park and dashed across the crispy ground to join the boy who'd saved a place in line.

It was time, though neither Millie or Guy needed to say it. Guy clambered out of the car and hooked his satchel across himself. He slotted the padded envelope inside and then walked in the opposite direction from the store. He looped around the bottle banks and then headed to the edge of the car park, making his way back towards the supermarket. He was moving slowly and deliberately, wanting to be seen, as he stopped next to a bin that was by the trolley park furthest from the store.

Millie started to see him as an old man that she'd asked to head into the cold on what suddenly felt like a stupid mission.

All for a hunch.

Barry poked his head through the seat again and then clambered across the gap, before plopping himself on Guy's driver's seat. He sat up tall and elegant, as if he was a driver, about to ask 'where to?'

Millie ruffled his ears as they both watched Guy from around fifty metres away. He was shuffling from foot to foot, trying to keep warm.

Millie saw the other man before Guy did. He was massive and wearing jeans with a shirt, and no coat. The sort who thought jackets were a bit girly. Guy was looking in one direction as the man strode from the other. Guy checked his watch but still didn't realise there was someone bearing down on him. Twenty metres away. Ten. The man was moving so quickly that Millie couldn't think what to do. Should she shout at Guy? Warn him? Even if she did, it was going to be too late.

Guy finally turned and spotted the other man when he was almost upon him. Millie's stupid plan, her stupid hunch, was going to end badly. Not only that, Guy had told her this wasn't what he did.

The man stopped a couple of metres from Guy and something was said between them. Millie was tense, ready for some explosion of violence... which never came.

Guy laughed and then the giant of a man did the same. He wrestled a trolley out from the train of others, said something else to Guy, and then turned and hurried towards the supermarket.

It was only a customer.

Millie had seen a big man and thought the worst. Except it didn't matter how big a person was: everyone looked stupid when they'd accidentally picked the trolley with the dodgy wheel. Millie watched as the man bumped and banged the trolley around the tarmac, trying to get it to go in one direction as it stubbornly tried to go in the other.

He wasn't a threat.

Millie had set up a second Instagram account, posing as a journalist from the *Sun*. She'd sent DMs to the mystery account, asking about the snippets of the main image. She'd asked what the full version showed and, when the person who had put it up proudly announced it was a full-length nude of Zoe from Girlstar, Millie had asked how much for it.

She'd not bothered to haggle on price. They'd agreed a time and place for the exchange – and here they were. Millie's silly hunch.

Barry sat up straighter in the driver's seat and Millie looked away from the man with the trolley to realise that someone else was approaching Guy from the other side. They were striding from the petrol station, heading directly to Guy, ready for a payday.

And Millie knew exactly who it was.

THIRTY-SIX

Guy removed the envelope from his satchel as the person approached. He clasped it under his arm, letting them see the shape and size. It really did look as if it might be packed full of cash, even if it was only newspaper.

Millie waited. If she opened the car door too early, it could be heard – or the movement might be spotted.

Zoe's mum was as inexperienced at all this as Millie. Her choice of bright pink coat and beanie hat was as conspicuous as the giant man with the wonky trolley. She strode towards Guy and, as she stopped a short distance from him, Millie made her move. She carefully opened her door, whispered a 'wait there' to Barry – as if he was going to drive off – and then closed the door as silently as possible, before setting off.

Guy was stalling. The envelope remained tightly under his arm as he said something Millie couldn't hear. She moved as quickly as she could, given the ground was coated with snow and frost. It would be quite the unveiling if she slid halfway across the car park and landed on her arse.

As soon as she was within earshot, she heard Zoe's mother give a crisp: 'It's in the car. Money first.'

There was a flicker of movement from Guy, a glance and a nod, and then Zoe's mum turned to see Millie almost upon her. She started to back away, towards the petrol station, but Millie held up her phone.

'It's too late,' Millie said. 'I've already videoed this – and everything you just said has also been recorded.'

It was a lie but Zoe's mother didn't know that. Underneath her coat, she was again wearing the pink tracksuit with 'Wendy' embroidered on the front.

'I guess I *am* a bit of an Inspector Cluedo,' Millie added. She couldn't resist. 'If you've got your daughter's print in your car, you can give it to me, and I'll make sure Zoe gets it safely, before anyone else *accidentally* sees it.'

Wendy turned between Millie and Guy. The game was up and she knew it.

'How'd you know?' she asked. 'I thought you were a joke when I saw you.'

Millie was short of words for a second. She wasn't used to being insulted quite so brutally to her face.

'It could only have been a handful of people,' Millie replied. 'I never thought it was someone from outside. Who would've known that picture was there? Even if the front door was unlocked, who'd have got past the gate? Why only take that one thing? It had to be someone strong to get that frame off the wall – and the first time I met you, you had those massive shopping bags. They were much heavier than I could lift. Whoever had the print wanted attention from papers and websites – which meant selling it. You wanted money – but there was no blackmail attempt, because you weren't after *Zoe's* money.'

'Pfft.' Wendy scowled between them and then focused on Guy. 'I've just realised who you are. You're that bloke with all the news and stuff. It was *my* idea to get Zoe to contact you. I thought you'd write something. Get a bit of attention. You couldn't even do that properly. I have to do *everything*.'

She reached for the envelope, which Guy let her take. There was a couple of seconds of confusion, in which she clearly believed she was holding thousands of pounds. Then she opened the flap and looked inside, before tipping the ripped newspaper pages onto the ground.

'Are you joking?'

'Were you *really* trying to sell your daughter's photo?' Millie asked. Even as she watched the papers tumble into a pile on the frosty ground, she couldn't quite believe it.

'I gave birth to her!' Wendy scoffed. 'She owes it all to me. There was a time when she realised that and was paying it back.'

Millie remembered Zoe saying that her parents had been on her payroll, when she'd been at the peak of her earning powers. With the crumbling house and the half-empty tour, it was easy to see that money wasn't as easy as it had been.

'You don't have children because you expect to make money from them,' Millie replied.

'Who else is supposed to pay for my car? Not Sharon. She's always been useless. Always asking for money, that one. I don't know where she gets it from. Do you know how much she owes?'

Millie stared, unsure what to say. She *did* know how much Sharon owed and she definitely knew where she got it from.

'That picture is stolen,' Millie said. 'You can either hand it over, or I'll show the police the DMs you sent, plus we've got you on camera trying to sell stolen goods.'

There was a stand-off as Wendy looked at the scraps of paper on the floor. Her hopes of swindling thousands were gone and she knew it.

'Fine!'

Wendy turned and stomped back towards the petrol station, with Millie a few paces behind. When she reached the pink monstrosity, she wrenched open the back door and pulled out a large, rolled-up canvas cylinder, which she shoved towards Millie.

'She's gone anyway,' Wendy said. 'Can't be bothered spending time with her mum, or her sister. Even at Christmas.'

Millie took the print, which was heavy enough that she felt her shoulders click as she clasped it. 'Zoe's gone to see her children.'

'You're her friend now, are you?'

'I know I don't expect my son to pay me back, just because I brought him into the world. Which he didn't ask for.'

That got a smirk and Millie knew the reason.

'Why did you send me that photo from the Bay Burning?' Millie added. 'What did you want to happen?'

A shrug, although the sneer said plenty. 'Because I saw you standing around, not doing anything, when you should've been doing something about all this.' She tapped the giant print in Millie's arms, which made it feel heavier.

'I was there with my son.'

'Ugly little thing, isn't he?'

She knew the reaction she wanted – but Millie was determined not to give it. 'Merry Christmas,' she said, through clenched teeth, before turning to head back to Guy. She'd expected him to be back at the car – but he was still by the trolleys. The papers had been cleared from the floor, though he was staring at the phone in his hand.

'I'd have picked all that up,' Millie said. She had to swap the print from arm to arm, because it was too heavy. Somehow, she was going to have to get it in Guy's car. She probably should have thought about that.

Guy didn't look up.

'Everything all right?' she asked.

He took a breath and then blinked up from the phone, as if only then noticing she was there.

'Guy...?'

'That was about Kevin Ashworth,' he said quietly, holding up his phone. 'He was found hanging in his prison cell this morning.'

THIRTY-SEVEN

Guy switched off the engine and reached across to place a hand gently on Millie's knee. 'None of this is because of you,' he said.

Millie knew that, and yet she couldn't quite take it all in. She'd seen Nicholas four days before – and now he was dead. She'd seen his father the day before – and he was also gone. She didn't know either of them personally and yet couldn't stop thinking about the speed of it all. A week or so ago, there was a father and son – and now there wasn't.

'Will you tell Victoria?' Millie said. 'I don't think I can be there.'

'I will.'

He tapped the rolled-up print that was resting on the hand-brake. The only way they'd been able to fit it in the car was lengthways through the centre. Barry wasn't happy at being confined to one side of the back seat.

'You've done well,' Guy said. 'You did all this – and Zoe will be relieved to hear that her picture is in safe hands.'

Millie didn't know what to say. He was probably right and yet it felt like such a small thing compared to what had happened with Ashworth and his son. She wondered how he'd managed to hang himself, then realised she didn't want to know. She thought about whether he'd planned it and then decided it didn't particularly matter.

'Did they say when it'll be made public?' she asked.

'It won't take long. I'd be surprised if it hasn't already leaked. That's why Zoe didn't want to call the police. Everything gets out.'

'I've got to go,' Millie replied. 'Jack and Rish are coming over with Isaac. We're swapping presents and then they're off to spend Christmas with Rishi's parents. Then it's Alex's wedding reception tonight, so...'

There was nothing left to say, so Millie opened the door and wished Guy a Merry Christmas. She again offered him the chance to come over for dinner but he said he was happy enough with just him and Barry.

The two of them battled the large print out of the car, via the boot, and then Millie said goodbye to Barry, before heading into her house.

The picture was too heavy to drag around, so she left it in the hall against the wall – and then sat on the stairs. She texted Zoe a photo of the rolled-up canvas and said that the picture was safe. It wasn't long until a reply came back.

> WHAT?? Where was it?

Millie didn't want to spoil Zoe's Christmas.

> We can talk when you're home. Have a fab Christmas with the boys

Dots appeared to show that Zoe was typing, then they disappeared. Millie waited a minute or so but there was no other response.

That wasn't the only active text thread. She and Luke had been messaging back and forth since the diner, mainly swapping pictures of dogs. He'd sent her something an hour or so before, asking what she was up to on Christmas Eve.

> Why don't you come over for dinner tomorrow? (If ur free). My friend says she doesn't mind cooking for a +1

It was true that Nicola had said she was happy to cook Christmas dinner for three instead of two – but that was when Millie had mentioned Guy coming over. She was almost certain that, as soon as she found out it was Luke instead, Nicola would be asking him if he had any single friends.

> RU sure?

Millie told him it was definitely fine and that he should come over before twelve. He said he was already looking forward to it – and then Millie left it at that.

It wasn't long until Jack, Rishi and Isaac turned up.

Jack bustled inside, away from the cold – as Isaac thrust a box-shaped gift into her hands at the door.

'Yours is under the tree in the living room,' she told him. 'But don't open it until I get there.'

She doubted he heard anything after the word 'tree' – and he certainly didn't hang around as he bounded past her, Jack following through the house.

Rishi air-kissed Millie left-right-left-right, which had become his thing in the past month or two. 'Are there definitely no nuts in the house?' he asked.

Millie had already assured him four times that morning – and three times the previous day – that there wasn't, but she let it go. 'I did another check five minutes ago,' she said.

'Good, it's just—'

'I get it.'

It felt as if he was going to say something else but he

stopped himself as Millie led him into the kitchen. She sorted out drinks as he talked her through the route they were going to drive to his parents' place. He was babbling in the way he did when he was nervous. Millie wasn't sure why at first – but then he placed what looked like a marker pen on her table. The cover was yellow and there was an orange nib on the end.

'This is one of Isaac's EpiPens,' he said. 'I wondered if I could leave one with you? Just in case Isaac's over one time and... you know...?'

'I'll keep it in my bag,' Millie replied, before taking it and slipping it in with the rest of her things. 'Either that, or I'll go to America and sell it for a grand. Have you heard how much they cost there?'

Millie had forgotten that Rishi didn't *do* jokes when the subject matter was serious.

'Obviously, I'm not going to do that,' she added.

'I keep one on me at all times, then Jack's got one. There's one in the car, two at the flat, and I'm going to leave one with Mum and Dad. You can never be too careful.'

'That sounds sensible,' Millie replied.

'The doctor wouldn't prescribe more than seven, although I might go back and see if I can get a couple more.'

Millie almost said, 'Best leave some for everyone else', though she stopped herself in time. Instead, she took him through to the living room, where Isaac was sitting on the rug at the back of the room, a large wrapped box in his hands. Millie still had the gift she'd been given, which she placed on the arm of her chair.

'You can open it,' she told him, although she hadn't finished the word 'open' when Isaac made the first rip. When he was through it, he neatly balled the paper and put it to the side, before focusing on the gift. The gift was identical to what Millie had bought Eric when he'd been the same age. It was a construction set that involved gears and pistons. Half puzzle, half building. The object was to slot everything together to create a large tower.

'Can I play with it now?' Isaac asked, talking to Jack. Millie knew it was because he'd already discovered Jack was the pushover.

Rishi was about to say something likely along the lines of 'saving it for Nana and Granddad's house' – but Jack got in first with a straight 'Yes'.

The two men exchanged a look that said all that and more – and Millie had known the pair of them for long enough to know what was going on.

As Isaac started banging things around at the back of the living room, a little in front of the bureau, Millie, Rishi and Jack sat at the other end. Rishi talked them through the journey to his parents', again, along with added commentary of how long he expected it to take. He said his parents were excited about a new grandchild spending his first Christmas with them, because his sister already had three children of her own. He was excited, because they were excited.

Jack was quiet and playing on his phone.

Millie opened her gift, which turned out to be a giant candle. Rishi told her he'd picked it, which had been obvious from the moment she'd smelled it. She thought she saw Jack gently roll his eyes, which made her effuse about how nice it was – and how she'd definitely burn it the next time she was in the bath. Things like candles were very much Rishi's domain – not Jack's and not hers.

'What time's the wedding?' Rishi asked.

'Just under two hours,' Millie replied. 'There's photos, then a break, and then the reception.'

Rishi glanced across to Jack, who was still on his phone. 'Are you sure you're all right going? It's a bit...'

'I know it's weird. It's not about me, or them. I'm only going for Eric. Plus he's going to be sleeping here tonight, then presents in the morning. Back with his dad for a few hours and then he's with me from Boxing Day while the newly-weds go on honeymoon. I've got him all the way through 'til he goes back to school.'

She considered telling them how Eric had said he wanted to live with her – but there were so many caveats she didn't want to explain. It wasn't as simple as what he wanted and what she wanted.

Rishi had started to tell her about how his sister was trying for a fourth child when Isaac's little voice sounded from the other side of the room. With Jack on his phone, plus Rishi and Millie chatting, nobody had been paying him any attention.

She did now.

The rug had been rolled back, the hatch that nobody else knew about was open, and Isaac was holding a white pill bottle in his hands.

Millie had never moved so quickly in her life. She was across the room in what felt like a single step. She snatched the tub from Isaac's hand and knocked down the hatch with her knee.

None of that mattered – because both Rishi and Jack had seen. Jack was slower in crossing the room but what he'd spotted, that Millie hadn't, was that Isaac had been holding one tub, while a second sat at his side. Jack picked it up and scanned the label, before Millie had the chance to say anything. He glanced to the lines in the wooden floor, where the hatch was now closed.

'I think Isaac needs the toilet,' Jack said.

'But I—' Isaac started.

'Rish! He needs the toilet now.'

Rishi didn't try to argue. He headed to the door and beckoned across his son. Their footsteps sounded through the house, leaving Millie and Jack sitting on the floor. He passed her the tub, making sure to rattle it as he did so. Millie took it and put it on the floor with the matching one.

'It's not—'

'I know what Hydrocodone is,' Jack replied. 'I know the brand name is Vicodin, I know it's addictive, and I know both your parents OD'd on it.'

Millie didn't know what to say. Neither did Jack for a short while.

'How did you get so many?' he asked eventually. 'They're a controlled substance. You've got two tubs and there must be a hundred in each.'

Millie tried to think of a response that sounded feasible. 'They were Mum's,' she said.

'So why are you hiding them? Why didn't you let the police have them?'

There was no answer to that – and Millie had been friends with him for long enough to know that he didn't believe her anyway.

She realised what was going to happen a half-second too late. Jack grabbed for the hatch and pulled it open, just as Millie tried to block it with her foot. He stretched into the hidden hole and pulled out both pairs of handcuffs. He held them up and tapped the metal, as if convincing himself they were real.

'Mill...?'

It was a question. The one people had been asking her ever since her parents had died.

She calmly took the cuffs from him and put them back into the hatch, along with the two tubs of pills. They wouldn't be there for long. She needed a new hiding place – and the spot in which her dad used to keep piles of cash was no longer going to work.

Millie rolled back the rug and pushed together the parts of Isaac's building set, so they could be packed.

'What's going on, Mill?' Jack asked.

'Nothing.'

Jack pushed himself up, so they were face to face. He tapped his foot on the rug: 'What about that stuff?'

'What about it? I guess they were Mum and Dad's.'

'Are you saying you didn't know they were there?'

It was the worst, most obvious lie Millie ever told. Her reaction at diving across the room was enough to tell anyone who saw that she knew.

Except she couldn't say that.

'I had no idea,' she said.

They both knew it was untrue – and yet she knew he wouldn't call her on it. He'd confided his feelings about Isaac and, without particularly wanting, or meaning, to, it was something she now held over him.

Rishi appeared in the doorway. 'I left Isaac in the downstairs bathroom,' he said, before turning to the floor. 'What was that?'

'Dad's hidden cubbyhole,' Millie said, which wasn't a complete lie. 'There's another in the bedroom. I've always wondered if there was another somewhere...'

She left it at that as Rishi and Jack eyed one another. She wondered if Jack would tell him later what the label on the pill bottle read, though she doubted it. It felt like their secret.

Jack was suddenly the Jack she'd become friends with. 'Imagine if there *is* another hiding spot,' he said, full of feigned excitement. 'Imagine if there's loads of money! You could be rich, Mill.'

Rishi didn't pick up on the fake enthusiasm, instead taking it at face value, and seeming remarkably calm. 'I'd have the floorboards up if it was me,' he said. 'Jack's right: you might be sitting on all sorts of secrets.'

Millie didn't tell him how right he was – and she didn't have to, because Isaac appeared behind him. 'I only had a number one,' he said.

'I think we should get off,' Jack said. 'Just in case there's traffic...'

The mention of potential traffic meant Rishi wasn't going to argue. He helped Isaac pack up his partially built tower, air-kissed Millie, and then headed off towards the car. There were goodbyes and happy Christmases. Promises to text and see each other soon. Millie went along with it but couldn't escape the sinking sense that there was no going back.

Jack was torn between too much eye contact and none at all – but she could see the doubt in him as he wondered who and *what* she was.

Unlike some strangers, plus numerous people on the internet, he had never once asked if she'd killed her parents. And now she wondered if this had made up his mind.

THIRTY-EIGHT

People started doing double takes at Millie before she was even in the venue. She had dressed down in a plain-ish purple dress and flats, something that wouldn't upstage the servers, let alone the bride. That didn't stop other guests looking.

Nicola was at Millie's side and leaned in to whisper an unhelpful: 'Everyone's looking' as they passed through the large doors of the converted barn. The inside was an explosion of gold and silver streamers and decorations. A floor-to-ceiling Christmas tree was in the corner, next to the stage, on which a series of instruments were set up. Circular tables were dotted around much of the rest of the room, with a long table along one wall.

The stares felt worse than Millie had known before. She had a degree of control if she was in a supermarket, or on the street, and someone eyed her. She could walk, or move, or leave. Here, there was nowhere to go. One giant room, hundreds of pairs of eyes. It was a *much* bigger wedding than when Millie had married Alex. At least twice the size, probably more.

And those eyes weren't looking at the bride.

Millie recognised so few people. A lot would be Rachel's

friends and family but it was hard not to wonder who everyone else was. Millie knew Alex's family, plus some of his work friends – but what about the others? Did he and Rachel really have so many more new friends?

'Do you want your photo—?'

A man in a suit with a camera in his hand stepped in front of them but was cut off by a curt 'No.' Millie hadn't meant to be rude but she definitely didn't want her photo taken.

It had never felt a good idea to come and Millie didn't know what she expected. There was always going to be people staring and whispering. She was always going to be stuck in a room for hours with people that didn't like her.

'Shall we sit somewhere?' Nicola asked.

She started picking up place settings from the nearest table, then returning each individually and checking the next. Millie considered hiding in the toilet until she heard people starting to settle – but then she remembered why she was there.

It wasn't about her.

'Mum!'

Eric appeared from nowhere and Millie melted at the sight. He was in a suit that she'd never seen before. It was grey, with a red tie – and he looked eighty per cent cute, twenty per cent micro estate agent.

'You're here!' he said.

Millie asked if he knew where they were sitting but he was already trying to drag her around the room.

'Come see the chocolate fountain.'

The last thing Millie wanted was for the other guests to see her arguing with her son, so she allowed herself to be guided. Nicola mercifully tagged along as he showed her the chocolate fountain, while grumbling that it was 'for later'.

There was a magician, who somehow made a chair disappear and reappear; plus an eight-tier cake, a photo booth, three professional photographers, and a videographer.

'There was a man with an eagle earlier,' Eric told her.

'Why was there an eagle?' Millie asked.

'It flew in with the rings. His claws were *really* sharp.'

With what she'd seen, plus the band for later, the DJ, the venue hire, and everything else, Millie knew the cost of this wedding was at least four or five times what hers had been. It wasn't a competition, she told herself that, but – if it was – she'd lost like a unicyclist in the Tour de France.

They eventually ended up back near the front, where Millie realised she'd walked past the table setting board without seeing it. She noticed what had happened almost immediately. Nicola did, too.

'There's nowhere for me to sit,' Nicola said, sounding slightly confused, as she pointed to the board.

'I told him,' Millie replied, unsure what else to say. When she'd talked to Alex about the reception, bringing a guest was one of her conditions. There was no way it could be an accident.

Alex and Rachel, bride and groom, were standing on the far side of the room. Rachel's dress was somehow both extravagant and elegant at the same time. It was simple and yet seemed to glow. The material must have cost a fortune – and it fitted perfectly. It looked so good on her that Millie almost said so out loud.

Almost.

The happy couple were busy chatting to a small group of people from Alex's work. Even if she wanted to, which she didn't, there was no way Millie could head across and ask where Nicola should sit.

'What do I do?' Nicola asked.

'Why don't you take the seat and I'll wait in the bar?'

'You can't do that. What about Eric? You can't have him in the bar with you.'

Millie looked to the tables, where the chairs were already tightly packed. There wasn't going to be room to slot another in.

He was across the room but Millie suddenly knew she was being watched. She looked up and Alex nodded the tiniest of amounts. The smirk let her know that it was all deliberate. Millie was there and couldn't leave.

'I'll wait in the bar,' Nicola said. 'At least I can have a few drinks. Do you know some other people on your table?'

Millie had been so busy looking for Nicola's name that she'd not noticed who she was with. She did now – and her face must have told the story.

'What?' Nicola asked.

Millie pointed to the name. 'That's Alex's grandmother. She hated me even before we got divorced. She reckoned he was marrying down and said I was just a "host".' Nicola seemed confused, so Millie added: '"Host for a baby". Like that was the only thing I was good for.'

Nicola turned towards the tables, her mouth open. 'She said that to your face?'

'Twice. Both times in front of Alex. Both times, he pretended it was a joke.'

Millie didn't find out what Nicola thought of that – because Alex's dad was on the stage, dinging a glass with a knife. He called for everyone to take their seats, which started the rush towards the tables as Millie, Nicola and Eric continued to stand near the board.

'Text if you need me,' Nicola said.

'I'm so sorry.'

Nicola gave a sad smile as she headed one way, with Millie and going the other. Millie wasn't at a table near the back, she was – perhaps predictably – somewhere near the centre of the room, surrounded by the most people.

She shrank as she sat, wishing she'd brought a big coat, or something else with which to cover up. Eric didn't notice the embarrassment as he sat at her side, swinging his legs under the chair.

Millie didn't know a single person at the table, except for Alex's grandmother. The older woman was the last to arrive, helped into her seat two chairs away by a man Millie didn't know. She called him a 'good boy', as if he was a dog that had sat on command. Then she told the couple next to her that the groom was her grandson.

'He's doing it properly this time around,' she said loudly enough for everyone – but specifically Millie – to hear.

As soon as she spotted Eric, Alex's grandmother began digging into her bag.

'I brought some sweets just for you,' she said.

'We're about to eat,' Millie replied, unable to stop herself.

Alex's grandmother made a point of shifting her gaze to Millie. The older woman glared, as if Millie had just done a poo on the floor.

'He wants sweets,' she said.

'What boy doesn't?' Millie replied.

Eric knew what he was doing as he quietly slid out from his chair and took the packet of chocolate eclairs from his great-grandmother. She gave him a kiss on the cheek for his troubles, which got an instant 'ugh'. Millie didn't tell him that it served him right when he sat back down.

Everyone seemed to be in their seats by the time the best man stood up. It was someone from Alex's work, although Millie couldn't remember his name. He was old money, so something like Hugo Glovingly-Muttington. Millie had learned long before that the more names a person had, the less she liked them.

'Here we go again,' he announced, which got an enormous laugh. Millie felt eyes on her as she smiled along.

She should never have come.

It took a good forty to fifty seconds for the laughs to die

down, and then Hugo, or whatever he was called, added: '...
Properly this time,' which got an even bigger laugh. Even
Rachel found it funny, which seemed absurd considering she
was partially the subject of the joke as well.

Millie fake-smiled as she dug her nails into her palm under
the table, while refusing to make eye contact with anyone.
There was a balloon hovering over the main table, so she
concentrated on that, willing it to pop. Which it didn't.

This wasn't only Alex and Rachel's wedding reception, it
was an organised humiliation for her. She wondered how many
people were in on it. How many times the happy couple had
discussed it.

Eric had noticed something wasn't right. His hand was
suddenly in hers under the table. She patted his fingers gently
as he whispered 'Are you OK?' to her.

'Yes, love,' Millie replied, even as she felt the anger burning.
She couldn't stand her eight-year-old boy feeling sorry for her,
and yet even he could sense this was a degradation.

The speeches continued and there were a couple more
cracks about 'getting it right', plus less direct ones about Alex
and Rachel being 'the perfect match'. The best man said he'd
never seen Alex so happy, then added for good measure that
'she makes him happy like nobody else'.

There were probably other things but Millie somehow
tuned out. She silently hummed to herself, while continuing to
focus on the balloon.

Pop, she willed. *Pop*.

It didn't.

Suddenly people were clapping and it was over. Servers
appeared and food was thrust onto the tables. There was lamb,
which Millie had never really liked, but that choice probably
wasn't a dig at her. The potatoes were underdone but the rest of
the meal was annoyingly pleasant. Red and white carafes of

wine were passed around but Millie kept on passing as she stuck to the table water.

It felt as if Alex's grandmother never stopped staring. Millie thought about asking if she was all right – but knew she wouldn't. People *wanted* her to make a scene, which was precisely why she couldn't let it happen.

The meal turned into dessert and, despite Eric eating the sweets, he'd managed all his dinner, at least half of Millie's, plus two sticky toffee puddings. He was one of those kids that somehow never seemed to put on weight.

Through the meal, Millie kept half an eye on the top table. Between the main course and pudding, Alex had headed across to one of the tables on which his workmates were sitting. They laughed and joked around – but then he returned to the main table, without visiting his son. Eric didn't appear too unhappy. He was busy trying to scrounge a third dessert off the woman sitting on his other side. When it became clear she intended to finish her own food, Eric looked back to his Mum.

'Can I say hello to Dad?' he asked.

A pang of sadness swept across Millie that he had to ask. He'd been shunted away from the main table and then ignored for more than an hour. The fact he'd sat largely still through it all was something of a miracle.

Millie eyed the top table, where everyone was in their seats, having mini two- and three-way conversations. A couple of slow eaters were still picking at the remains of their meals and Millie assumed Eric was going to check whether they intended to eat the rest.

'Go on,' she said.

He crunched back his chair and stood: 'Will you come?'

'You can go by yourself.'

'I've got something to show you.' He reached for her hand, wanting to lead her.

'What?'

'I'll show you when Alex is there.'

She almost corrected him to call Alex 'Dad' but Millie wasn't in the mood for defending her very much former husband.

She allowed herself to be pulled up and then followed her son around the tables to the front. Eric looped around the back of the main table, Millie a step behind.

And then they were behind the bride and groom. It was impossible for Millie not to picture her own wedding when she saw Alex up close in his suit. In the time that had passed, she could never quite remember why she'd been so keen to marry him – but it was impossible now to ignore his appeal. Despite his many faults, despite the reason she'd had her affair in the first place, he looked incredible in a suit.

Alex was looking one way, talking to Rachel's dad; while Rachel was turned the other, talking to Alex's mum. Neither of them noticed as Eric tucked in between them – but both jumped simultaneously as Eric spoke.

'How long does it take?' Eric asked.

Bride and groom spun towards each other and then Alex peered up to Millie, an eyebrow raised to silently ask why she – and Eric – were there.

'A few more hours yet,' Rachel said.

'It's so long,' Eric replied.

'Lots of people want to congratulate us,' Alex replied, nodding towards his new wife. 'Don't you think Rachel looks pretty?'

Eric didn't bother to turn. 'No.'

Millie bit her lip but Rachel didn't. 'That's very rude,' she said.

'*I* think she looks pretty,' Alex said. He glanced up towards Millie again and, with the merest inclination of his eyes towards the other side of the room, told her to move their son away.

Millie waited for a moment, fighting the urge to challenge

him. They hadn't wanted her to come as a babysitter, they'd wanted her to come to keep Eric as far away from them as possible. If it hadn't have been for how it would have looked, they'd have probably not let him come in the first place.

It was hard to know what to do. If they'd been anywhere else, at any other time, Millie would have told Alex that their son wasn't supposed to be an inconvenience. She almost said it anyway.

Almost.

Because she didn't get the chance. While nobody was paying him any attention, Eric reached forward, calmly picked up a glass of red wine, and then threw the lot into Rachel's lap.

THIRTY-NINE

For a second, nothing happened. The purply-red liquid seemed to hover before spreading across the white of Rachel's dress. The glass bounced of her lap and then rolled across her knee, before clattering onto the floor.

There was another second of silence – and then everyone started shouting at the same time. Alex grabbed Eric by the shoulder and hauled him away as Rachel called him a little shit. Alex and Rachel's parents were bellowing across each other, from both sides, asking what had happened. Millie stared, barely able to believe what had happened.

'What was that for?' Alex demanded of his son.

Eric looked him dead in the eye and didn't blink. 'She threw out my dress,' he said.

Alex glanced to his new wife over the top of Eric's shoulder and Millie saw a furious flare of horror pass between them. They'd forgotten and assumed Eric had. Instead, he'd been sitting on his young anger for six months.

'This is *not* OK,' Alex said. His face was burning the colour of the wine as he jammed a finger towards Eric's face. On the other side, Alex's mum was busy dabbing at Rachel's lap,

though, from what Millie could see, she was only succeeding in
further patting in the stain.

Chairs were scraping as people stood to try to see what was
happening and, as Eric glared unrepentantly, Alex looked up to
Millie.

'Can you *do* something with him?'

The image of Nicholas sitting with his chocolate cake
flashed through Millie's mind. Then there was the last time
she'd seen Kevin Ashworth, who'd given up his entire life to
ensure his son had one.

They were both now gone.

'He's *your* son, too,' Millie said. 'He wanted to see you but
you've dumped him on a different table, where there's nobody
his own age.'

'Not everything's about him,' Alex replied.

'He's eight years old.'

Alex twitched a fraction before he turned away. 'I can't deal
with this,' he said, as he reached for a napkin. He leaned around
his son and started dabbing at his wife's lap, before Rachel
pushed away both him and his mum.

'This isn't going to come out,' she said, sounding distressed.

More people were on their feet, trying to see what had gone
on. Rachel's mother had rounded the table to get to her daughter, where she stared disbelievingly, asking what had happened.
Everyone was asking the same thing.

'It was an accident,' Alex said, attempting to laugh it off
until Rachel's cold 'No, it wasn't' cut across him.

This time, Millie did guide Eric away from the top table.
His body was tense and he was breathing quickly as she clasped
him tight to her side.

'We can go if you want?' she said. 'We'll go to McDonald's
if you're still hungry, or—'

'Can I have a milkshake?'

'Whatever you want.'

Millie knew it wasn't the best of parenting. He'd already eaten enough and she was rewarding him for bad behaviour.

That was one way of looking at it.

The other was that she didn't care.

They took a long loop around the room, avoiding the tables as much as they could. Nobody paid them much attention, because everyone was focused on the top table, asking what had happened.

Eric was silent as Millie guided him through the main doors and into the separate bar. Nicola was on a stool, nursing a glass of wine – except she wasn't the only person there. As Millie had taken her time getting out of the main room, Rachel must have headed directly to the bar, along with her mum. The stain on the front of her beautiful glowing white dress had turned a browny-purple and had spread across the entire area around her crotch. Rachel's mum was asking the barman if he had any bicarbonate of soda and he said he'd check the kitchen. As he turned to go, everybody else focused on Millie and Eric.

Rachel's features twisted into fury. 'You put him up to it, didn't you?'

Millie took a small step forward, trying to protect her son from his new stepmum. 'Of course not,' she replied.

'I should've known to keep you far away. Should've known you'd pull this sort of stunt.'

Rachel's mother was clasping a cloth in one hand and a bottle of water in the other. 'Why don't you just go?' she sneered. 'Haven't you spoiled everyone's day enough?'

'We *are* going,' Millie said.

Nicola pushed herself up from her stool and turned between the warring parties. She stepped carefully across towards Millie's side.

'Oh look,' Rachel sneered, 'the two divorcees. You're both gonna die alone. You know that, don't you? No wonder you came together. Nobody loves either of you.'

Nicola had frozen as Millie sidestepped towards the exit. She reached for Eric but he was standing firm.

'I love Mum,' he said.

Millie's heart soared and sank at the same time. It was wonderful and joyous and everything she wanted. But there was a time and place.

Rachel's eyes were slits, her body trembling, though she was never going to give up the last word.

'You're never getting custody,' she said. 'You know that, don't you? Alex knows every judge in the county and, even if you do manage some sort of ruling, we'll tie you up in so much red tape that you'll have to sell everything to cover even half the costs. Meanwhile, Alex has friends that'll do it all for free.'

Millie was in the doorway, Eric behind her, Nicola behind that.

'It's the one thing you want,' Rachel added. 'And I promise you'll never have it.'

FORTY

CHRISTMAS DAY

Millie was sitting at her kitchen table as Luke leant across the counter and checked the sealant that was connecting it to the wall.

'That needs re-doing,' he said, as he stood back up. 'If you get water down the back of there, you won't be able to dry the wall out easily, then the whole thing will go mushy.'

'Is "mushy" a technical term?'

He grinned: 'I was dumbing it down...'

Millie smiled back: 'So now you're calling me dumb...?'

Luke laughed as he leaned back on the counter. He scanned the rest of the kitchen and Millie could see him making a series of judgements about what could, and should, be replaced. When his gaze returned to her, he didn't acknowledge it. Instead, he focused on their texts from the previous night.

'Just to recap, you went to your ex-husband's wedding reception yesterday...?'

'Right.'

'And you were on a table with his grandmother, who hates you...?'

'Correct.'

'And your son went up to the bride and threw a glass of red wine over her?'

'Also correct.'

Luke blew a raspberry to himself. 'Wow.'

'You said you wanted honesty.'

'Is there *always* this much drama around you?'

'Is that a problem?'

'Not necessarily... I suppose I'm just wondering what I'm getting myself into.'

'Christmas dinner,' Millie replied. 'That's all we're getting ourselves into for now.'

She said it to see how he'd reply, even though she had a sense they might already be past that. If that was a first date, then this meant their second was Christmas Day at her house. She could keep saying it was casual but she was kidding herself.

'How are your mum and dad getting on in Dubai?' Millie asked.

'They love it,' Luke replied. 'They go every year now. It's too cold here and they've got a bunch of friends who all go out at the same time. Dad'll have been on the golf course since first thing and Mum would've done yoga, or something like that. I'm going to FaceTime them later.' He paused, as Millie pictured him otherwise sitting in his house by himself on Christmas Day. The two of them had more in common than they wanted to admit. 'What time's your friend coming over?' Luke asked.

Millie checked the clock on the oven, in which the turkey was already roasting: 'About twenty minutes.'

That got a nod, without further comment. Luke was still leaning against the counter, looking down upon her. 'Was your boy in trouble?' he asked.

'Not with me. His dad picked him up this morning. Eric didn't want to go but his dad said he could only have his presents if he went, so that settled that. Alex didn't want to talk to me but just about said Rachel's calmed down after yesterday but...' Millie held up her hands. She doubted that very much.

'Eric's back with me tomorrow,' she added.

Luke had been nodding, although his eyes had shot sideways towards the sink a couple of times. He must've clocked Millie noticing it, because he laughed to himself. 'Sorry, I *was* listening, I just noticed how bad the limescale is on that sink.'

'You're such a smooth talker,' Millie replied. 'Does that work on all the girls?'

A laugh: 'Why do you think I'm single?' He paused momentarily and then pivoted in a way that left Millie needing a second to readjust. 'If we're talking honestly,' he added, 'I have to say I'm not really a drama person. I don't post on Facebook, I don't bother with cryptic texts or any of that. I'm not boasting, or anything, but I had a wild enough time in my twenties and I'm done with it all.'

Millie quite liked that he'd gone from joking to serious with barely a breath. 'Believe it or not,' she replied, 'I don't really *do* drama, either. Sometimes, drama kinda happens to me.'

It wasn't *quite* true. She chose to have the affair that had led to so much of what was happening now. She'd had her reasons but she wasn't blameless.

Luke didn't question it. He glanced to the microwave clock and then huffed himself up a fraction. 'There's something I need to tell you,' he said.

'That sounds serious.'

Luke gulped, and, suddenly, it *really* felt serious. 'I know you said not to but I asked my private investigator mate in Manchester about what happened to you. I couldn't stop thinking about how you said someone betrayed you...'

He was avoiding eye contact now. Millie had tingles.

'I said no,' she replied.

'I know. It's just... he said he knows someone who knows someone who works at the paper that put you on the front page.

They're the ones who bought the photos of you. I don't know what he did, or who he asked, but, he got a name...'

It felt as if someone was stroking the back of Millie's neck. She fought the urge to scratch. 'He knows who tipped off the photographer?'

A nod.

The kitchen was suddenly cold. Millie had suspected for a while that somebody she knew must have sold her out to either the paper, or a photographer. How else could the photos have been taken?

She wanted to know and yet she didn't.

'This isn't a good start,' Millie said carefully. 'I told you not to do something and, a week later, you've done it.'

'I know. I really do. I just...' He stopped, thought about what he wanted to say. She liked that about him too. 'You sounded so scarred when you told me and you'd obviously been thinking about it all this time. I figured I'd ask my mate and that I'd never hear anything again. If you ever asked me to do it, I'd already have the answer. I didn't expect him to come back with a name.'

Millie was staring at the clock on the oven, watching the vague outline of the turkey within.

'I don't want to know,' she said, although she wasn't sure she believed it.

'That's fine. It's just... I'm pretty sure you know this person.'

It wasn't fair, it really wasn't. Millie wanted to be told and then to instantly have her memory wiped.

She was about to tell him to give her the name when the doorbell sounded. It echoed through the house and, for a moment, Millie couldn't move.

'Nicola,' she said, as she pushed herself up.

Millie drifted through the house, wondering what name Luke was about to give her. Had she been betrayed by one of her parents? How could they have known?

Except, Luke had said he was 'pretty sure' she knew the

person, so it couldn't be family. It had to be a friend, or maybe a work colleague?

Millie opened the door, ready to welcome Nicola inside – except it wasn't her. It was a man that Millie didn't recognise. He was tall, with feathery, gingery hair poking out from underneath a beanie hat. There was something vaguely familiar about him that Millie couldn't place.

'Are you Millie?' he asked.

As soon as he'd said her name, Millie knew who he was. He was the man who'd been arguing with Guy at the Bay Burning. The one who'd been waiting on the wall outside his cottage what felt like a lifetime before. Millie had more or less forgotten about him.

'Who are you?' she asked.

There were footsteps from behind and she glanced back to see Luke at the end of the hall. The man noticed him, too, but didn't flinch or move.

'I'm Craig,' he said, 'and I'm wondering if you're the Millie Westlake who knows Guy Rushden.'

'Why do you want to know?'

'Because I'm Craig,' he said. 'And Guy Rushden is my dad.'

KERRY WILKINSON PUBLISHING TEAM

Editorial
Ellen Gleeson

Line edits and copyeditor
Jade Craddock

Proofreader
Loma Halden

Production
Alexandra Holmes
Natalie Edwards

Design
David Grogan

Marketing
Alex Crow
Melanie Price
Occy Carr
Ciara Rosney

Publicity
Noelle Holten
Kim Nash
Sarah Hardy
Jess Readett

Distribution
Chris Lucraft
Marina Valles
Stephanie Straub

Audio
Alba Proko
Nina Winters
Helen Keeley
Carmelite Studios

Rights and contracts
Peta Nightingale
Richard King
Saidah Graham

Printed in Great Britain
by Amazon

22758579R00179